Table For One:
The Standard

By

John Louis Lauber

This is a work of fiction. Names, characters, businesses, places, events, and incidents are either the product of the author's imagination or is used in a fictitious manner. Any resemblance to actual persons, living or dead, or actual events is purely coincidental.

TABLE FOR ONE: THE STANDARD

Copyright © 2022 by John Louis Lauber

All rights reserved. No part of this book may be used or reproduced in any manner whatsoever without written permission, except for brief quotations embedded in critical articles or reviews.

First Edition: January 2023

ISBN 979-8-9875228-0-6

Published by Properly Seasoned Media LLC
https://johnlouislauber.com

Acknowledgements

"Writing is a lonely undertaking," said Ernest Hemingway. He was right. My first novel is done and the sequel, nearly. But I found solace in the loneliness.

First and foremost, I wish to thank Laurel Siena, my dear friend, confidante and editorial soul. She told me to "just pants it," and start writing – no outline, no nothing. I did. It worked. Her encouragement and subtle pushes in better directions were invaluable and remain so. XO.

To Patti and Mike McDowell, who read those first chapters and gave me the support to get past the first stumbling blocks, leading to my "A-ha!" moment. It's been an easier walk down this path since.

To Pat Bailey, Jason Bartlett, Jim Boon and John Ziton, especially, and others; of all the friends one could have on this Earth, how bloody lucky am I?

To my sisters and brothers, Wendy, Steve, Charlie and Julie. The advancing years will never change those grand and golden memories and the bonds we once shared.

Especially for my sister Julie - though we never met, this book is dedicated to her and her inspiration to me…and what joy there might have been.

With deep gratitude and affection – I thank you all.

-Jack

Praise for TABLE FOR ONE: The Standard

"FIVE STARS...Unforgettable dishes, sterling reviews and those elusive Michelin Stars...in Chef Jacques Rousseau, Lauber crafts a character and cast as richly rendered as the menus Rousseau fashions. [...] His first installment, *The Standard*, sizzles and pops with bold flavor. If you love Fusilli-like plot lines served well-seasoned with political and Mafia intrigue, your reservation awaits. Bon Appétit!"
Laurel Siena, Editor & Member, The Writer's Guild of Texas, Austin, Texas

"Fantastic! I kept getting reeled in more and more. Well-developed characters, snappy dialogue and a plot that weaves and shimmers...and a stunning finish! This is a sharp beginning to the collection. Great work...and all that wonderful food! Superb book.
Professor Lisa Perlt Farley, Ed.D, Butler University

"One of the best, most gripping mysteries I've read in a long time. Lauber's menu is delicious - the finest cuisine, a hefty portion of police and political intrigue, throw in a stone handful of Mafia muscle and a sweet cliffhanger ending that is as good as it gets. John Louis Lauber sets a perfect table and all you have to do is pull up a chair and enjoy! Can't wait for the sequel!"
R. Scott Johnson, SVP, Alliance Bank, St. Paul, MN

"If you're a foodie, you'll enjoy this book! Lauber's prose is rich with description, and you grow to like Rousseau and his supporting cast. Being set in Chicago, it's almost natural to have the Mob involved in the plot where criminal activity is concerned. The Mafia boss and his cronies border on stereotype, but Lauber gives them enough personality to be believable. Once the characters are introduced, the plot shifts into high gear. The story becomes a page-turner with plenty of twists, turns, and surprises. Darn good for a first novel!"
Chris Norbury, Award-Winning author of the Castle Danger Series

For Julie

Part One

Chapter 1

Rudy Tufton awoke that morning, as he had every morning for the past 52 years—he just didn't know today would be his last. It wasn't God or Fate that cast death in his particular direction that day but a darker, more malevolent force than he.

Rudy was the sector health inspector for Cook County, and had policed Chicago restaurants since the 1990's; he dealt with people every day, but he was not prone to warm and fuzzy kindness, not a man to try work cooperatively with his restaurant owners — just the opposite — he loved bullying people in his job. Rudy Tufton was a five-star bastard and he couldn't care less about his bad rep. No one could touch him.

Later that night, Rudy would be collecting after-hours, because blackmail was always better done under the cover of darkness; it was the *only* reason Rudy kept his job. He was forced to give regular kickbacks to his own superiors, a deal they had made with him years ago after he was caught humping a plump waitress behind some trash cans one afternoon following one of his inspections. He was going to close the place down, and the owner's only move to prevent shuttering was to convince the waitress to have sex with Rudy, who had long coveted the buxom woman, and he grunted and sweated over her backside right up until a rookie beat cop busted him in the alley as he was finishing.

The bigwigs at the Health Department bailed him out on the public obscenity charge and let him keep his job after the dust settled, but their deal came with strings attached.

THE DINING ROOM at Chicago's *La Cantina Morelo* restaurant hummed with activity later that night, atypical for most Chicago establishments on a Tuesday. The place was jammed because diners knew the formula: great ambiance, convivial service, and the very best Hispanic fare.

La Cantina Morelo served the finest Oaxacan dishes in Chicago, and had ever since John Fitzgerald Kennedy blessed the place with his imprimatur in 1960 when he ate there during his first campaign stop. After he became President, JFK would drop by LCM whenever he was in Chicago and Jose Morelo, the current owner Mario's grandfather—his *abuelo*—served the President personally.

Tonight, though, the mood in the kitchen was tense.

Third-generation owner, Mario Morelo, was trying his best to placate the notorious food inspector, Rudy Tufton, who had popped in at closing time for a "surprise inspection."

"Please, Mr. Tufton. Don't shut us down. This was my papa's restaurant and my abuelo's before him," said a beleaguered Mario.

"What the hell is an abuelo?" the inspector asked, uncaring.

"My grandfather," said Mario. "He was a great man."

"Not my problem, Chico," said Rudy, fully knowing what *abuelo* meant.

La Cantina Morelo was an impressively clean place, but in the years since Kennedy, it had become harder and harder to run a restaurant in the city of Chicago; having a health inspector shaking you down didn't help matters.

Tufton thrust a hammy hand in Mario's face, a thick finger extended menacingly and growled, "You know what, Morelo? I've cited you twice before about those damn, dirty *planchas* of yours. Third strike and you're out. I'm shutting you down," he said.

It was a ridiculous remark. Every restaurant in America had little smudges here and there. Rudy was merely exploiting his position and tonight's mark was the kindly Mario, who ran a very clean and sanitary operation, just as his father and grandfather had done over the decades.

As Mario's fear rose, Rudy uttered his trademark line, words that had grown to a sick lore in the Chicago restaurant community, "And you know what, Chico? *There ain't thing one you can do about it.*"

It was Tufton's catchphrase. There was nothing any owner could do; no higher court of appeal was available, and he abused the notion constantly.

Mario stood near Rudy, leaning against a stainless-steel prep table and pleaded, "But Mr. Tufton, my planchas are absolutely necessary. We do our best to keep them clean when it's busy. You know how it is."

He waved his arm around to show Rudy his employees, all cleaning up for the night after a busy dinner rush. It was now 11 p.m.

"The planchas were slammed tonight because people like the grilled tacos and Cubanos and there's no time to clean during the rush...but we'll clean them now for you and we'll clean them very well," said Mario.

Rudy stared blankly. "Yeah? What else you got?"

Mario sighed. He reached into his front pants pocket and removed five $100 bills and held them out to Rudy.

"Here. Can we stay open? I'll make a promise to you...the planchas will be wiped down during the shift. We won't wait until the evening service is over," he said. "Good enough, Mr. Tufton?" asked Mario with a weary voice.

Rudy leaned in and his eyes moved from the sweaty money up to Mario's face. "Look at me, Mario." he said. Mario looked up - his humiliation was showing. Rudy spoke in a low tone.

"Next time, Morelo...there'll *BE* no next time."

He reached over and swiped the bills from Mario's hand and stuffed them in his pants pocket.

Satisfied, Rudy stood erect and shot the cuffs on his worn, wrinkled blazer and grunted. He wore no tie, which couldn't fit around his fat, perspiring neck anyway.

Mario breathed a sigh of relief and put both his hands to his face, his tears and sweat making his hands dripping wet and he rubbed them on the front of his chef's coat to dry them off and continued hanging his head.

Rudy smirked at this and turned to leave, then turned back. "Oh, one more thing."

He spat in Mario's face.

The timid Oaxacan merely wiped the mucus off with the sleeve of his chef's coat and said nothing.

Tufton did that sort of thing because he was a colossal dick and no one could stop him. The gesture revealed far more about him as a man than any tangible effect it may have had on Mario Morelo.

Rudy looked at Mario one last time and winked, then walked out the back door of the kitchen, his thick cigar smoke trailing behind him like a dirty, ragged blanket.

Mario simply went back to work, cleaning and thanking everyone for their efforts. Word spread quickly throughout the place about the inspector and their brush with closure. The business would continue unaffected as it always had, at least until Rudy's next "inspection."

He would worry about that when the time came, for Mario, in his calm and gentle persona, possessed the infinite patience of all of Mexico. Mario was a good man and he had many friends, some of whom he didn't even know.

OUT IN THE STREET, the inspector moved slowly and intently like a newly sated walrus, fresh from a big feed. This was his turf and he didn't move fast for anyone. Tufton had a certain power, or so he liked to think. He walked up Schiller Street toward Wells Street and turned right, heading for his favorite watering hole, McBride's.

The night was cool after an early evening spring shower and the air was freshened from its usual mix of dust and exhaust and urine and resignation. Rudy needed a drink.

Chapter 2

McBride's was the third building on Wells Street, and Rudy rolled through the open door to his usual stool at the corner of the bar.

There was a good, happy crowd on hand that night, but Tully McBride, the owner, spotted Rudy walk in and grimaced, narrowing his eyes from behind the bar. He despised Tufton and didn't want him in his establishment, but cash was king and he reluctantly turned and grabbed a bottle of Old Overholt whiskey and a lowball glass from the shelf under the antique mirror. He set it down in front of Rudy and poured a double shot.

"That'll be ten bucks, Tufton," Tully said.

"Jesus Christ, Tully, why do you always keep raising the price of whiskey?" Rudy Tufton complained. "Every other month, you jack it up, again, and you know I know you water the shit down. Don't lie to me either," he said.

Tully shook his head. "Tufton, I raised the price from $4.75 to $5 a year ago," he said. "You got a bad memory for a shakedown artist. And remember, that's a double," he said.

Rudy scowled. "I remember the important shit, and don't you forget it," he said. "You're lucky all you serve is peanuts and pretzels and those god-awful thin pizzas or I'd have shut your ass down decades ago." He tossed a crumpled $10 dollar bill on the bar.

Tully grabbed it with his thumb and forefinger and rinsed it in the sink before smoothing and flattening it on a bar towel to dry.

This irritated Rudy. "What the hell is THAT all about?" he asked. "My money's dirty?"

"In more ways than a hundred, Tufton," Tully said. "Drink your drink, asshole. I'm busy."

Rudy finished his Old Overholt and had another. He munched from the community bowl of free pretzels, licking his fingers before grabbing repeated handfuls. A half-hour later, sufficiently relaxed, he stepped off his barstool, left no tip as always, hitched his pants up to his huge belly, and moved toward the door and out into the street.

In front of McBride's, he paused and belched, took one last drag, and dropped his cigar on the sidewalk and smeared it into the concrete with the tip of a scuzzy loafer.

He fished another cigar out of the box in his shirt pocket, lit it with a beat-up Zippo, blew out a long snake of heavy smoke, spat on the sidewalk, and moved, turning north up Wells.

He had an idea. On his way home, he was going to drop in on old Sig Larson at The Sturehof Tavern before last call and shake him down from an earlier citation. The night suddenly buzzed with fresh anticipation.

The sick truth behind Rudy Tufton's "citations?" They weren't health violations at all, merely oversights of the flimsiest order. Was there a splotch or two of sauce on the steam table or a dirty plancha? Violation. Did the walk-in cooler handles sport any muck on them (they all did)? Violation. When was the last time the paperwork on rolling inventory was updated? NO ONE ever did this—it was just another flaccid government document. Sorry, strike three. Time to pay up.

Rudy Tufton had bled money from restaurants for decades. He did it simply because he could. He knew every health code by heart and could enforce them at his discretion. His superiors knew all about it, but they would never have stopped him, because he was making rain. Tufton was the food service equivalent of the slimy lawyer who litigated at will, making others go blind on paperwork, all the while lining his own pockets with bribes from helpless owners.

To be fair, some restaurants *were* filthy shitholes run by owners who couldn't care less about the dirty food they served from dirtier kitchens. In these, Rudy was doing a minimal public service to the people of the city by closing them down, but he took their bribe money right along with everyone else's.

If Rudy Tufton once had principles, they were long gone. He abandoned the ethics of his job eons ago, violating the oath he had once sworn to deliver worthy, decent, and fair inspections to places that served the public need and kept people safely fed.

Even as a child, Rudy never displayed any generosity of spirit. He was born with a huge void where his empathy should have been and family knew he was a bully from the age of 6. He had a brother and sister that lived right there in Chicago, but he hadn't spoken to either in over 20 years.

Rudy Tufton was a gold-plated prick and cruel to his core. No matter how many free meals he copped or how much bribe money he grabbed or whatever amount of suffering he inflicted, it would never be enough to fill that chasm. He had lived his entire life by taking from others and never giving back.

But the years had grown long, and Rudy was looking for a way out. Inspecting was starting to wear his massive body down. It was harder to move, to cover an expansive area of restaurants every week. His knees and hips roared after each long day. It was his own fault; he ate extraordinarily and hugely, his body ballooning from once-fairly-trim to a flabby, ultra-soft pile of crenulated fat.

On an inspector's salary, there was no possible way he could afford it, but it was no matter. Rudy hadn't paid a restaurant bill in a generation. It was the ultimate paradox: he fined restaurant owners for violations, then ate their free food anyway.

Chapter 3

Farther down the block, in an alley on Wells Street, a set of eyes carefully peered around the corner of a building and focused icily on Rudy the Inspector as he trudged up the street toward The Sturehof. The man took full note of the alley and the empty street both ways, scanning subtly for witnesses, especially in doorways. There were none. Chicago was winding down for the night. He and Rudy were alone.

The man wore all black: cuffless trousers, a long-sleeved spring jacket, and a tam o'shanter-style cap. He blended completely—he and the dark were one. In his left jacket pocket was a tiny spray canister, which the man now held in his hand.

He had been tailing Rudy Tufton for weeks, finding habits, determining schedules, travel patterns, and regular stops. The man had charted Rudy's daily life down to the last detail and had talked to many people in the restaurant community; not a single one had anything redeeming to say about the crooked health inspector—far from it. His reputation was unquestionably toxic. This was a man with no discernible worth to the human race—a net negative. It was time for Rudy to go.

As Rudy neared The Sturehof, he reached in his back pocket and removed the violation pad he loved to methodically and rudely tap it in his hand when he talked down to a prospective restaurant owner/violator.

Crossing the alley, he was suddenly hit by wetness that splashed the right side of his face.

Rudy wheeled and looked around and then up to see if a downspout was leaking after the earlier rain. He stopped and touched his moist face with his right hand, jerking it to his nose for a sniff. As soon as he did, he was hit hard by a shocking wave of dizziness. His vision swirled wildly.

Rudy took several lurching steps into the alley and tried to steady himself on a dumpster. It didn't help. He was losing his balance, feeling consciousness wane, and he knew it. A squeaky, desperate, "What the fff…!" were his last words as he slumped down to the ground and splayed out on his back.

Inside the tiny can was a mix of sodium cyanide, ethyl alcohol, and one other wondrous chemical. The canister sprayed a jet-clean line of liquid up to 30 feet. In the proper aerosolized concentration, sprayed directly in a person's face, the mixture took effect within seconds, absorbing instantly into the skin, going straight to the brain and central nervous system. It rendered a person completely paralyzed and unable to speak yet conscious and fully aware of their surroundings. The man in black had paid a lab tech from a pharmaceutical company to concoct it in a clandestine laboratory operation stashed deep in an old building on the city's North Side.

The substance was one of those chemical gifts from God — an extremely efficient method of control. The *pièce de résistance* of this lethal concoction?

Even an autopsy couldn't detect it.

It was a serial killer's best friend. The perfect weapon.

Chapter 4

Rudy Tufton shed no blood, broke no bones, and tore no clothing during his fall to the ground.

Seconds later, the man tailing Rudy emerged from the shadows behind the dumpster, pocketed the tiny canister, and removed a 6" puntilla knife from a sheath inside his jacket.

The knife handle was made of white bone ivory and had been scrimshawed with great care. It was a very old instrument and very loved and had been used many times. Its severe sharpness was an exact measure of the man now holding it.

He moved over to Rudy, quickly, and observed a completely conscious man who could fully see and hear and feel. But Rudy could not move an inch even if he were on fire. This is exactly what the man wanted—a docile and helpless Rudy Tufton.

He knelt next to Rudy, leaned in, and whispered, "Hello,
Rudy. I'm a friend of La Cantina Morelo."

Rudy's eyes and body language registered nothing.

Slowly, the man pressed the puntilla into Rudy's abdomen, just above his groin. The blade punctured his flesh and slid in slowly.

Rudy's mind exploded in hot, naked fear, though his eyes and face showed nothing more than a blank screen.

No matter—nothing could help Rudy Tufton now.

The chemical was truly a wonder, thought the man in black. Rudy should be in beautiful, exquisite agony and it would only get worse—his pain was about to multiply exponentially in the next few seconds, with nary a whimper of protest from the bully.

The man paused the knife and spoke a sinister finale into Rudy's ear. "You know what, Tufton? *There ain't thing one you can do about it.*"

The man pulled hard and strong on the knife, cutting upward in one smooth line through Rudy's abdomen—bisecting his upper and lower intestines and fileting his stomach. Out spilled the entire cargo of Rudy Tufton's last food and drink (An Italian roast beef sandwich with peppers and onions, French fries and onion rings, chewing gum, and a beer and Old Overholt whiskey). It all dumped out of him, accompanied by an impossible amount of blood.

Steam rose from around Rudy in the cool air, like a griddle full of hot Italian sausages, and the man stopped his cut exactly at the sternum.

Rudy's eyes were exploded wide in his head—they glowed fire red from a deluge of burst blood vessels, and, though he hadn't moved a muscle, his eyes had begun robotically blinking when the knife slid in. Now, the blinking slowed, and Rudy's eyes became resigned; defeat was near.

The blinking then ceased, much like that of a dog that dies by the side of the road, having been hit by a car whose owner had no intention of stopping.

Rudy's eyes blinked for the last time, and the lights went out and fogged over into oblivion. Rudy Tufton was no longer a health inspector. He wasn't anything; he never was, really.

The man reached over and put two fingers on Rudy's neck and checked for a heartbeat. Nothing. Dead. *Muerto*.

He studied Rudy for a moment more and then used the knife to take care of one final item on his checklist, before he wiped the puntilla blade carefully and slid it back into its custom leather sheath.

He removed a bottle of water from another inside pocket and splashed it over Rudy's face and head, stood up, looked around once more, and turned soundlessly back into the shadows of the alley and vanished.

Chapter 5

The man in black used his key to let himself into the basement apartment of the house near Wicker Park. The old duplex, built in 1892, was owned by a Mrs. Dominia Chlopicki, an elderly Polish woman who, at 96, still lived in the house, although she had spoken to her new tenant only twice—when he first moved in, carrying a steel toolbox and three days later, when he gave her a year's rent in advance.

She had robotically taken the rubber-banded wad of money he gave her and wedged it in the front pocket of a threadbare housecoat that had survived four presidencies. She then handed the man a single key and a hand-scrawled receipt, smiled an ancient smile at him, and turned and went back in the house without another word.

They hadn't seen each other since.

The man had scouted the neighborhood for weeks, taking note of the streets and alleys, storefronts and foot traffic, visible landmarks and—most important—escape routes. He also did a thorough background check on his new landlord. By all appearances, Mrs. Chlopicki lived like a hermit. When she did appear, it was only to trudge her walker down a couple blocks to a small corner grocery. Her eldest daughter lived in Connecticut, and she had no immediate family or friends. No one ever checked on her.

Dominia had a kitchen radio that was tuned—loudly—to a classical music station and was never turned off, even in the small hours after midnight. Any normal person couldn't possibly stand the incessant classical dirge, and there hadn't been a tenant in the upper unit for years. The duplex was the perfect safe house.

It suited the man's needs perfectly. Mrs. Chlopicki never bothered him once. In fact, it was possible she had forgotten he even rented from her. Mid-stage Alzheimer's and her daily arthritic battles may have explained her lack of attention. Obscurity was the man's ally, and though this place was a conveniently placed stopover, the man kept another location, well-equipped and designed for some of his more rigorous lunar activities.

The other location housed a large stainless-steel table, ample refrigeration, and a wide assortment of other necessary tools of his trade, which included a huge, locked cabinet containing hammer drills, reciprocating saws and several cases of knives and other cutting paraphernalia, stacks of polypropylene tarps and yards of rope, and many aprons and gloves and face shields, which were discreetly disposed after each use.

Like the basement unit in Wicker Park, the second property offered silence, seclusion, and avenues of escape.

The man pocketed his key and walked through the living area to turn on a single, low-watt ceiling light in the kitchenette. He opened the freezer door atop a 1960's-era Kelvinator refrigerator and reached in his pocket for a hand-sized plastic Ziploc bag. In the bag was a token from Rudy Tufton. He placed the bag in a small cooler with some dry ice and stashed it in the back, behind two frozen baguettes and a bottle of Ketel One vodka.

The man turned from the kitchen and walked into the adjacent bedroom. In the back of the closet, behind a steel filing cabinet, he knelt and removed a small section of wood baseboard trim and placed the sheath containing the puntilla knife in the makeshift cubbyhole. He took the spray canister from his pocket and set it next to three others like it and then replaced the baseboard section and returned to the kitchen.

He poured a glass of vodka and sat down, removing his jacket and cap. He shook his head, ran a hand through his hair, took a long sip, and set his mind to replaying the events of the past hour and a half. This was his ritual: To analyze (and beat to death) every detail he could imagine. To determine if there had been anything, anything at all that could trip him up and lead the authorities to his door.

These were his thoughts at the completion of each retirement. Did he leave a fingerprint? Was he witnessed or followed? Did he leave any evidence, either at the actual scene or travelling back from whence he came? These questions percolated over and again each time because his continued freedom was paramount.

There could be no mistakes. It was a wicked game of chess he played, and he had done well thus far in his career, which is to say, he still stood on the other side of the prison bars in glorious, anonymous freedom.

The man knew no one would miss the departed food inspector Rudy Tufton. Indeed, there would be dozens, if not hundreds, of the joyfully thankful, and they would dance a jig when the news broke the following morning. The man relished his brief time with Rudy, not because it closed the loop of association, but because of the clear reality that the world was rid of an evil person. Right had been done. It was that simple. Hundreds of lives would live a cleaner existence because one dirty soul was no longer there to create spiritual havoc. The Standard had been maintained and the universe always answered.

Satisfied with his project analysis, the man finished his vodka, washed and dried the glass, and placed it back in the cupboard above the sink. He dutifully wiped down every surface for fingerprints and pocketed the paper towel to dispose of later, thereby removing any traces of his DNA. He then checked the fake rubber soles attached to the bottom of his shoes. These were vital: they stamped a footprint for a man wearing a size 10 shoe—even though the man in black wore a size 12—and gave him an added inch of height. It was yet another way to throw police investigators off his scent. Ingenious. The soles were intact.

He turned off the kitchen light, walked through the living room, locked the door behind him, and made his way silently back into the Chicago darkness.

Chapter 6

St. Bernard's Parish, Louisiana. Christmastime, some years earlier.

Jacques Rousseau was locking up his restaurant after a busy Saturday night when he heard the echoes of a loud commotion from far down the street in front of Ripp's Bar. He pocketed his keys and turned toward the street.

Ripp's was one of the bars in St. Bernard's Parish that was a good place to go while the sun was up—they served an excellent shrimp Po'boy—but as each day descended into twilight, the place transformed into a dark den. Ripp's was where many of the local Cajun men went to get drunk and brawl after a day on the waters or in the woods. Most had police records and wearing a clean t-shirt to Ripp's was considered dressing up.

Most of these rough-and-tumble Cajuns made their money in a variety of ways, with a good percentage by illegal means. They worked as little as possible and spent a large portion of their time at Ripp's—blowing money they hadn't really earned. Each evening there was a fight, always beginning from the flimsiest of pretexts and fueled by alcohol.

On this particular night, 6 men had appeared in the street—four on one side, two on the other— and somebody was about to get their ass kicked. It was the same Saturday night's faux-machismo played out a hundred different times in a hundred different bars in Bayou country.

"Come on Thibodeaux! I'm done hearin' all the women talk about how pretty you are…sumbitch…and you ain't lived here for two years!" said a tall, scrawny Cajun named Davey Johnshoy. Davey was typical Louisiana pride-and joy, missing a tooth from a fight two years ago and a blood alcohol level in the high teens.

Tonight, Davey was once again smashed, but that didn't stop him from shooting off his mouth, so here he stood in the street, ready to brawl. He rarely won any of these fights, relying instead on his bigger friends to bail him out when the fight turned against him and his big mouth.

Tonight's target was a friendly, well-liked local boy named Remy Thibodeaux, who was home visiting family for the holidays and had come to Ripp's with his cousin Doyle for a couple of quiet beers.

Remy's family had come to Louisiana in the mid-19th century and was known throughout the generations as a nice, quiet, and resourceful Cajun family—everybody's friend—at least, until someone picked a fight. The legend long remained that the Thibodeauxs never started a fight. They finished them.

Davey took two steps forward and launched a flailing overhand right at the head of the tall, muscular Thibodeaux. Remy did a nifty double-step and slipped the hook by a good foot. Remy had done some fighting in his time and was a formidable opponent.

Undeterred, Davey wheeled and came back at Remy again, throwing wildly with another punch, but staggered over his own boots and sprawled to the ground. Remy moved in and was ready to make it a quick *adios* for Davey.

Suddenly, there was a loud CLICK! and another drunk friend of Davey's stepped forward, a switchblade poised low in a hand obscured behind his right leg. The gesture turned the adrenaline up to a 10 and now Remy was outnumbered. The only man on his side—Cousin Doyle—had come out merely to watch Remy's back and suddenly grasped the gravity of the situation.

Oh shit, he thought to himself, and he wracked his brain for a plan. Cousin Remy was a damn good fighter, but 4–against-2 were crummy odds.

"Put it away. Put it away right now," a firm voice said from down the street. "You don't want to do that," said the voice, coming closer.

Light from a street pole above showed Jacques Rousseau walking into view toward them and the action paused for a moment. While everyone in Louisiana had a bayou lilt in their accent, this sound was clean, pure, *parlez-vous-Francais*.

"Aw, who is this? The chef?" slurred Davey. "Go back to your kitchen, now…pussy."

Davey's lowbrow buddies thought this was funny and started laughing. In their mirth and inebriation, it took them a split-second before they realized Jacques had closed on Davey and, before anyone could react, Jacques leveled him out with a hard, single tomahawk fist to his mouth. Davey timbered down to the ground and didn't move.

Jacques turned and focused on Knife-Man, who went by the name Dougie. "Will you put it away now, please?" he asked calmly. "Or do I have to deal with you too?" Jacques stood firm, ready to defend himself on the drunk holding the blade.

Before Dougie could answer, Jacques noticed that Remy had joined his side. The two could have been from the same family; they looked so much alike, except for their hair color and their eyes. Remy's were hazel with flecks of green, which turned to dark ash when his anger was stirred, while Jacques' eyes were as achingly blue as a June sky in New England.

"I'm Remy," he said out of the side of his mouth to Jacques.

Jacques glanced sideways at Remy and said evenly, "My name is Jacques Rousseau. *En guarde, mon ami.* Now we have a fair fight."

Remy stepped forward. "I got this one," he said to Jacques and for the others to hear.

Dougie stepped forward as well and slashed once, then back again with the knife, missing Remy by a hair. It was like lighting a fuse.

While Jacques and Cousin Doyle kept a close eye on the other two bandits, Remy staged a street-fighting clinic, disarming his assailant with a powerful leg sweep, sending the switchblade scattering, and then putting his fists to work on his opponent's face. In 20 seconds, Dougie looked twice as bloody as Davey and the fight was over.

Dougie lay on the ground after taking a crushing roundhouse right straight to the nose from Remy. He sat up on one arm, swept his coat sleeve over his mouth, and drawled slowly through the blood, "Y'all just leave Davey alone now. He don't mean to start shit when he's drunk. He just ain't got a good set of brakes on his yapper."

Remy scowled, "Hey, Dougie? The next time Davey tries this shit, you better clam him up. And if you ever pull that switchblade on me again, I'm not stopping at your face. They can dredge the whole bayou and they'll never find you again. You read me, buck?" asked Remy.

Dougie put a hand of surrender up and nodded at Remy; he motioned to the other two and the three of them slowly gathered themselves and Davey up, dragging and slouching their way toward a pickup truck in the Ripp's parking lot.

Remy stood in the street, hands on his hips, gathering air as he began to lower his adrenaline. He looked over to see Jacques still standing there, as calm as a Hindu cow.

Jacques quietly asked Remy in his unmistakable accent, "Are you alright?"

Remy nodded and said, "Yeah, I'm fine. Those guys pull that shit every now and again but pulling a knife...you're kinda forced to deal with it," he said, chuckling. "You know what I mean?"

Jacques smiled for the first time and said, "You are a better man than I." His eyes grew dark as he continued, "If it were me, I would cut his ass and chiffonade it," and said so with animated, thrusting arm motions.

This struck Remy as extremely amusing, and he started laughing. He mimicked Jacques' French accent and said "You would 'chiffonade his ass'? Oh, man, tell me you're not a cook, with a line like that!" and his laughter grew.

Jacques was amused at Remy's impersonation and started grinning at the caricature, and then he, too, was laughing. Both enjoyed the humor after such a display of raw violence.

Jacques stepped toward Remy and put out his hand. "Jacques Rousseau. Chef Jacques Rousseau."

Remy stepped toward the hand and gladly offered his own. "Remy Thibodeaux. I'm a cook, too."

Jacques nodded and pointed down the street. "That's my place—Le Feu Follet."

Remy smiled. "Now I remember the name! You're the man who gives my Uncle Tibay all that frog leg business! Well, let me shake your hand again. It's nice to know you, Jacques. And thanks for backing me up just now. You might have saved me a stitch or two…or ten," he said gladly.

"It's no problem, Remy. People like that don't scare me at all," said Jacques.

****

TWO WEEKS into the New Year, police investigators pulled a body from a remote backwater of Lake Charles. The medical examiners from St. Bernard's Parish Police later identified the victim as Douglas "Dougie" Conroy.

His body had been partially consumed by alligators and other denizens of the bayou, and, along with natural decay, no actual cause of death was able to be determined. Although, given his activities in and around St. Bernard's Parish, foul play was not ruled out by SBP police investigators; Dougie had a police file since age 10.

Although both Jacques Rousseau and Remy Thibodeaux were questioned in the matter, Remy was back in New York at the time of Conroy's disappearance and Jacques was not detained due to numerous witnesses who claimed to have seen him at Le Feu Follet on the days in question.

The case remains an open investigation to this day.

Chapter 7

Jacques Rousseau had first arrived in Louisiana as a young adolescent, after his family suffered a devastating tragedy. Jacques was raised in the port city of Marseilles, France and began working the docks by age 11. After his mother and father died, he came to America to live with distant cousins on his mother's side, always helping in the kitchen, with the garden, or with the harvest. He had decided early on in life that the kitchen was his favorite place. It was where his true soul existed—cooking and food were his sustaining passions.

While it was the place he felt the most comfortable, and certainly the safest, a shadow of the tragedy lingered long with him. Even his smile held a thin veneer of sadness. Or, perhaps, it was quelled anger.

He stayed in and around New Orleans as a young adult, cooking at restaurants, honing his growing talent and skill sets, and partnering with the right people at the right time until it became obvious that he needed to set off solo and open his own kitchen. He opened Le Feu Follet Bistro not long after. The new venture, and the first generation of his now-famous restaurant, Chez Rousseau, had been named Le Feu Follet Bistro, after the famous Louisiana legend.

Also known as "The Cajun Fairy," Le Feu Follet is a local legend going back over a hundred years. It is said to appear as a phosphorescent ball of fire in the swamps and marshlands of Louisiana that represents both the light and the darkness of nature and of life itself. The spirit sometimes takes the form of loved ones, and given his early life in France, this theme, both the good and the evil, resonated strongly with Jacques.

Jacques' new friend, Remy Thibodeaux, was born and raised in St. Bernard's Parish, an outlying community of New Orleans with fiercely traditional Southern ways. His family roots grew back to the early 1800's, and Remy was always proud to add the tagline of "Old School Cajun" to his family history. He, too, was an exceptional cook, and had trained as a teen in numerous kitchens in and around New Orleans; as his acumen gained strength, he eventually transitioned north to the world's table of New York City.

He had heard there was big money and big adventures to be had in the big city as a cook, and, while there were adventures, money was always tight.

Remy had come home for the holidays to visit family for a few days' respite from his job as sous chef at the highly acclaimed Pinchot, an urban haven of haute cuisine on NYC's Upper West side. It was this auspicious Yuletide timing that had led to his and Jacques' dubious introduction on the street and the fight outside Ripp's Bar. Since then, they had learned much about each other. Physical similarities aside, they shared the same attitudes on the work ethic and the value of loyalties.

Rousseau's customers at Le Feu Follet Bistro were first intrigued at its special name and the honoring of the legend; they found the tall and reserved-but-amusing French owner pleasant and soon realized that he knew his food exceptionally well. His superb dishes quickly gained him a following and even stout, lifelong Cajuns admitted his simple, but flavorful offerings of etouffee', remoulades and gumbos brought back fond generational reminisces.

An example was Jacques' clever jambalaya recipe, which used both smoked sausage *and* smoked frog legs and it began to earn Rousseau a growing respect within the community.

His imaginative treatment of rice dishes especially impressed his clientele. Something as simple as a grain of rice, and its importance to Louisianans rang true. This was never lost on Jacques, as he sought and bought only from the best suppliers, and conjured recipes from deep in his mind, then transformed them into wondrous dishes; Rousseau went much further than your standard red-beans-and-rice in the Southern cuisine tableau.

His mentor in France had been the famed culinary legend Pierre Letreuce, and Rousseau was the mirror image of him in that his attention to the most infinitesimal detail was a marvel to see and a joy to savor. Jacques, like Pierre, was a ferocious businessman as well—to him, the dollar ruled. After all, if there was no stable, healthy revenue stream, how could the business prosper? Jacques knew early on that success depended upon consistent money.

After two short years, Jacques sold Le Feu Follet for a tidy profit and opened another restaurant. He named the new place after his mother: *Clarice*. This time, his menu brought a complete departure from the board of fare at Le Feu Follet Bistro, and Jacques fiercely embraced his Marseilles heritage and his mother's talent of serving anything and everything from the waters; seafood was the singular focus and with his executions at Clarice, Jacques Rousseau earned his first Michelin star. He was on his way.

Certainly, some of the credit for the success at Clarice was attributable to his new sous chef, Remy Thibodeaux. Since their daring introduction in the street, Jacques had kept ties with his new friend and, when the time was right, he wrote Remy and convinced him to leave New York and return home to Cajun country. The financial offer to Remy had much to do with the decision, but it was a win-win for Remy because now he could forge ahead with a new business and a reputable partner *and* be close to home again.

The two cooks emphasized each other's talents seamlessly—brothers from other mothers. They worked well together and enjoyed a friendship that included a great deal of hunting and fishing after working hours, often with numerous family members from the Thibodeaux clan. Jacques and Remy were a sterling partnership and, though neither knew it at the time, their efforts were leaving a mark on the culinary realm in America.

The Jacques Rousseau brand grew and expanded into a vibrant new voice in food in the South, and he would soon realize greater challenges beckoned. After some hefty due diligence and smart money movement, Jacques decided to take his ambitions and his brilliant sous chef north, to the city of Chicago, and a space near the historic Miracle Mile district downtown. Chez Rousseau was born.

Chapter 8

The morning kitchen at Chez Rousseau was bustling. Chicago's newest hot dining trend had evolved in its first year to do an amazing amount of business since Jacques had moved north from Louisiana and opened the doors with his new sous chef, Remy.

Now, Chez Rousseau was known as *the* great French restaurant in Chicago, and a true destination for gourmands around the country. Its eponymous owner had earned a reputation, beginning in his late teens, as one of the most astute students of French cuisine and then one of its culinary scions. He had taken his cuisine in directions few chefs had ever dared on American soil. A few short months later, Jacques achieved his *second* Michelin star and *Chez Rousseau*'s place in the culinary pantheon of American foodie-ism was locked. Rumor had it a third Michelin star was in the offing.

At a stainless-steel prep table, the chef stood, admiring six gorgeous salmon. They were beautifully formed, having developed their musculature by swimming in the rugged waters of the North Atlantic Ocean for at least 3 years. The Chef liked to imagine them in their natural state navigating the cold waters back to their native breeding grounds, making the circle and cycle of nature complete. Jacques had just put *"Chopin's No. 2 Piano Concerto in D"* on the sound system and the notes moved gracefully around the kitchen, swirling with his captivated thoughts of the salmon lying before him.

A new salmon dish had been tested and approved by Jacques and the entire Chez Rousseau staff and was moved to the regular menu. It sold so well on its premiere night that Jacques headlined it as the signature entrée for April.

He named it *Poisson d'Avril*. The dish was poached in lobster stock and Pouilly-Fusse wine, served adorned in a luscious sorrel sauce heavy with butter, cream, salt, and a secret herb. Early diners all took advantage of the offering because it sold out every time Jacques prepared it—another bona-fide money maker.

Remy walked by, whistled, and said, "Beautiful. How many salmon for tonight? Wait, let me guess—36 portions?"

"I thought we'd try for 36, yes?" said Jacques. "And that may not be enough," he said with a smile, knowing they would sell out.

"Why *Poisson d'Avril*? I know what it means—'fish of April'—but it's going to be May soon and then June and July. What do we do then?" asked Remy.

"We keep the name."

"Why would we do that?"

"Superstition, *mon tati*. How do you say in America? 'Never mess with a winning streak.'"

"*Tati*? You're calling me 'little one' again?'" asked Remy with fake incredulity. Being Cajun, he obviously knew his French well. "Tati" had been a long-running joke between the two.

"Little only above the shoulders, my friend," said Jacques stifling a laugh.

Remy raised his eyebrows at the joke and snapped his hand towel at Jacques, catching him a good one on the fanny.

"Hey! That hurt! No horseplay in the kitchen now...*Tati*," said Jacques, smiling at Remy and shooing him away.

Continuing his work, Jacques slid the Henckels boning knife straight through the salmon's midsection at a downward angle toward the gill and then back on a straight plane deftly through the entire length of her backbone to the tail. Jacques flipped it over with his free hand and manipulated the other side—a perfectly skinned filet.

Through years of handling knives and cleavers, and hauling carcasses, sacks of grain, and potatoes over his shoulder, Jacques' forearms and torso were like that of a blacksmith. He had bull-strength, along with a surgeon's touch. Jacques knew his anatomy well.

Remy walked by and patted the chef on the shoulder and said, "Nice! Bravo!" and then moved on to continue supervising and assisting with the ongoing food prep.

No more horseplay now. There was work to be done.

Jacques continued, repeating his flawless technique on five more salmon and slicing them into exact 6-ounce serving portions without needing a scale.

Prepping for dinner service was Jacques' daily joy and he seemed to levitate through the kitchen. His employees' movements inside the musical backdrop provided a muslin of daily memory of his dear mother, Clarice. This was his favorite time of day in the morning kitchen's hustle...all the veggie, fish, meat, and sauce prep leading up to service and an always rigorous dinner rush.

The daily preparation and assembly of each cooking station's *mis-en-place*: Olive oils, walnut oils, and truffle oils, varieties of vinegars, and champagne, red, and white were all placed in speed bottles for a quick dash of flavor at a second's notice. Shallots, along with perfectly minced parsley, thyme, chives, basil, rosemary, and tarragon were all expertly minced and stored, along with red, grey, and coarse sea salts, and mounds of freshly cracked black pepper—each of these were loaded into striking white ramekins for easy access during the frenzied dinner service. Every prep chef moved with measured purpose around the kitchen, in perfect choreography.

Chopin played another lilting concerto on the stereo, and now the *Nocturnes* drifted, joining the emerging scent of spice and herb as they began their warm melding.

Jacques stood sharpening his Henckels boning knife and then used the sharpening steel as a conductor would a baton; one of his assistant cooks, Jaime, danced alone in the middle of the floor, one with the music. It was inspiring, this creativity of muses-within-muses and it spurred the growing anticipation.

And on that subject, anticipation, be it food, sex, or a physical challenge, anticipation in and of itself is a living thing. It is a breathing, eating, and growing organism and a source of beauty once a kitchen begins physically heating up and throwing off delicious scents.

This morning at Chez Rousseau, that very anticipation was present in the kitchen; it was moving toward something. It spurred everyone, adding that extra *soupçon* of focus and enthusiasm to each duty, and even that dullest of kitchen duties—chopping carrot, onion, and celery for daily mountains of *mirepoix*—now allowed them to absorb the energy from the anticipation. It made the chore not a bore at all, but an invigorating harmony within the performance itself.

Each and every morning, this identical scene was reprised in the Chez Rousseau kitchen.

Chef Jacques Rousseau believed with his entire *métier* that anticipation was a real and true ingredient in good cooking and eating, and in, well, anything. *You have to let it build*, was an oft-uttered mantra, like the constructed layering of flavors in a dish.

The universal difference between truly great versus merely palatable food: a chef blessed by the gods knows how to take a carrot or some salmon or anything edible and turn it into magic. If things are treated things with respect and intelligence, certainly with a splash of love, the very best comes back. A cook might appear to have talent, but the devil was always, invariably, in the details and Jacques Rousseau was its master.

His laser-focus was the very heart of what drove his excellence. That, and simply…food was so utterly fascinating to him. It was more than a filling of the belly or fuel or a repeated exercise of fork-to-mouth. It was the taste of the air and the essence of the soil—how a tomato picked in full sunshine tastes sweeter; why it was better to blanch Frenched green beans before sautéing. He foresaw so many nuances in the foods grown for him and then transformed them into perfection.

For instance, why is the sense of smell the guardian of all things culinary? How could memories that were 20 years old be sealed in amber and then arbitrarily released in a simple whiff of rosemary or roast chicken, and why did those memories appear as visually stunning as they had 20 years prior?

These were the many, endlessly fascinating things about food, cooking, wine, cuisine, and service that inspired Jacques, to such a degree that he sometimes felt as though his spirit may fly apart at any moment, his joy and awe were so great. Then the little chef deep within him would give a mental nudge to turn the hanger steak *now* or it would be ruined.

Jacques Rousseau had been this way ever since he stood as a young boy at his mother's side in the kitchen, taking notes; it showed in his work when he began unloading fisherman's boats at the Marseilles port, and it especially revealed his unique talent when he began working with Pierre at Letreuce. His education had begun in earnest and remained, even as his body entered and passed 30 years of age.

Letreuce was the only 3-star Michelin restaurant in France outside of Paris. Pierre Letreuce, the owner, also possessed deep emotions toward food that verged on the Biblical, emotion beyond obsession.

He was pious about his preparations, knife skills, and flawless technique; all of these, especially his recipes, were constantly copied and emulated by youthful chef-wannabes of the French populace, male and female alike. The fact that Pierre was so strikingly good-looking no doubt added to his mystique and allure as a *bon vivant* and world-class chef. Though only 5'8", he carried himself with the assuredness of a lion. Still, he was the gentlest of souls to those who needed it most. With a wave of once-black hair now infused with a dashing salt-and-pepper look and a genuine, inviting smile that could make the perfect woman melt, Pierre exuded a presence of spirit that was inspiring to be near. Even so, one was wise not to ever cross him, for he was passionately protective to those he cared about. No one wanted to be on the wrong side of Pierre Letreuce.

He never married, nor had any children. As best as anyone could discern, he carried on a years-long relationship with Claudette, the Letreuce hostess, and they would spend time off together. While their trysts were of the utmost discretion, it was obvious the two cared deeply for one another, though it never developed into anything beyond sharing a fine meal and dancing together to a favorite Edith Piaf recording. Nevertheless, he loved her by his own deep and abiding standard.

Pierre's truest love, though, without a doubt belonged to both food and his namesake child, the Letreuce restaurant and its clientele. He lived for the place, working 18-hour days with joy. The Food Network was years away from airing and revolutionizing the perceptions of food as that seminal connection between people, but Pierre Letreuce was Europe's first, true superstar chef, far ahead of his time, and he epitomized everything a young Jacques Rousseau ever wanted to be.

Chapter 9

The dinner rush at Chez Rousseau was insane, per usual—even on a Tuesday. Their hostess, Patti O'Brien, a smooth veteran of culinary service, had received 50 additional reservation calls for evening service by 3 p.m. alone, all of which had to be turned away. Chez Rousseau served 32 tables, and each expected to flip once, which meant some 200 potential meals might be served. Tips were a part of business, but bribes were not. Patti O'Brien made it a firm policy that hostesses and hosts alike were to rebuff any hand with a folded bill tucked into it.

Chez Rousseau's massive foot traffic was due to its perfect location in the highly fashionable Rush and Division neighborhood on East Oak Street, just off the Mile. People regularly stood outside for an hour or two every night on the off-chance they might be seated through a rare no-show and many sought one of the two tables situated on either side of the kitchen door. These were a coveted spot for the gourmand, allowing the diner to see inside the high-frequency kitchen action and occasional flashes of the owner himself, while he and Remy quietly and confidently managed the chaos within.

The Chez Rousseau kitchen was unlike most professional environs in that it was eerily silent. Only the wafting of classical music could be heard mingling with very quiet commands. Jacques or Remy would utter at the pass, "May I have that cassoulet for Table 8 right behind the Veal Blanquette, please?" "Yes, chef," or *"Oui,* chef," would be the quiet reply from the team of *commis*.

Jacques shut the kitchen down each night at precisely 9:30 p.m., because it took customers a minimum of two hours' time to stroll, frolic, savor and swallow their way through the supreme food and incomparable wine selections. This generally took the close of business up to the 11 o'clock hour, which was why the tables flipped only once or twice each night. Dessert and cheese courses, served cold, did not apply to the regular kitchen schedule, as these could be handled easily by a single *garde manger* (a cold foods' cook).

Chez guests loved to linger dreamily over more wine and coffee and aperitifs while they relived, discussed, and debated the culinary delights of the evening with their dinner mates. It was wondrous conversation and the whole recreation of the meal was a separate course in itself. The entire evening was intoxicating theatre easily worth the price of admission.

Jacques wished his American clientele could have at least three or four hours devoted to dinner, just like Europeans. In France, a two-hour dinner is considered fast-food. Why rush, especially after all the pre-dinner dressing, perfuming, cocktailing, and perambulating? A mere two hours dedicated to dinner, after all that extensive preparation, seemed a complete waste of time. Good food, like good sex, is best enjoyed when the anticipation is allowed to build and bloom and burgeon to its eventual glorious climax.

For centuries, the French, Italians, Spanish, Greeks, and many others in Europe, anyone other than Americans, really, have known the secret to making food a memorable, daily event: *savoring their time.*

Eating—true dining—should take a relaxed, yet meticulous management of time without thinking about pace during a leisurely lunch or dinner. Each mouthful is to be analyzed like a theory and digested like a song. Certainly, the food itself is the center of attention, discussed *endlessly* with lunch or dinner partners, and spirited talk always sets its own table and puts the food in its rightful center stage. Jacques Rousseau's diners now paid a top dollar for the privilege of eating his creations, and his customers had begun to learn the worldly manner of luxuriating in their food by taking the necessary time, if only in the American way.

Near the end of the dinner rush, things got interesting.

At 8:12 p.m., Rodrigo Alberto, a kitchen runner and polished expeditor, came bolting back to the kitchen from the dining room in a state of semi-panic with a plate containing a lovely Dover sole, minus one petite bite.

"Remy!" he called out, "Table 6 says it isn't cooked through!" Rodrigo stood at the service pass panting for air and waiting for guidance.

"Let me see it," said Remy calmly.

The service pass in any kitchen is a one-way-only superhighway for food going out into the restaurant. Each chef or cook places a finished dish in "the pass" and servers and expeditors, hosts and hostesses, take plates from the pass and hurry it to the dining room. In its truest sense, it is a ballet—there is no other word—the timing of the performance results in food that is warm and inviting when presented to the customer.

Imagine driving the Autobahn in Germany at 140 miles per hour and suddenly encountering a huge truck coming the wrong way. Sending food back does the very same thing at the pass. Disaster.

Hard rule: One simply doesn't send food back in a Michelin-starred restaurant unless they are rude or pretentious or spiritually compromised...or they're a Dick or a Karen. It bothered Remy none in the least; he had nerves made of Kevlar—literally impenetrable.

He eyed Rodrigo with a wry, amused wrinkle from the corner of his mouth, took the Limoges plate of Dover sole off the pass and eyed it deftly. The fish was perfectly cooked. Remy gazed upon Rodrigo as his beneficent and wiser older brother.

"Who is at Table 6 tonight?" Remy asked quietly.

"Mr. and Mrs. Baldwin. It's Mrs. Baldwin sending it back, *again*."

This was the second time in the past two weeks she had done that. Remy registered it; she knows where she's dining, and two Michelin stars were no deterrent. She simply had the hots for Remy.

Earning two Michelin stars means the entire restaurant team put months of pure toil, blood, effort, and imagination into their work and occasionally took some insane risks.

Remy calmly mused about Genevieve Baldwin. She had been making subtle passes at him the past two months by sending food back and dropping clandestine notes to the bartenders to be delivered to the object of her fantasy. Sending food back tonight was merely her curious way of saying hello—only without the benefit of Remy getting to see her magnificent figure and stunning auburn hair. For observant gentlemen, Genevieve Baldwin could turn a simple smile-with-a-hair-flip into an enchanting moment.

Remy said, "Rodrigo, tell Mrs. Baldwin it'll be 90 seconds. Ask her to enjoy a long sip of her Cakebread chardonnay and she'll be eating again in no time. She won't miss a thing," and the runner disappeared through the swinging doors to deliver the message.

Remy knew there was an additional reason the food was sent back: *Mister* Baldwin, as in Richard W. Baldwin, the uber-wealthy real estate developer in Chicago. He had a reputation for playing a humorless game of hardball in all business matters; he was a frequent visitor to Chez Rousseau with his buxom wife, though he knew better than to take his other paramours there.

Baldwin had recently solicited Jacques about starting a new restaurant on freshly acquired Baldwin property in the lower annex in downtown Chicago near more foot traffic. Jacques had demurred at the first offer, which was nothing more than passing conversation one night as he visited with guests during the dinner hour.

The second meeting went poorly. Baldwin wanted a 60/40 revenue split in *his* favor and veto control over the menu. Baldwin said this in the Chez kitchen during morning prep not long after his first attempt; he had dropped by uninvited, and Jacques had shut him down.

"It's a standard business practice, Jacques," Baldwin had said, lying. "I have this split with all my restaurateur partners," he said with an air that reeked of arrogance.

"No *monsieur*, you don't have this split. Not with me," said Jacques, extending his hand. "Thank you for coming by today, but my answer is no."

"You don't know what you're doing, Rousseau," said Baldwin, taking a hard line. "I know the restaurant business, and you are WAY out of your league," he said.

"Monsieur Baldwin? Let us try 70/30 MY way, and," he held up a large stainless steel spoon for Baldwin to see, "as for the menu, you may take this spoon, drive yourself over to the Lake Michigan shoreline, and pound all that sand up your ass. *Au revoir.*" Meeting adjourned.

When Baldwin stood his ground and didn't move, Jacques snapped his fingers. Two very large kitchen employees materialized, ready to escort Baldwin out of the restaurant while Jacques simply turned and walked away, leaving Richard Baldwin to look like a perfect idiot.

It was the smart move by Jacques to cut him off. Baldwin was not a man to be trusted, and taking this deal would have been the beginning of a painful relationship. Unfortunately, Baldwin didn't earn his millions by taking *no* for an answer, and he wasn't about to leave the matter alone.

Chapter 10

Baldwin broached Jacques again exactly one week later, fortified with a double dose of Macallan bravery.

Baldwin barged his way into the Chez Rousseau kitchen during the height of dinner service looking for the chef with a waiter tailing close behind, trying to mollify the inebriated customer. This time, Baldwin severely crossed the line, invading the kitchen at the very worst time during service and Jacques fired back a proportional response.

"Jorge!" Jacques shouted to a massive Salvadoran dishwasher, "Get this flounder out of my kitchen, *now*! And use his head as a door-opener!"

Baldwin didn't get the message and kept braying, "Let me tell you something, you pansy frog piece of shit!" Baldwin yelled loudly and drunkenly. "You won't last two more months in this location! Anthony Cribaldi and me are partners and youuuuu....," Baldwin wailed as he was lifted straight off his feet by the giant Jorge, who tossed Baldwin over his shoulder like a sack of rice, then carried him, struggling and squirming, to the open alley door, and pitched him onto a pile of filthy garbage bags, then slammed the door closed and returned to his dishwashing duties.

Meeting adjourned, *Part Deux*.

Baldwin and his ruined Brioni suit didn't attempt a comeback, but Jacques knew he wasn't finished either, especially with his line about involving Don Anthony Cribaldi, who was the head of organized crime in Chicago.

Richard Baldwin had once sold a property and made a good profit for the Cribaldis. Although it had been a number of years ago, that tiny sale made him mobbed up.

That was Baldwin's twisted, gorilla thinking on the matter, but the truth was, it made him no more connected than the local barista, but that wasn't the way Baldwin saw it. He namedropped the Cribaldis constantly, as a veiled threat to anyone who dared cross him in a real estate transaction or anything else.

In reality, the Mafia Don of Chicago, Anthony Cribaldi, held a genuine affection toward Jacques Rousseau. He lived to eat at Chez Rousseau and particularly for their incomparable *L'angoustine a la Marseilles* and his supple risottos. Anthony said to Jacques the first time he ever ate there, "...their langoustines remind me of my dear grandmother Luisa," and then shook Jacques' hand rigorously.

So, Anthony Cribaldi favored Jacques over Baldwin in this tete-a-tete and revealed he was a true fan, and, while Jacques never collected on the implied goodwill, it was reassuring to know a powerful man like Anthony Cribaldi cherished his food so much.

The third and final time Baldwin proposed business, he went around Jacques and tried to bribe Remy with a very thick envelope. Baldwin waited on the street and confronted Remy on the sidewalk, unannounced, under the broad red awning of Chez Rousseau. He promised Remy a great fortune—never disclosed— to come aboard as his *chef de cuisine*, without Jacques.

"I'll make you a star in this town, Remy! You'll be the biggest chef with the biggest kitchen and a bank account to match!" bragged Baldwin.

"I'm a sous chef, not a star, you pretentious D-bag," Remy responded, "and I've got all the money I need.

You're mucking with my best friend," he finished, as calmly as he could muster, "so take a hike."

Remy considered Jacques his brother. Loyalty ran through the fabric of their days like breathing and cooking. So, yet another encounter ended with Baldwin left standing in the street looking like an asshole, and this was precisely why Baldwin had had his wife send her entrée back to the kitchen—just to be a churlish pain in the ass. He did not know his wife's ulterior motives, which was just as well.

It didn't matter. Remy took the plate and gracefully slid the sole onto a lightly olive-oiled saute pan over a medium flame, gave it several moments of heat, then somersaulted it onto the other side for another few seconds. He threw in a quick splash of Muscadet, a gob of butter, the lightest pinch of fresh tarragon, and slid it back onto a fresh Limoges plate.

This did not cook the fish, merely rejuvenated the Dover sole, and did not alter its light texture. It was a perfectly executed re-fire, and no one did it better than Remy.

He smiled and dispatched the perspiring Rodrigo back to the Baldwin table with a wave of his hand and in less than the promised 90 seconds, and, with that issue resolved, the sous chef turned his attention to more pressing matters as dinner tickets continued to pour off the speed-printer.

Later, Remy stood at the pass observing a new apprentice *commis* as he confidently plated the last entree of the night—Rousseau's luscious version of *Poulet Fricassee*—when Jacques appeared at the pass at exactly

9:30 p.m. with a silver tray containing two glasses of Port and a sizeable wedge of Stilton cheese on a tiny teak cutting board.

The kitchen family, as always, had already noted the exact time and began breaking down stations to clean for the night. Servers had also noted the time in the front of the house and ceased taking any more entrée orders for the remainder of service.

"Ready for a little recharge?" asked Jacques.

Remy smiled and turned to his boss, his truest friend, as he took a glass and tore off a huge chunk of the bleu cheese. He popped the Stilton in his mouth, raised his glass to Jacques in salute, and took a generous sip of the Port. He smiled as the flavors sashayed around his palate, giving him immense joy. This was their nightly ritual and the reward for hard work.

Jacques chewed his cheese thoughtfully before asking Remy, "We did well tonight, no? Any problems, hmm?" in his striking French accent. Jacques walked the dining room each night as a matter of course, gauging the pulse of the room, pressing the flesh, and making certain his diners were satisfied and inspired and happy. He missed nothing in the subtle nuance of feedback and was an impresario of the unspoken word or gesture.

"No, it was fine. Busy, but smooth. No issues," said Remy.

Jacques grinned slyly, "Except for Table 6, no? Genevieve Baldwin now dares to shit on our blessed Dover sole? I missed the action doing my nightly rounds in the dining room, but Patti laughed when she mentioned it," he said.

Remy laughed as well, avoiding any further commentary about the Baldwins, and then regaled Jacques with a story about what they used to do to food sent back to the kitchen when he worked in New York.

"I was a bit of a prick back then." Remy said, as he concluded his tale.

Today, he wouldn't think of sabotaging a dish, even if the sadistic diner deserved it. After years of rigorous meditation and tai-chi, Remy was the master of his emotions. Someone could detonate a flash-bang in the room, and it was highly unlikely Remy would even register it. The energy within the pressure of dinner service was something that both engaged and motivated him.

But, if one dared to work hard and truly piss him off, their affairs had better be in order. At 6'2" and 200 pounds of trim, lethal muscle, he could disarm two men simultaneously, without blinking and without a weapon. He knew how to handle himself, something that had been proven time and time again since his youth.

Jacques had divined that Richard Baldwin made yet another move at forcing a partnership by bracing Remy in the street. How Jacques procured his intelligence was uncanny. Yet even after three horrendously failed attempts, he knew Baldwin wasn't done. When he wanted something, he fought like a bastard for it, which was why Jacques was *en guarde*—he was waiting to see where and how badly Baldwin crossed the line the next time. Baldwin had a nasty streak in him, but Jacques had his own method of dealing with bullies.

When Remy had had enough Port and cheese, he embraced Jacques and kissed him on both cheeks,

Eurostyle, and moved around the kitchen to personally thank each of the kitchen staff for their hard work that night, giving hugs and handshakes and slaps on the ass and Euro-style kisses to both male and female alike. Once again, service had been a great team effort.

Jacques picked up the tray and bottle and poured a glass of port for Jaime Rodriguez, his lead *commis* and the kitchen's next in command to Remy.

Jaime was a sharp Panamanian who was being mentored and groomed in the Rousseauvian Way; this meant he was deathly loyal to both Jacques and Remy. It showed in the long hours Jaime logged in the kitchen and his willingness to help others.

Jacques took note of this; it was like reliving life with Pierre Letreuce, who had taken Jacques under his aegis years ago. Jacques predicted, with quiet pride, that Jaime's good heart and monster work ethic would one day allow him to run his own restaurant, and successfully.

Daily gratitude for the hard-working staff at Chez Rousseau was *de rigueur*, along with the regular bonuses that magically and regularly appeared in envelopes placed in each employee's locker. It was a generous way of doing business, and he and Remy had the most loyal kitchen staff in Chicago, if not all of America. There was no revolving door at Chez Rousseau.

Jacques finished his thanks in the kitchen and headed downstairs to change out of his sweaty checks and chef's coat and shower the grime from his body. After a long, full, and very good day, it was time to go home to a warm bed and a warmer Lisette.

Chapter 11

Early the next morning, Elizabeth Keller, a junior medical examiner (ME) in the Cook County, Illinois Coroner's Office, was hurriedly scribbling notes on a clipboard when she looked up and jumped at the sight of the Senior ME standing in the doorway to the autopsy room. Dr. Del Clayton was the Senior Medical Examiner of Cook County and Keller's superior - in every possible professional and scientific configuration.

Liz Keller hated it when her boss appeared unannounced like that. She swore the man could materialize or vaporize at will, something that disturbed and perplexed her to no end, especially after she had been eating a chorizo breakfast burrito, something that was high on Clayton's list of no-no's in the autopsy room.

"What do we have today, Ms. Keller?" asked Clayton. He took notice of the junior ME's discomfort and notably, the telltale scent of onion and cumin in the room. "Someone is field-dressing the good people of Chicago in the streets and alleyways now?" he mused.

For 25 years, Del Clayton had earned a spotless record as a forensic medical examiner through cultivation, peerless execution, and more than a little political manipulation. He was the acknowledged expert in the City of Chicago, if not the entire Upper Midwest. The fact was, every ME within 2,000 miles knew the name Del Clayton, as did those special law enforcement groups that forever made a great effort to remain invisible.

Del Clayton was a master of pathology, a pure instrument of the scientific—completely robotic in his analysis, but with an artist's touch when the situation beckoned. Clayton was the ultimate forensic weapon. The sheer exactitude of his diagnoses was legendary and he was a special asset to the police force. Every officer in Chicago PD considered Clayton the best in his field; even in private consults within their ranks he was respectfully called The Freak of Nature.

Liz Keller knew she was completely out of her league in Clayton's universe.

Keller had visibly swallowed with cold discomfort at the "field-dressing" comment a moment ago. She regained her voice with, "Good morning, Dr. Clayton!" She continued, "Uh, yes, right...we have an adult male, approximately 52 years of age, a height of 6 feet, and morbidly obese. Cause of death is obvious."

Clayton moved over to the table where a fully naked Rudy Tufton lay, white as the underside of a bloated cod.

The odor of post-mortem deterioration and expended gases had spread throughout the room, and Clayton assessed the air with his considerable olfactory powers. The mineral odors mingled and jogged his memory of the abattoirs outside Pamplona, Spain, where he had once run with the bulls back when the Earth was younger. This new smell was potently more disagreeable, though it fazed Clayton not in the least.

There was something present in this new waft, however, and he gave it notice...tincture of steel? Oil of clove, perhaps, but something synthetic stood out in the scent as well. Clayton gave the air a final sniff and turned back to Keller.

The rookie ME continued. "Other than the GI wound, there is one slight mark on the back of the head, but no blood, other marks, or ligatures. There's no sign of struggle, but there *is* a slight abrasion on the right hand, front," she rattled off the list. "Victim was found by passersby who alerted Chicago PD. They marked the body in the alley on Wells and called us," said the rookie ME with as much professionalism as she could project.

"Ms. Keller, may I remind you that nothing is obvious until we've examined the victim completely?" said the senior ME. He had seen this sort of imperfect dilettante nonsense in her before and was not pleased. "We are not 'CSI: Chicago.' We must determine any and all evidence of a cause of death," he said, not with the air of presumptive arrogance, but with the voice of practiced scientific perfection.

Clayton continued, "This is a serious matter requiring a serious approach at *all* times and, if you wish to remain in your position, I suggest you take a more calculating and professional attitude."

The senior ME lifted the clipboard from the rookie as if it were a rotted prawn. "What was the estimated time of death?" he asked.

Liz, rattled by Clayton's admonition, stammered, "Uh, I guess from around 9 to 11 last night…maybe a little later?" she offered meekly.

The Senior ME frowned. He despised those who covered their asses. He ran his department eternally by the book, without humor or guesswork. "What else have you found?" asked Clayton. "Is there any other possible evidence to consider before we proceed with final dissection?"

Keller replied, "Not exactly." She reached for a crumb of theory. "However, upon arrival, the victim's hair did appear to be...wet," she said.

Clayton pinched the bridge of his nose and sighed. "That's why your time-of-death stinks, Ms. Keller," said the senior ME dryly. "It rained last night."

At that, Liz Keller hung her head and embarrassingly reviewed her shoes. Her style of dress was as random and haphazard as her pronouncements. Under the requisite white smock of a junior ME, she wore stained beige cargo pants and an untucked black t-shirt, with her hair tied back roughly in a knot, secured with a black scrunchie.

Clayton jotted a terse note, handed her back the clipboard, and turned to leave the autopsy room. As he glided toward the door, he called over his shoulder, "Let me know when you've concluded your prelim so we can finish opening this lad up. Oh, and the next time you bring burritos or any food into the autopsy room will be your last day in this department. Get on it, Ms. Keller."

Chapter 12

Carmine Tratella picked up the tray and walked from behind the bar over to a table at the back of the room and set down two saucers with cups of strong espresso for his boss, Anthony Cribaldi. That morning, Don Anthony was having his daily consultation on the family business with his oldest friend and family consigliere, Silvio Arradondo. Each took their cup of espresso and slurped.

Carmine Tratella was a captain in the family and commanded the largest Cribaldi crew, some 150 soldiers strong. As Anthony's most trusted muscle, he wore the stripes and the requisite pistol, a cobalt 9MM, which he kept neatly secured in a shoulder holster and loaded, ready to fire at all times. Carmine was a particularly nasty and brutal man in the organization. He dispensed orders to kill with pleasure and the head Mafioso often used an old La Cosa Nostra line to describe Tratella's taste for killing: "This one has a bloody mouth,"

Today, he served cappuccino to his boss on a tray, like a new blood-recruit off the street—a task he masked with secret disdain. After he placed the saucers in front of each man, he walked back behind the bar, returning to his cup of coffee laced with a healthy dose of Sambuca Romana.

Anthony and Silvio sat in large, comfortable upholstered armchairs at a massive, round oak table far at the back of the room but facing the windows and the entrance to the club on Dearborn Street. A single, fresh red tulip stood in a Baccarat crystal stem vase placed in the middle of the table.

The Dearborn Social Club was a members-only society, and had occupied the building since 1920, just as

Prohibition had become the law of the land. The Cribaldi family had made a fortune during that volatile time by running watery beer and Canadian whiskey in and out of every speakeasy on the North Side of Chicago. They had operated successfully, and without fear, under the protection of Dean O'Banion and his horde of violent, bloodthirsty Irishmen.

Vito Cribaldi had run his business sharply, religiously making sure O'Banion received his weekly cut, adding slightly to the agreed-upon 10 percent vig, which the Irish boss discerned. O'Banion's men stopped by the Club every Friday like clockwork and got their envelope for Dean-O from Vito Cribaldi. Through this association, Vito had deftly sidestepped Johnny Torrio and later, Al Capone and that other nasty cadre of organized crime—under O'Banion's protection, the Cribaldis weren't to be touched.

After the infamous St. Valentine's Day Massacre, the Cribaldis were immune from the other families, and they entrenched their grip on the North Side, slowly gaining more and more real estate thanks to the hand grenade, the Tommy gun, and the envelope. Vito had eventually expanded his nefarious operation to include prostitution, heroin distribution, illegal gambling, and loan sharking. The one business Cribaldi stayed away from was the labor unions.

Vito's philosophy on this business move had been simple— "We make our money from what men do after work; there's no sense screwing them *at* work."

Over the decades, the family had gained increasing power by quietly policing the other families and secretly working as informants for the Chicago Police Department and the FBI by carefully surveilling and feeding information.

"Power was a carefully manufactured tool," said Vito Cribaldi many times over the years, and political power especially had given them a sharpened advantage over the other families. He was proven right, time and again.

When murder caused an otherwise good robbery or other nefarious plan to go awry, it paid to have the law on their side. Other families doled out piles of money to defense attorneys to keep their criminal asses out of prison. Vito Cribaldi never worried; if a Cribaldi associate were arrested or otherwise detained, he called the chief of police, who in turn took care of the district attorney. Occasionally, that phone call would go to the mayor and the matter was quietly resolved. Gunplay and knifings had become commonplace, for murder was a regular part of the business day in the neighborhoods throughout Chicago.

However, those days had long since passed. In the present, murders were serious business. DNA was a bigger bitch than karma, but Anthony Cribaldi knew how to avoid trouble as his father and grandfather had done. He did so by embracing technology.

Sitting in the social club that morning, Anthony Cribaldi looked over at the many framed photographs that adorned the walls of the club. They were taken throughout the decades starting in the 1920's. One memory was captured in a picture of the famed St. Valentine's Day Massacre. In the foreground could be seen a smiling Vito Cribaldi, who had been photographed looking down at the bullet-ridden corpse of Bugs Moran. Vito had good reason to smile that day.

Anthony absently twisted the signet ring on his pinky and gazed fondly at the hallowed, framed timeline. Stunning actresses of the era stood out, along with sports figures, politicians, musicians, and other members of their secret society, yet one photo always made Anthony's throat tighten: his grandmother, Luisa Cribaldi.

In her day, she had been a stunning vision of Sicilian loveliness and charm, and a doting mother to Carlo and his siblings. As a grandmother, she spoiled Anthony and the other grandchildren silly with love and lavish attention.

In this particular picture, his grandfather, the otherwise vicious Vito Cribaldi, was standing next to his new bride, Luisa, in front of the freshly christened Dearborn Social Club, an arm wrapped around her shoulder. In her arms, Luisa Cribaldi held a large, overflowing bouquet of her favorite flower—red tulips. The picture showed Vito Cribaldi planting a joyful kiss on Luisa's cheek, and her eyes shined brightly as the camera clicked; it captured a perfect moment in Cribaldi time and was Anthony's most prized possession.

Anthony swallowed deeply and turned his attention back to the table and Silvio, who now had a fresh piece of information for the family patriarch. It concerned a series of images that had been picked up by one of the many cameras situated in and around the city of Chicago, installed by Cribaldi henchmen throughout the years in such quiet, clandestine fashion that it puzzled the authorities to no end.

The Cribaldis had such cameras installed everywhere by the hundreds, each one equipped with high-tech audio. The family was plugged into the city from nearly every vantage point, and each camera beamed a clear, wireless signal back to a large bank of computers and digital recorders housed neatly in the rear card room of the Dearborn Social Club, far away from the prying eyes and clumsy reach of cops.

This particular camera, state of the art, even by CIA standards, was embedded atop a light pole looking down on the Sturehof Tavern. The camera clearly showed the street and alley adjacent to the Sturehof.

"Anthony, you should look at this," said Silvio. "That fatass inspector, who got knifed the other night, happened right in the alley next to Larson's place—the Sturehof," he said, as he slid the laptop computer over to Anthony and hit play.

The video clarity and resolution was incredible, even at night. It showed the entire murder of Rudy Tufton from beginning to end. When the man in black pulled up on the knife, essentially cutting Tufton in half, even old Anthony Cribaldi uttered a shimmer of shock.

"Jesus Christ...he cut him right open," Anthony whispered, and then waved the laptop away for Arradondo to take back.

"Anthony, you missed the best part," said Silvio, glancing at the screen.

The killer had turned around to look for witnesses and the camera got him.

"There!" exclaimed Silvio. "We got a partial shot of the guy's face. You can almost make it out," he said.

"*Marrone*," said Cribaldi, looking away from the laptop. Silvio spoke, his voice tentative. "Are you thinking what I'm thinking, Anthony?"

Cribaldi nodded. "Save that file onto a flash drive and put it in the safe. We'll give that over to the FBI boys or those *pezzonovantes* in the Justice Department when the time is right," he chuckled. He already knew Silvio would do just that. It was like money in the bank.

Anthony Cribaldi and Silvio Arradondo had used scores of video clips over the years to feed the Chicago PD or the FBI whenever they needed more political leverage, and it worked like a charm. Here, they had evidence of a stone cold killer doing his business and Anthony was 100% certain Chicago PD didn't have a clue as to the killer's identity. Due to Anthony and Silvio's ties with the FBI, CIA, and NSA, they knew the agencies had facial-recognition software of the highest technology. While unavailable to the public, it could pick a flea off a dog's ass from outer space. They weren't going to have any problem making this killer.

"There ain't been nothing in the paper about this since yesterday. Chicago PD ain't got dick. This is a good one to hang onto, boss," Silvio said with a wink.

Anthony laughed out loud, raised his cup of espresso, mixed heavily with sugar, and took it down in one huge, sucking slurp. He smacked his lips, dabbed his mouth with a napkin, and stood up. He leaned over and patted Silvio's cheek with the back of his fingers, before he made his way to the front to go outside, with Carmine Tratella leaving his Sambuca and moving ahead of his boss toward the door.

Anthony never went anywhere without some nearby protection, and today was a beautiful day for a stroll.

Money in the bank always made Anthony Cribaldi very, very happy.

Chapter 13

Jacques' pretty girlfriend, Lisette D'Argent, sat quietly alone at a table off the bar at Chez Rousseau, staring at her glass of cold Sancerre. She looked at herself in the antique mirror that adorned the bar, lost in thought. The night before last, she had awoken in the middle of a deep sleep to find the other side of the bed empty.

Jacques had not yet come home, and the clock read past midnight. Dinner service would have ended hours ago, and, even if Jacques had lingered with Remy and the staff at Chez Rousseau, enjoying a glass or two of finery and bites of leftover *Crab Roulanne*, he should have been home by now.

Hours later, when he did come home, and join her in their bed, he went immediately to sleep, without so much as even a whiff of sexual overture, just a quick kiss goodnight. Making love was a nightly enjoyment for them, occasionally bordering on a wildly athletic event.

Strange, she thought, then turned over, and dismissed it as much as she could. Ah, perhaps Jacques had been truly tired. She drifted off reluctantly to sleep.

****

Tonight, Lisette was thoughtful, meandering over her wine. Jacques' lateness and distance the night before last had remained in the back of her thoughts. Jacques startled her out of her trance with a whisper kiss on the back of her neck. Her slight shiver caught Jacques by surprise.

He said as he sat down, "Something wrong, *chérie*? You are someplace else, no?"

She reached for his hand and held it in both of hers, quickly cleansing her eyes of concern and meeting his. "Not at all," she smiled. "I was thinking of you just now. This Sancerre is good, but not superb. I thought you should know. Remember, we discussed the 2020 vintage should be much better, but I'm afraid it is not. Very flabby fruit notes and the finish is…hmmm…uninspired," she said.

Jacques smiled at this. Lisette was an honest and straightforward judge of wine and her palate had long been trained to sniff out more mediocre vintages. "Yes, I'm going to talk with the importer. He needs to observe his wines more thoroughly when he goes back to France on scouting trips," said Jacques, wondering if he should just take Lisette and himself on a long vacation through the Bordeaux region and personally make the large purchase.

He reached over and took Lisette's glass, swirled it, and held it under his nose, inhaling the fragrance before tipping a small amount into his mouth. A quick taste-check confirmed Lisette's assessment to the letter.

Remarkable, thought Jacques. Flabby, indeed. The wine laid on his tongue like a wet rag, not the fruity, flavor dance it should have been.

Chapter 14

Lisette D'Argent and Jacques Rousseau had met at a huge food and wine convention in Chicago at the massive McCormack Place complex.

Lisette had recently been promoted to an executive management position for a large family-owned agricultural concern that was expanding hugely from simple vegetables and a few herbs to now offering those and a whole new line of mushrooms and other edible fungi, including both black and prized white truffles. Their trademarked 'Endless Season' line of heirloom tomatoes was the toast of Midwest restaurants and discerning chefs like Jacques were clamoring to get their hands on the bounty.

Lisette had been with the Bailey Farms family for years, having come to America as a high school exchange student and living in the Bailey home during her externship. She had come from France to study horticulture at the University of Illinois, earning a Bachelor of Science degree in the discipline, and afterward, securing a permanent position at Bailey Farms. Her breadth of knowledge of growing and marketing edibles was supreme and fueled by a near demonic work ethic.

Jacques sought her company's booth at the convention and was conversing with a colleague of Lisette's over a huge assortment of fresh Porcini and Morel mushrooms when she noticed the strikingly handsome man.

"Tracy, be sure to show the gentleman the baby greens," said Lisette, and then to Jacques: "We have micro-potted greens you can grow right on your restaurant property using very little space!"

Jacques, who had been giving all of his attention to the very-attractive red-headed Tracy, now turned toward the person speaking.

Lisette D'Argent was a true, classic French beauty: 6' tall and slender, with a lightly athletic build and a stunning head of shiny, straight, jet-black hair set off by a pair of eyes as crisply blue as the waters of the Mediterranean. Jacques literally caught his breath for a second, for Lisette's loveliness had the power of rendering men silent in her aura.

Jacques recovered his romantic French charm and extended a warm hand. "Jacques, at your service, *mademoiselle*," he said. He then leaned in and whispered, "It is *mademoiselle*, no?"

Lisette nodded, smiled, and extended her own hand to entwine briefly with his, giving it a purposeful grip. She had learned long ago how to hold her own in the presence of any man, be it business or leisure.

"Tracy was showing me these fine mushrooms. I can tell they are of excellent quality. May I order a test batch of a few pounds? I'd like to experiment with them in my kitchen," Jacques said as he took a bite from one of the raw Morels and chewed. The texture was firm, and the aroma was pure essence of dried oak leaf, fine April air, and dense carbonate from the fertile soil. A true specimen, it was.

The smitten Tracy was about to answer when Lisette fully inserted herself into the discussion, taking Jacques gently by the arm in a close-the-deal move and smiling cheerily at Tracy as she maneuvered the man over to a table to sign sales paperwork.

Jacques was enjoying the attention of these two vibrantly attractive women and let Lisette direct him at will.

He thanked Tracy with a brief kiss of her hand as he was led away, and the woman's face blossomed crimson at the action.

As Jacques signed off on the purchase order, he handed the pen back to Lisette and held onto it as their fingers remained touching. He looked at her for a few seconds and then smiled at her, announcing happily, "I'm starving! Let's go to my restaurant and I'll cook for you."

Lisette began to protest, but Jacques paused her with a finger in the air. "Please," he begged. "I haven't cooked a meal for two for myself and a guest for a long time. It would give me the greatest pleasure to make you something memorable. And we all must eat, yes, Lisette?" he asked genuinely.

As with all women, Lisette was not immune to Jacques' charm, his gentle directness, and his devastatingly handsome face. "Yes, we must all eat, Jacques…and please call me Lis," she said.

"Lis, with an 's' or Liz with a 'z?'" Jacques asked.

"Spelled with 's,' but pronounced with a 'z,'" she said smiling. "Lizzzzzz….." she purred. She took his arm and told Tracy she was escorting Jacques to his restaurant for further negotiation. As they walked off the convention floor and out of the building onto Lake Shore Drive, Lisette asked her guide, "Where is your restaurant, Jacques?"

Jacques turned and pointed his finger north. "The great French lady," he said proudly.

Lisette registered real surprise. "Chez Rousseau? You work there!" she exclaimed. "Do you know how long I have tried to get a reservation? Your owners really should allow more walk-up service for the neighborhood!" she teased. "I hear your fish dishes are sublime. What is the one...*Poisson Avril*? I'm so jealous! But how can you cook for me when you have to work in a few hours?" she asked.

Jacques turned to her and smiled wickedly. "But you see, I can do whatever I want; I own it!" he said winningly.

Lisette's mouth dropped open. "You're Jacques *ROUSSEAU*?" she whispered. Her eyes sparkled.

Jacques loved hearing her say his name like that.

Chapter 15

Lisette D'Argent—Lis—grew up in France, just as Jacques Rousseau had, though their hometowns were nowhere near the other. She was born in Lyon to Simon and Julia D'Argent, he a senior partner in a law firm and she a homemaker and cook extraordinaire.

Julia D'Argent was not only an excellent cook, but she was an expert gardener as well. Her passion was growing a symphony of herbs and vegetables in a simple, but widely squared and well-planned, garden in her backyard. Julia also rejoiced in Lyon's vast string of markets, which included daily seafood shipments from nearby ports. Her *Sole Meuniere* was a dish of inspiration, a slight departure from the classic French standard; she added a spritz of Prosecco to the abundance of butter, parsley, and lemon.

The seasons of the year were a wonder to Julia, for she grew and harvested an astounding variety of greens along with radishes, carrots, potatoes, haricot verts, Swiss chard, tomatoes, a wild array of other vegetables, and herbs. She cooked superbly, with measured confidence, and with her husband's salary as partner in the 100-year-old law firm of Cournoyer, D'Argent and Germaine, the D'Argents entertained richly but smartly.

Dinner parties of 16 were not uncommon in their fine home, replete with Julia's cuisine, prepared artfully and accompanied by the finest French vintages Simon could collect, and collect he did, procuring the very best offerings of Rothschild, Margaux, Le Coin Perdu, Moet & Chandon, and anything Grand Cru, as long as it was at the right price. Simon was a great lover and student of wine and a generous host with his discoveries.

Lisette would set herself for hours at the top of the long staircase overlooking the grand foyer and listen, mesmerized, to the dinner discussions and the loud, pleasing exclamations uttered forth by her mother and father's guests as they were treated to marvelous, succulent, and memorable course after course after course.

She knew as a young child what joy the dining experience could bring to the typical day. Food was the great communicator, the conduit of souls which brought people together, lowering their walls in a single meal.

Lisette learned early on about the beauty that each day could bring through a celebration in food. Even something so elemental as an afternoon snack prepared by her mother—a slice of chewy baguette topped with cheesy French butter, thinly sliced radishes, and a sprinkle of chive and freshly ground Malabar pepper—evoked pure wonderment in little Lisette. She was a very willing and adventurous eater.

During her senior year in high school, Lisette announced to her parents that she was going to America, to Illinois, as an exchange student with a local family. After graduation, she would stay on in America and attend the University of Illinois to study horticulture. The family in America with whom she was corresponding was engaged in a large agriculture concern—Bailey Farms was the name—and Lisette had done exhaustive and impressive due diligence in her research. This, she told her parents, was what she wanted to do with her life: work with plants and dirt and weather, growing the food people would eat and enjoy each day. Perhaps she would make the next great American wine, or create a new hybrid of basil? Time would tell.

While it pleased and warmed Simon and Julia that their willful daughter was so organized in her dream plans, they nevertheless expressed to each other behind the closed bedroom door, that if their beloved child ever went to America there was a fair chance she would never come back. More than a few tears were shed at this thought.

Such was the bittersweet reality of parents: at some point, their child, raised with love and tender care and nurtured dreams, eventually leaves, seeking their own path, leaving the parents behind with proud, yet quietly breaking, hearts. The D'Argents' had indeed given their daughter a firm footing as she started down her own road.

Chapter 16

The first meal Jacques ever prepared for Lisette the day they met was a simple *Cod au Calvados*. It was his beloved mother's recipe of a whole Cod, sliced on the sides and stuffed with shallot and garlic, seasoned heavily, seared in a cast iron pan with butter and thyme, and finished in a scorching hot oven, the browned butter basted over it again and again to give it a marvelously crispy skin.

Out of the oven, it was adorned with a sauce fortified with lobster stock and Calvados, finished with wads of thick French butter, and served on a huge oval platter. Lisette's first bite was a gift of crunch and a silky texture in the flesh; the depths of the salty ocean reverberated on her palate.

It was a breathtaking presentation, served with a large bowl of haricot verts, a French variety of the American green bean; these too were laced with cheesy French butter, green salt, and freshly cracked pepper. Fine dining, prepared simply with quality ingredients, could be a thing of rare beauty.

This Jacques Rousseau was certainly talented, she thought. It was an understatement, and Lisette would soon find out his true depths as a chef.

Lisette had not eaten anything so rich and glorious as the *Cod au Calvados* since she was a child. It conjured again her mother's own wondrous cooking and rewarmed crystal memories, certainly endearing her to Jacques before she even knew where her heart was taking her.

Jacques was forceful and dynamic, yet gentle in all the right places. He could be funny one minute and then his eyes would open wide with a wild passion whenever he spoke of preparing *Oysters a la Brocende*. In his quieter moments, though, he seemed in animated suspension, as if something remained cloaked. He was a most versatile and interesting man and, with his jet-black hair and strong jawline, a very good-looking one, Lisette thought, as she adjusted herself in her chair.

It was no surprise to her when Jacques called the next day. She answered on the third ring, not wanting to sound too anxious. Very French.

"May I cook for you again?" he asked with a confident voice. He then turned playful as he said, "I have something new I wish to try with some Morel mushrooms I found in a trash can in a dark alley."

Lisette feigned insult and gasped, "Are you talking about MY Morel mushrooms from Bailey Farms?" She enjoyed the little jab from Jacques.

"Oh, I'm not sure where they came from, but I am sure I can make something out of it," Jacques said alluringly. "In fact, I could put...how they say here in America...'I could put cheese on a shoe and make it taste good.'"

At this, Lis burst out laughing, "Oh, Monsieur Jacques! You certainly know how to entice!" she teased. She liked saying his name like that. It rolled off her tongue. *Monsieur Jacques*. Mmm.
"What time would you like me, and where?" asked Lisette.

"Here. At the Chez. Seven o'clock," said Jacques.

"It's a date, then," said Lisette. "I'll be there in a very nice dress and on my best behavior. See you then," she said and hung up.

Jacques smiled. He liked this woman more than he cared to admit.

****

For her second dinner, she was seated at Chez Rousseau at the special table next to the kitchen. Remy and Jaime had taken command of the kitchen for the night, leaving Jacques to focus on the dinner menu for his special guest. He would join them on the line later.

Jacques prepared Lisette's first course of the Morel mushrooms by slicing them in half and stuffing them with a mixture of shredded blue crab, sautéed minced radish strips, a baby dab of pureed sweet potato, and two secret herbs. He capped the mixture with the other Morel half, secured and closed them with a scallion strip, dipped them in egg wash, and then potato starch and shallow-fried them in a thin layer of rich beef fat.

He completed the dish by constructing a final garnish of dried Portobello mushrooms (delivered by courier that morning from Bailey Farms) mixed with a whisper of spicy ancho chile and white pepper, pulverized in a spice grinder, and dusted atop the three stuffed Morel halves, which rested between scattered dots of a warm Pouilly-Fussé wine, butter, chervil, and cream reduction. It was spice and heat, paired with sweetness, salt, and a creamy umami-ness—a remarkable execution.

Lisette's first bite of the mushrooms was as tantalizing as a first kiss. She was completely overwhelmed by the imagination behind this reverential treatment of her mushrooms.

Jacques kept his foot on the gas and continued the ride with a main course of *Venison Tenderloin a la' Vinaigrettzia*, seared for 45 seconds on each side and served ultra-rare, sliced against the grain, and fanned on a bed of mesclun and dandelion greens mixed with several ribbons of fresh mint. He dressed the greens in roasted walnut oil, maple essence, and lemon juice, then generously seasoned them with Himalayan grey salt and freshly ground peppercorns.

Lisette's palette couldn't keep up the pace, this bombardment of flavor and sensation Jacques was unleashing upon her. The natural taste in the venison was accentuated by the rare cooking, releasing the flavor of acorns and wild vegetation the deer fed upon.

Concluding the rapturous symphony was a coda in the form of a simple, classic dessert— a baked, perfectly shaped Honeycrisp apple, heavy with Ceylon cinnamon, adorned in a caramelized-sugar mixture, kissed with a friendly splash of Grand Marnier, and topped with crème fraiche. It was like having a light, soft, caramel apple and orange-scented blanket wrapped around her at bedtime after a long, blissful day.

She had never had a meal captivate her so fully in her entire life, although those words should never be revealed to her mother. Lis was falling in love with each successive course.

Jacques was indeed a true romantic in the kitchen, knowing how to coax and lead the food and, equally vital, knowing when to let the food lead; it was as fresh as new love, and it all went straight to Lisette's heart. In all the excitement, she found she could trust Jacques completely wherever he took her during this journey through the senses. He was a master at the wheel of this ship; he didn't miss a single detail. An extra herb or seasoning would have been disaster.

She sipped a strong Robusta coffee with Amaretto liqueur at the end of the meal and waited for Jacques while he concluded service for the other fortuned Chez Rousseau diners. She had never heard such a hum in a dining room, such anticipation and enjoyment! It was like listening to the ocean: the waters would be quiet, and then a wave of anticipation would gather itself and build, and, as bite after bite was absorbed, the wave would grow and peak before finally exhausting itself on the sandy shoreline in full capitulation. Chez Rousseau had become the waters of Marseilles herself.

Jacques presented himself to her shortly after dinner service concluded, immaculate in his street clothes after changing out of his dirty-from-battle chef's whites and taking a quick shower. They shared a single glass of Pernod at the end of the bar, their heads hovering closely to one another, and Jacques finally walked her outside to her car, as she took his arm in hers on the sidewalk.

There on the street, under the wide, red Chez Rousseau awning, as the Chicago skyline bid *adieu* with one last glimmer from the sunset, a light breeze crescendoed and they turned to each other to share a tender, succulent first kiss. They embraced deeply.

She longed to show Jacques her gratitude, having been served the meal of her lifetime, and one kiss soon became two and then more. The kisses were a rapturous encore and the perfect finale to the night, but she was careful to set down her sensual fork at the right moment and quell her appetite. Jacques felt it too. More would be too much. But something was definitely happening. Something was building. Something *extraordinary*.

Love always begins that way—as a tiny, needful kernel. If given earnest care, good nourishment, and waters of positivity, the kernel's growth can be fruitful and endless through the seasons. So it was with Lisette and Jacques on this fine, rare evening.

Lisette did not yet know Jacques' history, nor that he was branching out onto new *terroir*, taking careful steps with a heart that had been broken and then repaired and then nearly destroyed outright. Though his childhood had been anything but idyllic, in an ideal world, even love should be able to repair or revive certain things. With Jacques, perhaps it could.

Tonight, love had come back into his life and it felt wondrous, like putting on brand new clothes. Lisette had done that for him.

Chapter 17

A few short months later, Jacques and Lisette were returning from a walk, something they loved to do in the early morning hours after making love and before Lisette went off to work at her spacious Bailey Farms office in Lincoln Park Square. More often than not, she slept at Jacques' place, a handsome turn-of-the-century walkup house off Madison in Oak Park, just a quick 15-minute drive from downtown and the Chez. Jacques jumped in the shower following their walk, but not before he placed an envelope with Lisette's name on the dining room table.

He was a minute or two into showering when the shower curtain suddenly parted and he saw Lisette standing there with the unopened envelope in her hand. Jacques stood, naked, while Lisette eyed him cautiously. She was not accustomed to this thing called trepidation and her face showed it.

"What is this, Jacques?" she said quietly.

Her reaction was the exact opposite of what Jacques wanted. "Lis, wait," he said quickly. "It's good news...I hope?" he offered with a reassuring smile and a shrug of his shoulders.

Lisette opened the envelope, eyeing Jacques once, and read his note. She touched her hand to her throat and then to her eyes, shielding them. Jacques couldn't tell if she was happy, sad, pissed off...nothing. And then, Lisette emitted a tiny squeak as her body began softly shaking. She was crying the happiest of tears. It *was* good news.

"You like it, then, yes?" grinned Jacques proudly, obviously pleased with her reaction. He leaned down and offered his face to her and she gazed into his eyes with pure adoration, smiling as she raised her face to his. She softly thanked him with her lips, again and again and again.

Within the crafted and embossed envelope laid cream-colored linen stationery. The words adorning it were written in Jacques' flowing hand.

My Darling,

I invite you to join me here in Oak Park. I want us to live together…and have wanted so since we first met. It will not be my place. It will not be your place. It will be <u>our</u> place. Come live with me and be my love, and we will all the pleasures prove. I want nothing but you…for the rest of my life. I love you, Lisette Christine D'Argent.

Yours,

Jacques

A key was included next to the envelope. Lisette must have overlooked the tiny, square, wrapped box behind the centerpiece on the kitchen table. She eventually found it and they, the *boudoir*.

Chapter 18

Jacques sat at one of the dozen tables outside the corner coffee shop, Beans/Beans, with Remy and Lisette. It was their Sunday ritual, they enjoyed superb coffee, the finest patisseries, and sparkling good conversation. Remy often joined them. It was a good chance to play catch-up with their personal lives, and it allowed them to leave Chez business alone for a day to enjoy camaraderie.

Both Remy and Lisette had become fast friends once she and Jacques had begun seeing each other and, strangely, it soon became obvious that food was not their primary bond. They were both sports nuts.

"If Lankinen doesn't make that save on Ovechkin and our winger doesn't flick that beautiful pass at the other end of the ice for the score, the game's over!" said Lisette to Remy. "It was great transition hockey!" she exclaimed.

Jacques laughed at Remy because Lisette knew her hockey, and Remy hated seeing his Washington Capitals lose on Chicago ice. The sous chef may have been born and raised in the warmer climes of the bayou, but, once he migrated to a hockey-mad town like Chicago, he had taken to hockey like a fish to water,

In her first year in America, as a high school senior, Lisette had taken a strong liking to American ice hockey, a faster, more physical style of play than European. Thanks to the Bailey family, and especially their eldest son Michael, who was Lisette's age and had been a die-hard Chicago Blackhawks fan ever since he was in diapers, Lisette was introduced to the popular sport.

The entire Bailey clan would load themselves up in a huge custom van that seated all 10 of them comfortably and make road trips several times a year to downtown Chicago to see the Chicago Black Hawks' games at the United Center. Of course, they brought their new French charge Lisette along with them. Hockey wasn't just a sport—it was a lifestyle.

At first, Lisette didn't understand the game, particularly the violent brutality. She had thought the fighting men should be arrested after one particularly disturbing display, even more shocking to her was seeing the stark contrast of red blood on white ice. But through careful, patient instruction from Michael Bailey, she grew to appreciate the intricacies and strategies of the battle on the ice; it was then that Lisette saw how sports could often be like fine ballet. Both displayed strength and grace, mixing the forces to create pageantry. It was a wonderful combination, just like good red Zinfandel wine and deep dish Chicago-style pizza. This was when Lisette began to love America and when her roots began to grow.

"Okay, okay," said Remy. "Here's your $20. But I'm still betting against Chicago when the Bruins come to town," he said, handing the money to Lisette.

Jacques enjoyed the repartee, taking advantage of the back-and-forth between Lisette and Remy to wolf huge bites out of a deep-fried apple fritter, a Beans/Beans specialty, and gulp his Peaberry coffee. It was a beautiful Sunday morning, and the sidewalk café was full of people enjoying another picture-perfect day.

Lisette took a sip of her double-espresso and changed the subject. "So, did you ever have dealings with that food inspector, the one that was killed over on Wells?" she asked.

Jacques and Remy exchanged a fast glance and shook their heads. The police had released an updated story in the paper earlier in the week, although the inspector had been murdered some time before that.

"No, he covered a different sector," said Jacques.

Remy added, "We've always had others inspect us at the Chez, but not him." He shrugged, "He was a big prick, from everything I've heard. A real mean fucker."

"On the take and everything," Jacques offered. "Word is he got what he deserved."

Lisette gave Jacques a glance, "Well, I'm sure he was no pleasant man, but no one deserves to die like that, love, don't you agree?"

"You don't know the stories about him," said Jacques. "He terrorized restaurants for decades. He took piles of extortion money from them and, one time, he tried to shut down a place during dinner service, took a big bribe, and spat in the owner's face. And he's gotten away with abuses like that for years," Jacques finished, "but no more, it seems."

"Jacques," Lisette said quietly. "The man was *eviscerated*."

"Okay, okay…I'm trying to eat, Lis. Can we drop this?" asked Jacques. "*Pas plus s'il vous plait*. No more, please," he said.

Remy switched the conversation with his bent brand of humor. "Hey, speaking of gutting people…what should we do with that asshole, Baldwin?" he asked. "I'm telling you, we should '86' him from the restaurant, permanently," he added. "I mean, what the hell was that all about? I checked the fish Rodrigo had brought back. It was perfect."

"I'm glad you brought that up," said Jacques, as he was now officially fed up with Richard Baldwin's shenanigans. "I think we might need to send up a rescue flare to Don Cribaldi the next time Baldwin pulls anymore nonsense," he said.

This brought silence to the table. Anything having to do with the Mafia boss of Chicago was to be taken seriously. A single phone call of that sort usually carried a menacing weight. It meant someone was going to get the crap beaten out of them—or worse—depending on the Don's mood and if his button men followed orders properly.

"Hold on there a minute," said Remy. "Just because Anthony Cribaldi likes our prawns and risotto doesn't mean you're connected. You're starting to sound like Baldwin himself."

"The hell I am," Jacques defended. "The Cribaldis detest Baldwin going around Chicago trying to pass himself off as a connected guy. He's lucky he hasn't wound up in the Chicago River in cement shoes," he said jokingly. "All the attorneys we feed at the Chez talk about him and you've heard the same stories as me."

"Hey, boss, I can tell when someone's pissing on my boots and telling me it's a rainstorm," said Remy. "Lawyers gossiping while drinking is the second oldest profession," he chuckled.

Lisette responded with her father's philosophy: "'A lawyer is incapable of telling the truth, especially when drunk.' Jacques, who cares if he sends the food back? It's only because you won't go into business with him," she said.

"Yes, *chérie*, but that's the point," said Jacques. "Why should I have to explain at all why I will or won't do business with someone, especially the likes of Baldwin? I don't trust him at all, and he's not done yet. I can feel it."

Lisette thought about this carefully and said, "In the business world, Jacques, my darling, that is what is known as a hostile takeover. Richard Baldwin likes your business model so much that he wants in on it and he'll use whatever means at his disposal to get what he wants—right or wrong. If anything, take it as a compliment. You've created something of real value," she said.

Jacques said nothing.

Remy interjected. "I hear what you're saying Lis, but let's set all the Wall Street and Wharton School lectures aside. We don't want to do business because he's not a good person. I won't even go into the rumors swirling around him." "What rumors?" asked Lisette.

"You don't want to know," said Remy. When Lisette started to protest, Remy continued, "Lisette, I'm serious. You really don't want to know. It's bad."

"I'm a big girl, Remy," she said, glaring. "I can handle it."

Jacques stepped in. "You do *not* want to hear this," he insisted, hoping she'd back down.

But Lisette simply sat back and crossed her arms. "Let's hear it," she said.

Remy shared a glance with Jacques, who gave a subtle nod of his head. He exhaled before he spoke, saddened by what he was about to admit. "Almost two years ago, two girls were found in a shallow ditch, dead. They had both been raped repeatedly and then strangled," Remy paused, struggling to finish. "Lisette...these were *girls*. One was 14, the other only 12," he said. "Now do you believe us?" Lisette's face registered the gruesomeness and she shifted in her chair uncomfortably. Her throat caught for a second and she asked, "What does this have to do with Mr. Baldwin?"

"The girls were buried on Baldwin property. It's all fenced off and highly secure," said Remy. "There are video monitors installed outside...outside! No one goes there unless they're looking for trouble. Or hiding it," he said with disgust.

"Well, the surveillance footage would have captured people on the property, wouldn't it?" asked Lisette, her voice wavering with emotion. "Didn't the police investigate this? I mean, how could they not? What a horrible thing to do…"

Jacques finished the story. "Baldwin told the police his computer system had been hacked. The footage was stolen or compromised and presumed deleted," he said, shaking his head and looking away from the table.

"Oh, for Christ's sake!" said Lisette, coming out of her morne. "And they believed him?"

Remy said, "Well, if they hadn't, Baldwin's ass would be in jail now. Instead, he keeps pressuring your boy and me by sending perfect Dover sole back to the kitchen and making insane business offers. Damn I hate that guy."

"Jacques? Where are you, love?" asked Lisette. "You're scowling. Are you thinking about Richard Baldwin?"

"No…I was thinking of someone that reminded me of Richard Baldwin," said Jacques, his voice trailing off like a passenger train moving away in the distance.

Chapter 19

The seaside port at Marseilles, France was where Jacques Rousseau and Pierre Letreuce had met many years ago. Pierre used to scour the market early, each and every morning, for his restaurant's daily needs.

Jacques had secured himself a job at the port, getting up before the crack of dawn each day to help unload the navy of boats that came in with the morning's catch. Every day was a fresh surprise in the glory of the ocean: One hour, he might be unloading a fisherman's catch of sole. The next, it was wire-mesh sacks laden with briny, succulent oysters or clams. Squid and octopus, fat monkfish, spiny lobsters and langoustines, sturdy mackerel, striped sea bass, and light, fragrant sardines. Jacques was right smack in the middle of the freshest sea treasures most of mankind would never know.

He was 11 when he got his first job at the port. His family needed the money.

Jacques was a quiet lad. Everyone warmly called him *Tati*, and he was quickly accepted by the local fishing community. Jacques worked hard and talked very little for a boy his age, which was unusual, yet prized; he also did not engage in laziness or hijinks. He was remarkably wise for his 11 years—why carry two sacks of 40-lb oysters when one can throw them in a plastic tub and haul two tubs with a hand truck instead? Jacques wasted no muscle or movement.

Pierre observed the stringent work ethic in young Rousseau and took note of it during one of his visits to the market.

Letreuce personally made the daily trip to the seashore market to pick carefully for his restaurant what he had conjured in his mind the day before. Creating these extravagant menus required deep pondering; he considered all the possible taste and texture combinations and did so while simultaneously making mind-love to a buttery, elegant glass of '87 Montrachet paired with a chive-laden *chevre en croute*.

Other times, he could be found sucking down a dozen oysters he had hand-shucked at a prep table, a sweating bottle of Perrier-Jouet's stunning Belle Epoque champagne nearby. The salty brine of the oysters and the shivery mouthfuls of crisp, pear-like champagne made a superb marriage of taste and éclat.

This was how Pierre Letreuce planned his menus. ®He needed a muse—a spark of culinary inspiration in the form of food and liquid refreshment—while he crafted his clientele's next daily bread. Eating and drinking triggered those multiple flavor and texture pairings inside his mouth, firing his labyrinthine imagination like nothing else could. A bite of food or a sip of wine was all it took and his mind became a food super-collider.

This daily exercise by Letreuce gave rise to new combinations of taste. Pierre was a brave chef—after all, who else would put strawberry, orange, and bay froth on a huge, single salt-encrusted sea scallop? For loyal Letreuce customers, it was yet another revelation from Pierre, and, consequently, they came to expect this ongoing, inspired, hand-of-God genius from the chef, which was why it was getting harder and harder—and more expensive—to dine at Letreuce.

Pierre knew his food cost to the bare franc, as all good chefs must. Better, he knew the power of perception-to-value and how to parlay that into streams of money. Pierre was a formidable businessman. It was as if Madame Eugenie Brazier and Warren Buffet had been brought together to fuse their DNA and create a singular masterpiece of the culinary milieu—this was Pierre Letreuce, and it defined his powerhouse reputation throughout all of France.

Jacques Rousseau worshipped Pierre. There was no other word for it. Pierre was the only man he had ever trusted, and he loved him unreservedly. It was his dream to one day stand as a recognized cook in that sacred kitchen in Marseille, France, cooking alongside and replicating the dishes of his mentor.

He would make it eventually, yes, but it would come at a great sacrifice.

Chapter 20

Young Jacques had just finished another long day's work, which had started in the small hours of the Marseilles seaside morning. By 10:00 a.m. he had offloaded seven boats' worth of golden bounty from the ocean and then delivered three huge sacks of oysters to the Letreuce kitchen.

Not too long ago, Pierre had taken young Jacques under his wing and began teaching him the ways of the professional kitchen. Daily, he would demonstrate the techniques needed to properly dress and prepare the myriad seafood offerings brought in each day at the port. Jacques was small, but soon his hands and arms gained added muscle and dexterity from scaling fish, shucking oysters, hauling heavy crates, and using razor sharp boning knives.

The great chef was pleased to see Jacques' progress; he was a remarkably quick study.

Pierre walked by the steel table where Jacques had just finished shucking the last of the oysters and inspected his work. The chef was amply satisfied with his young pupil, who left each new shucked oyster quivering inside a clean half-shell. Perfectly done.

"You have done well, Tati!" said Letreuce proudly. "Tomorrow, I show you how we take the cheeks from the burbot—it is easy enough to do, but easier to ruin if you are not careful," he said. "I have every faith you will do well!"

With that, Pierre turned and loudly announced to the others in the kitchen, "Everyone! Tonight, we will be serving Jacques' oysters!"

There were a few shouts of hurrah and even mild applause and Jacques smiled awkwardly at first, his face beet red, but then he beamed brightly as Pierre nodded and laughed.

Pierre sensed something in the young boy, a talent beyond his solid work ethic, because he could see ahead of the game while it was in progress. These were Jacques' first rites of passage in the kitchen, and he had done amazingly well. Pierre had seen this potential in apprentices before, but not from one only 11 years old. Jacques Rousseau had a true gift and Pierre recognized it. It had also earned him tribute from the others. A professional kitchen is a reputational battleground and Jacques was establishing firm footholds at a very tender age.

Jacques was tired but energized by Pierre's recognition. He had never been given credit before…or applause. What in the world was that? The chef ruffled his hair affectionately and sent him on his way with a warm baguette filled with smoky ham and soft Brie de Meaux. The boy's heart sang as he pedaled his bike toward home, a burlap sack strapped to the back of his bike rack and containing a fat, whole golden Bream from the market.

Bream is a fish comparable to the American bluegill, though it is a much larger version. For tonight's dinner, Jacques' mother would sauté the whole fish in a cast-iron pan with a layer of angel-slivered shallots spread across the skin. Garlic, tomatoes, and fresh sprigs of thyme were added to the pan, and she would finish it in a hot oven before drizzling it with virgin olive oil. Jacques knew the clean scent of the ocean and the aromatics would fill the

Rousseau home from that evening well into the following day.

Jacques rode home, bicycling one-handed while he wolfed down large bites of the delicious baguette. The brie was so good, creamy and fantastic, blending with the ham and crusty bread. It filled him quickly. Jacques was happy, a rarity in his life. Today was good and it made it easier to smile. The action felt nice on his face.

He hummed a little as he pedaled and had scarcely turned the corner on his street when he heard the shouts echoing from his house. His father's voice barreling out into the street steeled him immediately, as it always did.

"I saw you! I saw you with my own eyes!" Gilles Rousseau screamed at Clarice Rousseau. "Oh, Henri is so funny, yes? Henri is so nice, eh?" It was barely past noon, but Gilles Rousseau was already quite drunk.

Clarice Rousseau, Jacques' soft-spoken, kindly mother pleaded with her husband. "No, Gilles!" she said. "I was only talking to Henri! Talking! And with the others, too! You are my husband, my *amour*! I would never be unfaithful!" she finished with growing alarm.

She was a petite woman. Her best feature, other than her kind demeanor and radiant smile, was a light and glimmering array of sienna hair that draped around her shoulders, bordering soft face in a pleasing corona.

"You were standing close to him outside the patisserie and smiling! Don't deny it! You are a WHORE!" Gilles bellowed.

This accusation was common in the Rousseau household. So common, in fact, that Jacques could only wait for what would come next—a single, savage slap.

Jacques knew the routine well and the concluding, sick, wet packing sound his father's hand made when it struck his mother's face was nothing surprising.

Gilles Rousseau was a burly man with strong, stout arms. He was a stone mason, with gnarled hands to prove it, but he could never keep regular work. A foul attitude and his devotion to drink ensured his scattered employment. As much as Jacques wished, he was too small at 11 to protect his mother or himself. His father had a mean heart that became even meaner when he drank; it was a never-ending tale of constant abuse in the Rousseau home.

Jacques approached the front door. The bag of bream hung heavy on his shoulder. Without realizing, he had squished in his hand the baguette he had been eating on the way home from the restaurant, a tense reaction to his father's voice. The gravelly, penetrating baritone had cut through him like a knife in softened butter.

Jacques opened the door and stepped into the house, setting his rumpled sandwich on the sideboard. His father stood in the doorway to the kitchen, a large, weathered glass containing a cheap *vin rouge* in his hand. Lately, he was more irritated with his son, jealous of Jacques' happiness after a day's work. It was a stark reminder that he himself had not worked that day, or even that entire month.

"What are you looking at?" barked the elder Rousseau. "What's in the sack?"

Jacques stared at the floor and answered quietly, "It's a bream, Papa, a good one, from Monsieur Rolet. It is still fresh," said Jacques. He asked timidly, "Where is maman, papa?"

Gilles Rousseau swallowed from the glass and said nothing, but Jacques could hear sniffling sounds behind the closed door of his parents' bedroom down the hallway.

He called out to her from across the front room. "Maman, I am home!" He started toward the kitchen and tried to slide past his father in the doorway, but Gilles put out a hand and blocked him. He looked down at the boy with eyes that burned with hot disgust; he could not hold regular work and he had no money. Yet here was his hardworking son, standing before him, having brought home dinner.

While it was possible that Clarice Rousseau still loved Gilles (and she did), Gilles could neither feel nor express the emotion. Life to him was a series of transactions. He could not give; he could only take what he felt was owed to him.

Inside Gilles Rousseau's heart lay a vast, gaping, black hole. He did not think his drinking and violence mattered, though a good husband and father certainly would have. That was, perhaps, Gilles Rousseau's greatest sin—he passed misery onto others without a second thought. Introspection was a stranger to the elder Rousseau, and he often used the phrase "if-only." It fueled the self-loathing deep within.

"Please, Papa…I need to clean the fish before it goes bad," Jacques spoke softly.

"Then let it go bad. This is my house. You will move when I tell you to move," Gilles slurred in a cool, dead voice. "Leave the bag and go down to Montreaux's and get me a fresh bottle. This one is finished."

"But Papa, Monsieur Montreaux won't let you have any more credit," said Jacques earnestly.

Gilles swung out his left hand and caught the boy hard on the side of his face, roaring at Jacques, "Then pay him with what you have in your pocket, *bâtard*!"

The blow sent him sprawling to the floor along with the sack containing the bream. His vision was dizzy as he looked up to see his father towering over him. It always hurt Jacques' heart when his father hit him—the emotional pain was far deeper than any physical wound—but it hurt more to be called a bastard, even though Jacques was indeed Gilles' biological child.

This was often how the nights went—Jacques having to buy his father's wine with his hard-earned money. But having to go through the emotional and physical battering, along with seeing his poor mother abused in the same way, burned a scar on Jacques' psyche that never fully healed. He was forced to know true injustice at far too tender an age and he hated it like nothing else in the world.

Jacques Rousseau was a kind, dutiful boy, always eager to help others. Why his father chose to be so brutal created a crack in the boy's perceptions. Jacques felt his face with his hand as he looked up at his father, then got his feet under him and stood up and walked out the door to the wine shoppe. The bag of bream lay, wet and stiffening, on the floor.

****

As he walked down the street, Jacques passed three men sitting, smoking, and conversing at a table outside Café Athene. They were all drinking glasses of chilled Chablis along with several fist-size hunks of dense Beaufort cheese, a variety from the Gruyere family, all the while deep in discussion about who caused the car accident near the square two days earlier. The afternoon sun was blazing in the center of town, which was now filled with luncheoning diners.

One of the men, Andre Gaston, noticed Jacques as he passed by. Andre was one of Pierre Letreuce's trusted cooks—a sturdy *commis* of considerable talent and generous spirit. Andre called out to Jacques with a buoyant smile on his voice. "*Bonjour*, Tati! Where are you going this beautiful afternoon?" he asked.

"To Montreaux's," said Jacques quietly, without turning his head. The welt on the side of his face was growing and he did not want the men to see his humiliation. He kept walking.

"Eh! Tati! Come here!" called Andre. Jacques always stopped and visited when they were enjoying their wine, cheese, dominoes, and talk. He loved the animated banter of the big men, all good friends, so he often stayed long with them, and they enjoyed his quiet company. Andre rose from the table and caught up to the boy a few steps ahead.

Jacques stopped but did not look at him, his humiliation growing.

Andre reached over and gently took Jacques' chin in his calloused hand and turned his head to see. The red welt on his cheek was clearly visible and the eyelid had begun to turn black from the blow his father had dealt. Andre had seen this before. "Tati, where did you get this?" he asked.

Jacques did not answer.

"Did your papa do this, Jacques?" Andre asked softly.

"No, Andre," said Jacques, quickly. He sensed why Andre was asking. "I fell off my bike. I was carrying too many sacks of oysters for Monsieur Letreuce," he said. "Ah," said Andre. "And Monsieur Letreuce did not give you ice for it when you were at the restaurant?" he tisked. "I will have to speak to him about that—Monsieur is usually very good about tending to injuries."

"No, Andre! Please don't say anything to Pierre!" he pleaded. "It was my fault for falling with my bike!"

The big commis moved his hand from Jacques' chin to his shoulder and gave him a few reassuring pats. He was gentle with the boy despite his anger growing from within. No grown man should ever raise his hand to a boy, especially a soul as kind as Jacques. But Andre did not voice these thoughts. He only spread his hands to the child as a sign of peace and spoke in a low tone so only the two of them could hear.

"Do not worry, *mon ami*," said Andre. "I will say nothing to Pierre. It will be our secret." Then he took a knee in front of Jacques so their eyes were dead level with each other. "But Jacques?" he asked, as he looked squarely and seriously into the boy's eyes.

Jacques raised his head and met Andre's gaze, his lower lip quivering as a single tear moved down his soft cheek.

"The next time I see your face like this, I am going to talk to your papa. It will be a very short conversation. I will bring Monsieur Letreuce with me. He would not enjoy seeing his friend like this, no?" he said.

Jacques nodded but did not reply.

With that, Andre stood up and gave Jacques his handkerchief, four francs from his own pocket, and another few pats on the back before sending him on his way to Montreaux's.

As he returned to the table, Andre's friends quieted — noticing his hands were red from clenching.

"Gilles hit him again, didn't he?" one of the men said.

Andre stood at the table, reached for his glass, and took the last sip of his wine before muttering, "It is not my secret to tell."

The third man, Oscar Merieure, a retired *gendarme*, said flatly, with a determined grimace, "One day, someone will teach that damn Gilles."

Andre said nothing. He gave his share of franc notes for the wine and cheese to the men at the table, shook hands with each of them, and moved off quickly down the street, heading back to Letreuce.

****

Andre Gaston was very angry with Gilles Rousseau. His mind burned at the image of the bruised face, and he discovered he was clenching his fists again as he walked. Andre had once killed a man in defense of his family. That man was his father.

Bernard Gaston was a violent man who often beat Andre's mother and sisters. One night, very drunk, he tied Andre to the corner leg of the kitchen stove and, using the fire poker, beat Andre's mother to death in front of Andre before he fled the town and disappeared. Andre and his sisters had gone to live with their mother's brother after her death, and that was supposed to be the end of that.

A year later, Bernard Gaston was found dead in a small flat in Montmartre. He had died from what the police called suspicious injuries, particularly a blow to the back of the head the coroner had claimed was fatal. This would normally be *de rigeur* in a murder investigation, except for the fact that Bernard Gaston had been found with a noose around his neck, strung up in his closet like a coat.

15-year-old Andre was never questioned during the investigation due to a lack of evidence, namely the missing object which fractured the back of his father's head. The coroner made the claim it had to have been a thin, weighty object, like a fire poker. No such implement was ever found, and the case was closed.

Gilles Rousseau and Bernard Gaston were both very much alike in their treatment of weaker, dependent people and this disturbed Andre. It brought back memories he had fought for years to bury. He would find a way to stop this violence against his young friend, and the boy's family, but that must come later. The dinner hour was approaching, and Andre was never late for service. He was loyal that way. Andre Gaston was a good and decent man with many friends. Jacques Rousseau was one of them.

Chapter 21

The scanner on the desk crackled to life: *"Chicago 14 Dispatch! Chicago 14 Dispatch! This is Unit 27! Come in!"*

"Go, 27," said the Command Center dispatcher for Precinct 14. "What's happening, Jeremy?"

"Backup! Get me some backup, NOW! The St. Sylvester School on Palmer! Send backup and ambulance!" shouted officer Jeremy Fitzpatrick.

"Jeremy, what do you got?" asked the dispatcher. "You're only 3 blocks away."

"Jesus...we've got a body parked on one of the playground swings, sitting up...he's...he's missing both hands! No pulse...I'm administering CPR now!" Officer Fitzpatrick cried and then the radio went silent.

"Officer! What's your status, Jeremy?" said Dispatch. "Unit and ambulance are on route. They should be with you
on the scene now. Officer! Respond!"

There was nothing for over two minutes.

Officer Fitzpatrick had pulled the body, still limp, off the swing set and laid it on the ground before he began administering CPR. He kept on for nearly two minutes with chest compressions but could register neither a heartbeat nor breath sounds of any kind.

Call the code, his mind said, for, even if he wanted to keep trying, he knew it was too late. The man was dead.

Jeremy stepped away from the body and forcibly calmed himself. He spoke into his shoulder radio, "Dispatch, cancel ambulance and notify Cook County MEs. This guy is dead on the scene. Repeat, this is a 10-45d. They'll have to take it from here."

"10-4," said Dispatch. "Detectives will secure the crime scene. Dispatch out."

The victim was later identified as one Dimitri Vasileyich, 26, a member of Moscow Night, the notorious and violent crime gang that trafficked in small-scale armed robberies. Their calling card, however, was contract hits where the victims had been done in by shocking methods and then left on public display.

Vasileyich was a rising star in the outfit and had already notched 5 murders on his belt, the most notorious being a woman in her 50s who had been hung in her own backyard from a post on her porch. The woman's adult son had been over a month behind on his weekly vig, fueled by a hefty $50,000 debt he had accumulated through his heroin and gambling habits.

Dimitri was dispatched to send a message to the son, which he had done by hanging his mother with her bathrobe sash so that her unsecured robe flapped open as she swayed, revealing nothing underneath. Dimitri was a violent, despicable criminal with no desire to change his ways and who was beyond formal rehabilitation, even if the police and their callously political poster boy, District Attorney Joseph Ellison, could ever mount a case to get him off the street and behind bars.

The man in black had surveilled Dimitri. He knew him well by then, having tailed him during the spring, spotting his habits, peccadillos, and nightly stops. All he needed was darkness, opportunity, and a bit of luck. Tonight had turned out to be perfect timing.

Vasileyich had just come out of The Music Lounge on Armitage, stone drunk, and had crossed over and careened his way down Whipple Street. He was on his way over to pick up a clean Tech-9 pistol from another Moscow Night member a few blocks away. He cut through an alley past Dante's Pizza on Whipple and, though the moon shone through wispy cloud cover, he was suddenly hit in the face by water, except...it didn't seem like water, and...Dmitri soon felt very woozy.

Dimitri hit the ground. *Hard.*

The man in black waited a few seconds until the Rocurium from the tiny aerosol can had sufficiently subdued the assassin, then checked the alley. With no one in sight, he walked over and knelt next to him.

"Previet, Dimitri. Kak dela?" the man asked him, as if he truly cared about Dimitri's health.

It was such a friendly, benign greeting for the malignant and befitting end the criminal now faced. Dimitri could not respond and simply stared straight ahead, fear bubbling under his skin.

The man shot out, grabbing Dimitri's right hand and severing it at the joint. He worked the puntilla knife through the lunate tendon, bisecting the ulna and radius bones, and then quickly performing the same procedure on the left hand. He removed a gallon Ziploc and stacked both hands in it, prayer-style, sealed the bag, and stashed it inside the large inner pocket of his jacket.

At the first cut, blood had shot out of Dimitri in pulsing, rapid bursts. But, as his heart stuttered, the blood slowed, like someone pinching a garden hose on and off. The thug bled out in less than a minute and expired while both soaking *and* soiling his trousers.

The man put two fingers on his neck, which registered no pulse, no breathing—nothing. Dimitri Vasileyich's last utterance on Earth was a frapping peal of flatulence.

He had been a killer of high-performance for his job and had caused much suffering in his short life.

Not anymore, thought the man in black. *He met MY standard*, and the idea was satisfying.

As for what to do with the body, the man already had a plan in place. Showtime.

Chapter 22

Liz Keller was just finishing up the final autopsy notes in the Chicago Medical Examiner's Offices for her boss, Dr. Del Clayton, on the Rudy Tufton case. The remaining dissection, blood, and chem panels, and an acutely thorough examination of the body, had been concluded quickly. Publishing the findings, while fairly academic, often took longer.

Synopsis: Rudy Tufton died in a Chicago alley via evisceration and loss of blood. He was gutted from stem to stern. The event occurred in the exact place his body had been discovered, so he had not been moved post-mortem. The scene, and method of death, bares evidence of murder, along with the fact that his anus had been removed immediately after his passing.

Clayton knew full well that any murder contained at least 25 mistakes on the part of the killer, and this is where he focused his superior acumen, particularly something as glaring as a missing sphincter. The actual gutting of Tufton was incidental to how it came to be. Victims always put up a struggle during an assault as personal and intimate as a stabbing. Strangely, though, Rudy Tufton had not protected himself in any way. There were no defensive cuts on either hand, nothing on his arms or his face—other than his midsection, there were no marks of any kind on his body. This was a huge red flag to the senior ME.

Since her auspicious beginning on the case, Elizabeth Keller had taken advantage of the second chance from Clayton and immersed herself in her work, demonstrating a far more serious approach to her boss from her earlier clumsy and casual attitude. Liz was no dummy, having graduated with honors from the University of Chicago with a double-major in biology and organic chemistry.

She had been through a few rough months with the passing of her mother and the end of her first true romantic relationship. She had been in love, and the break was brutal on her soul. Then, her mother had died in a car crash right after Christmas and Liz felt as if she could never recover.

Liz's job as an assistant medical examiner in the forensics lab had become merely a place to go and get out of her apartment; it was somewhere she could simply exist and escape her thoughts. She had essentially floated through life these past few months– like a specter— but now she seemed to grasp a purpose once more. Clayton's stern warning had pulled the young examiner out of her freefall.

The Assistant ME had also begun appearing for work much more presentably. She now sported pressed chino slacks and clean, buttoned oxfords, with an impeccably neat hairstyle tied off with a simple gold-colored barrette. No other jewelry, no earrings, just straight-up Liz, the way she had been in college, with gutty street-smarts and strong intelligence to boot.

Clayton knew all this, which is why he had hired her in the first place. He took note of the new changes and allowed her to author and file the report findings under her name and write the conclusion on the Tufton case when they had one.

The move was a positive step, and Clayton insisted she start finding her own solutions, her own answers to the riddles on future cases. As it turned out, Liz Keller was about to score a big one all on her own.

Rudy Tufton's hair had been wet upon discovery and transport to the ME's office, not unusual because of the rain. What was unusual, though, was a slight film and sheen on the victim's facial skin that Keller had detected with magnification and pointed out to her boss. Clayton analyzed it, and had a hunch, as did Keller.

Keller paused her typing and shifted gears. "What should I write in the report about the missing anus?" she asked.

Clayton didn't miss a beat. "Report that the anus was suspected to have been removed during the crime. If you want an actual wording, simply put 'anal tissue excised' and leave it at that," said the senior ME. "Be straightforward. Eventually, we might arrive at *why*. For now, we keep the *what* as simple as possible. Report the facts Ms. Keller and leave the conclusions for when we have more evidence," he concluded firmly.

"Absolutely. But, Dr. Clayton," she continued, "What about the residue? The slight film on the skin that's not on his arms or hands—that's definitely a compound." She reached for a swab and swiped the face in both directions, placed it in an evidence pouch, and sealed it. "I'm taking that to the lab for spectrometry," she said flatly.

Clayton nodded his agreement, and for the first time, he concurred with his new assistant ME on several key scientific matters. "Put a rush on that, Ms. Keller. I want to see that analysis in one hour," he said.

Keller began labeling the pouch hurriedly.

"Oh, and Elizabeth?" said the senior ME.

Keller turned back and looked at her boss, who had never once addressed her by her proper name in her first months on the job.

"Yes, Dr. Clayton?" she said. "You can call me Liz."

"Good work here. Carry on…Liz," said Clayton with a brief upturn of his mouth—his version of a smile. "Call me Del, if you like," he said as an afterthought, as he gathered his papers and left the room.

****

55 minutes later, a senior analyst named Adam Ziton came to Liz in the autopsy room with the lab results. They had a new compound, not yet discovered by Chicago PD, but known to the feds.

"It's a combination of sodium cyanide and ethyl alcohol and something else," said Adam. He scratched his head. "But what's odd is why the cyanide is there in the first place. It's not at a high enough concentration to do any real damage. It certainly wasn't enough to fatally poison someone."

Keller pondered this for a moment and then asked Ziton, "What about the other chemical? Why can't we identify it?"

Ziton grimaced, "We know the cyanide plays off this new one as a catalyst, but it evaporates when it comes in contact with water. But not completely—that's the film you saw."

Keller straightened and said, "What makes this dry itself, but not completely?"

"It's obvious the rain washed it off, but not all of it. We can't get a pinpoint on it chemically, but it might be evaporating the other chemical in the *presence* of water, but then we're back to square one," Ziton said.

"Adam, nothing is obvious at this point," said Keller, quoting her boss. She stopped with a jolt. "There are certain toxins and alkyds that will combine in one state, but not another. There are only two or three possibilities with liquids," she said, turning over in her mind the question of why cyanide *and* ethyl alcohol were present. Then it hit her. The first anesthetics from centuries ago were created by mixing these exact two chemicals.

She went on. "What if this mystery chemical AND the cyanide mixed with the ethyl alcohol in such a way that," she paused for a second, collecting her thoughts, "That it could paralyze them, yet leave them conscious?"

Ziton raised his palms at Keller and shook his head. He didn't know.

Keller swallowed hard and said, her voice rough, "It means Rudy Tufton knew he was going to be gutted...before and during. And..." she trailed off with a shudder.

"And there was nothing he could do about it," said Ziton, "except watch and die."

Liz's stomach began bobbing and weaving. The nausea was overpowering. *Oh hell*, she thought, *Not here!* Then Liz Keller did what most rookie MEs do in their early careers: she vomited, hugely, leaning over and chucking into her wastebasket, the stream barely making it in the container as she slumped to her knees.

While her head hovered above the receptacle, one hand holding her hair out of the vomit's path, Keller screeched to Ziton, "It's Rocurium! Rocurium!" She stood up and steadied herself, wiping her mouth with a paper towel offered by the man.

She continued, more in control now. "Rivetti over at the FBI Crime Lab told me last week that they were working on a series of burglaries where the suspects were putting liquid nitrogen on deadbolt locks and then shattering them with a hammer to gain access to whatever building they were robbing. But they were using dish detergent to make it stick more. So, Rivetti explained there's this new compound that *evaporates* liquids by chemical reaction within minutes, so they could tell that it was a planned robbery and not just some dipshit spilling detergent around. Rocurium!" shouted Keller.

She knew, as sure as she'd known anything, that this was no random murder. It wasn't a crime of passion or a card game beating or a knife fight gone wrong or stupid people doing stupider things. This was chilling and sinister. There was a stone-cold killer running around Chicago, massacring people, who had a new method of getting away with it. Chicago PD had had motives in the killing, or better still, a way to stop them before they killed again. But now they had a means, a tracking device, something to go on, however thin the new evidence might be.

She stood up and thanked Ziton for the test results and the towel and then excused him. She scrubbed out the fouled trash can in the mop sink and returned to her office to work out the last of the report. She hoped Ziton could keep his mouth shut about the Rocurium before word got to her boss. She also hoped her boss wouldn't find out she'd puked.

Chapter 23

The air in the room was filled with the unmistakable scent of spent sex. Hazy morning sunlight drifted through the long window curtains as smooth jazz from a Chicago FM radio station emanated from wireless speakers embedded in the walls and ceiling throughout the room. The area appeared to be a very large combination bedroom and sitting room, decorated lavishly and expensively—complete with a full bathroom down a long hallway.

On a large bed of ruffled silk sheets lay a young woman, panting and sweating. She had been crying a moment ago because she was frightened. Now, she tried to clear her mind as she sat upright and began to piece together why she was in the bed, or, worse, what may have happened to her.

Her recollections were fuzzy at best, although that was more attributed to the drug that had been given to her. When prompted, she had asked the nice man for a diet root beer. The first sip tasted funny. By the third, she began feeling dizzy and then she had lost consciousness. The next thing she knew was this moment, laying there in the satin, her mind flying everywhere. It was difficult to think. She was still trembling.

She knew something was terribly wrong…down there. Her vagina ached horribly. There was some blood, and this frightened her even more. She breathed rapidly, in and out through her tears, trying to calm herself. Her mind raced.

Why was this happening? she thought. She wanted to go home. She wanted her mom and she wanted to play with her dog, Jenny.

Small wonder—she was only 13 years old.

There was a knock at the door and a man entered the room. He was not the same man who had given her the glass of root beer. This one was taller and far more muscular. He was bald and wore a black turtleneck, with an equally dark expression on his face; he spoke softly, nonetheless.

"There is a shower in the bathroom over there. Why don't you gather your clothes and clean yourself up. Someone will be here to take you back when you're finished," he said calmly and walked out the door closing it behind him.

The girl heard the deadbolt lock snap back into place and she began to cry again.

Chapter 24

Del Clayton stared at the final autopsy report Liz Keller had authored for Rudy Tufton, deceased food inspector. On his desk was a new case file.

Liz walked into Clayton's office as he grabbed his phone and punched in a number. Someone at another desk deep in the recesses of One Police Plaza picked up the call.

"Get me Johnson at the FBI Crime Lab. Tell him to call me right away," Clayton said, hanging up the phone with a dull click.

He turned and looked at Liz. "This is good work, Liz. Solid reporting job, with one wrinkle—Rocurium makes sense, but it's a protected compound. No one can get it unless they're a registered law enforcement or intelligence agency, and no illegal lab anywhere has been able to replicate it, yet." said Clayton. "Yet. Maybe they finally found a way. Thoughts?"

Keller nodded. "Agent Rivetti was certain this matched the characteristics of Rocurium, and he would know."

Clayton nodded, "I'm inclined to agree with you on that, Liz. But we've got another one," he said.

Keller's face went dead serious, and she pointed to the file on the desk. "Is that the Russian case?" she asked.

Clayton's radar shot up. "How do you know about that?"

"I heard the crosstalk on my police scanner last night," she said. "I was going to ask if we had the body, but I knew you wanted to see the Tufton report first thing, so I made that a priority."

Clayton paused and kept his eyes at the report in his hand. Liz Keller had just scored major points in his book. If she were listening to the police channels on her own personal time, particularly the wee hours after midnight, that meant she was more than just a clock-punching, 9-to-5 forensic technician. Del Clayton also kept a scanner in his home, as he had from his first day on the job so many years ago.

Could Liz Keller be this good? he wondered.

He handed her the file as he said, "Ms. Keller, meet one Mr. Dmitri Vasileyich, former member of the Moscow Night gang."

Liz took the file and began reading. One line on the police report jumped out at her. "Oh my God," she said.
The phone rang and Clayton grabbed it on the first ring.

"Clayton here. Hey, Jim, your guy Rivetti had better be damned sure about this. No one is supposed to know about Rocurium other than us and the other agencies...Yeah, I know some of the riff-raff has managed to get some, but let's stay on point here. Has anyone done a rat test with it?" He paused and listened, his face a solid block of granite. The gears were grinding. He said, "And paralysis was registered within seconds? How many replications did they do? Three? Okay, that's good enough for me. No, wait, don't hang up, Jim, we've got another one," said Clayton.

"Yep. Russian mob guy," he continued. "Got both his hands clipped off. I'll get back to you, but he's got the same damn residue on his face that the Tufton guy had. They brought him in overnight and we're doing the prelim this afternoon." Clayton listened some more. This time, Johnson's voice over at the FBI had risen in volume. Even Liz could hear it.

"Jim, you let me handle the science, goddammit. And just so you know, I've done this for so many years, *I've* even got cop blood in me. So when I say we're looking at a probable serial killer, it's better if you just take my word for it," Clayton said snappishly, only pausing to listen once more, before cutting Johnson off. "Tell your guy Rivetti to send 12 vials of Rocurium over to my assistant, this morning," he said, and hung up.

He got up out of his chair and stretched for a moment and turned to Keller. "Okay, Liz. We got ourselves a ball game. I'm backing you on the Rocurium theory." "What now?" she asked.

"Get back to the lab and make up 12 field tests to verify the presence of Rocurium. From now on, any suspected cases, we're going to do a double-blind test on each. We need those tests right now," said Clayton. "And if you don't get the vials from the FBI by noon, let me know. I'll be damned if I'm going to let Johnson make this political, no matter what the FBI thinks they have." "On my way," Liz said.

When Del Clayton had momentum on a case, it was best for everyone to keep the hell out of his way. And now, it looked like he had a very competent adjutant in Liz Keller.

Clayton could sense it. This case was moving. His juices were flowing—they hadn't had a case this scintillating since that sketchy double-murder of the two girls over in Oak Park last year.

The decayed bodies had been found on a wooded, vacant property owned by one of the shell companies of real estate mogul Richard Baldwin, but the evidence never amounted to anything and, while the case was still technically open, the trail had gone cold. Baldwin had had a verified alibi for the murders. In Clayton's opinion, the alibi was no doubt manufactured, but he kept that to himself because there was no proof. Verifiable proof was everything in Clayton's world.

Clayton suddenly noticed Liz still standing there. "What do you need, Liz?" he asked.

Keller had been off somewhere else, lost in thought, lost in the new case. Both the Russian and Tufton's faces and hair had both been wet, she remembered.

"The police report, Dr. Clayton. The victim's hair was wet," said Keller. "Just like the Tufton case."

"I noticed that, as well, Ms. Keller. It didn't rain last night. We'll get to all that in due course. Get on those tests. We'll need them now," said Clayton.

She nodded, turned, and left the office briskly. Her brain had been running scenarios at warp speed on this new would-be killer ever since Clayton showed her the case file. Out in the hallway, Keller pumped her fist, twice. They just scored a big one. Rather, *she* had.

Chapter 25

The next afternoon, Jacques and Remy were sitting in the office discussing menu possibilities, while sharing a huge plate of osso buco, freshly cooked by Jaime. They paired it with a sturdy '04 Lafitte Burgundy, and it was a sublime combo. They both considered themselves the kings of all they surveyed, enjoying such a sumptuous, decadent lunch.

Tonight's menu was already fully prepped and ready for the upcoming dinner rush. Jacques and Remy often selected this time in the mid-afternoon to enjoy a bite and peruse menu possibilities for the coming days. The kitchen air was quiet, yet dense with so many delicious aromas, the men could almost feel it on their skin.

Patti O'Brien came fast around the corner and approached the two as they sat in the office with the door propped open, stuffing osso buco into their faces. She had an alarmed look on her face.

"Jacques? I'm sorry to bother you, but this envelope was just hand-delivered by a….well, a pretty nasty looking man," she said.

Jacques turned toward her. "Did this nasty man leave a name?" he asked.

"No name. Just to tell you that Richard Baldwin sends his regards," said Patti. "He then spat on the floor and walked out," she scowled. She handed the envelope to Jacques.

Jacques took the envelope from Patti and passed it to Remy. "Open it," he said.

Remy grabbed the letter and tore the side off, blew into the length of envelope, and fished out a single piece of paper. He unfolded it and read the entirety of the letter in 10 seconds and passed it back to Jacques.

Remy's brow furrowed, registering anger. "You're not going to like this, Jacques." Using each other's proper first names was an urgent code, a private signal requiring immediate attention.

Jacques read the letter and said nothing, folding it in half and stuffing it in his breast pocket. He stood up and said to Remy, "Let's go. We'll take my car."

As Jacques passed Patti, he looked back over his shoulder and said to his hostess, "If Remy and I aren't back in two hours, tell Jaime and Rodrigo they're in charge of dinner service."

As if he could sense Patti's response, he added, "They'll be fine. I trained them," and as he sped through the back door, finished, "Besides, Remy will flatten them if anything goes wrong."

****

Two hours later, Jacques pulled his Audi A6 into his designated spot in the alley lot behind Chez Rousseau and shut off the engine. He sat there, staring ahead, while Remy, who sat in the passenger seat, applied a wet cloth to his nose and eye Remy checked his face in the sun visor's mirror, nodded once and flipped it shut.

"You going to make it?" asked Jacques.

Remy scoffed. "Shit, this makes a Friday night brawl at Ripp's feel like a massage, amigo," he said. He turned to Jacques and chuckled, "Damn, I bet it felt good hitting that fucker Baldwin when you caught him. If they really had done something to Lisette, we'd be in the slammer, and then we'd *really* need Don Cribaldi."

The letter Patti delivered from Baldwin's messenger had contained a picture of Lisette. It said Jacques could "Choose business or love, but not both," with instructions to meet Baldwin at his office in Cicero, about 11 miles outside Chicago proper. The image of Lisette was one taken earlier that morning on the street outside her office building and time-stamped at 9:27 a.m. Baldwin's men could easily have abducted her, doing God-knows-what. Jacques' mind burned glowing red coals at the thought, and what he was going to do to anyone who touched her. He had appeared centered and calm, but really, he was ready to kick someone's ass—that someone being Richard Baldwin.

Jacques and Remy had driven in silence all the way to the little theatre in Cicero, where Baldwin kept some swank office space on the mezzanine level, including a large combination bedroom and sitting room for resting and relaxation. Two calls to Lisette's cell went straight to voicemail and the tenseness in the vehicle was palpable.

As they pulled up in front of the theater, Jacques had shut off the ignition and said, "Let's be ready for anything. We don't know how many men Baldwin will have for this."

"Fuck that. I'm punching out the first cocksucker I see and I'm not stopping. We can ask questions later," Remy had snapped.

"If we see her first, we grab her and get the hell out of there. We'll figure everything out later, but she's my first concern. *Our* first concern," Jacques had told his friend, who was in disbelief at the man's calm tone.

They had both gotten out of the Audi and walked up to the front doors. They were unlocked and the two walked in and surveyed the empty lobby. Remy smelled stale popcorn.

Jacques' calm air lasted only until he saw Baldwin, then it broke with a fury.

Baldwin had stood at the top of the mezzanine and yelled, "Well, look at the heroes!" before he turned back and ran down a long hallway leading to his offices.

Jacques had roared, "Baldwin!" and shot across the lobby and up the stairs, taking them two at a time in a dead run to find the man who had taken his Lisette.

Remy was left to deal with the goons.

Usually, their size alone was enough to intimidate, but when Remy saw the first thug emerge from a side door into the lobby, he simply laughed. "You wanna dance, *chérie?*" he mocked. When the stout lout lunged a big swing at Remy's head, he had simply sashayed left and counterpunched to the man's right temple, spinning him around.

After that, Remy proceeded to punch him at will, three more hits to the face and a slick spinning kick to the midsection. Then, Remy was struck hard from behind. Another goon had come from the side door and blindsided him with a small, concealed police baton.

He then swung and thumped Remy again, hard on the back, and sent him staggering, while the first goon had gotten up and delivered two solid jabs to Remy's face. As Remy regrouped, the goon with the police baton tried to get greedy, grabbing his hair and going for another shot, but Remy was ready. He kicked straight up with his left leg, connected with the man's balls, and toppled him over like an unstable wedding cake; there the second thug lay, groaning and holding his crotch, rocking slowly in agony. With only the first man left standing, Remy had gone into autopilot mode, his fists creating a bloodbath, and the wetness of the blood made hard packing sounds on the goon's face.

Remy was an especially devastating fighter not only because of his brutally strong body, but also because of his large hands. This explained how he could hold sheet pans two at a time in the kitchen without squishing anything. Paired with his cast-iron jaw and a body made of granite, he was ferocity personified and impervious to pain.

It had only taken two shots to the face for the last goon to do down before Remy began kicking both of their midsections at will, beating them into submission and cracking rib bones. They were no match for his savagery.

Meanwhile, Jacques had caught up to Baldwin by diving headlong in the hallway and tackling him hard to the carpet at the entrance to two oak double-doors leading to the offices. Later, when asked to recall what happened, Jacques could only say the next moments were a blur as he rained damaging blows on Baldwin's jaw, nose, eyes, and temples. He, like Remy, was a devastating fighter when sufficiently provoked and unafraid of getting his hands dirty.

When Jacques landed the last punch, he grabbed Baldwin by the lapels and screamed into his face, "WHERE IS SHE?! WHERE IS LISETTE?!!"

Baldwin was only able to sputter, "Not here...she's in her office...I never...did...anything...I just wanted...your attention."

Jacques released him, then drove his foot deep into Baldwin's groin, brutalizing his testicles. Baldwin, the master of all land deals and self-professed Mafia attaché, had laid on the ground with a high-pitched mewing sound coming from his pursed lips. His face was swollen, and one eye was unrecognizable under the blood.

Jacques had turned and went back the way he had come to find Remy dealing the last kicks to Baldwin's bodyguards, who were also emanating forth a series of soft cries and whimpers. Tough guys, reduced to rubble.

Jacques then signaled Remy with a single, piercing whistle and he ceased his onslaught.

Suddenly, Jacques' phone pinged, and he tore into his pocket to retrieve it. A single text message from Lisette appeared, reading: "I'm sorry, darling! Meeting ran WAY too long :-(Everyone jammed in a lower-level office with no cell coverage in Lake Forest. See you after dinner tonight!"

Upon reading this, Jacques bent over at the waist and put both hands on his knees, releasing massive breaths of relief. He stood after a moment and texted her back a single red heart emoji and pocketed the cell. He loped down the stairs and helped Remy gather himself. The two then left the lobby of the theatre and got into the car for the drive back to Chez Rousseau, both quiet the entire way.

They arrived just as dinner service was about to begin, completely calm and satisfied with the justice they dished out to Baldwin and his goons.

"You going to make it?" asked Jacques.

Remy scoffed. "I've had worse, believe me. This ain't nothing compared to what those three are going to feel tomorrow. Bastards."

Jacques hummed his agreement, lost in thought.

Remy started to get out of the car, but Jacques put a hand on his shoulder and stopped him. "I have an idea. Let's see how they handle the dinner rush without us, eh?" he said mischievously. "What do you think…a little baptism by fire for Jaime and Rodrigo? They'll either step up or fall flat on their faces. Let's let them give it a go?"

Remy rubbed his chin and said, "We never did finish that osso bucco, did we?"

Chapter 26

Mornings at Chez Rousseau were as busy in the front of the house as they were in the kitchen; servers set fresh linens and place settings and arranged colorful flower blossoms in crystal bowls for each table. The place was made to sparkle. Every day, the sidewalk was swept and power-washed spotless, and along with the massive red awning, it gave off a Hollywood movie-set feel.

Once again, anticipation was building for the evening service. The day had arrived beautifully, with plenty of sunshine and warm August air.

Jacques and Remy sat at a table in the large front window of Chez Rousseau, sipping glasses of iced tea with lemon and mint garnishes as they assessed the upcoming evening service and business in general. Last night went splendidly. In Jacques and Remy's absence, Jaime and Rodrigo led the team like warriors, as if they had been doing it all along. It was a fine performance, accomplished without a single glitch and Jacques was immensely proud.

A very inebriated Remy had taken an apron and rolled it into a makeshift diploma and gathered everyone in the kitchen, whereby he bestowed upon Jaime the newly minted degree of 'Sous Chef 2.0' to wild applause. Jaime and Rodrigo's faces were flushed throughout the "ceremony."

Upon their return from Cicero, Jacques and Remy returned to the office and finished off the plate of osso bucco and the bottle of Lafitte. The osso had had a chance to sit and "haunt" for a couple hours at room temperature, and it was spectacular. Gluttony seized them and the two also attacked a large rondelet of a soft, triple-crème

Camembert cheese, spread on crusty baguettes. Then, they grabbed a sack of oysters and shucked a massive pile of Bluepoints, teaming them with a crackling cold bottle of Veuve Cliquot and ate like Hector, reborn.

It was a needed release of silliness for the pair after the Baldwin donnybrook, and, while both were a tad fuzzy this morning, it was nothing too terrible. The tea with lemon was a refreshing salve.

Remy said, "Have you heard any rumblings about our little visit to Cicero yesterday?"

Jacques looked out the window and said, "Oh yes. I called our friend Marge at Chicago Mercy and asked if, by chance, three large men happened to stop by last night. ALL had shown up in Baldwin's Mercedes, and all had injuries bad enough to admit them overnight. For 'observation,'" he elaborated, smiling as he held up his fingers to make quotations. He clearly enjoyed beating the daylights out of Baldwin and his thugs with Remy; the smart money said Baldwin wasn't likely to respond after such a beatdown.

"Observation. Yeah, observe this, Baldwin, you dick," said Remy, displaying his middle finger. "That idiot doesn't know how lucky he was that he didn't do anything to Lisette. I honestly don't think I could have stopped you if he had."

"I wondered about that myself."

"Did you mention anything to her about it?"

"No, and I won't. It's done," said Jacques. "But I am going to pay a call to Anthony Cribaldi soon. I'll let him deal with that prick Baldwin, because I don't trust myself anymore, Tati. I almost killed the man yesterday. Baldwin saved his own ass by confessing...but enough is enough." Remy nodded. It was a good idea that they direct the Baldwin heat away from themselves.

Jacques took a sip of tea and looked at his companion. He said, "There is one more thing, *mon frère*. I've heard a rumor we may soon have a visit from The Queen."

Remy sat up and said, "Oh, hell no. Are you kidding me? The Queen of Mean? Barnes?" Remy was referring to the highly popular and incendiary food critic, Priscilla Barnes. She had originally dubbed herself 'The Queen of Cuisine" on her food blog and website, but, given her reputation for acidity, the "mean" moniker was far more apropos.

Priscilla Barnes had worked for years as a hostess at the finest high-end restaurants in New York City and thoroughly knew the front-of-the-house as well as the back of-the-house kitchen business. No one was going to put anything past her. Her cachet and reputation grew at these elite, tony establishments and she did well financially. Apparently, that wasn't enough to keep her happy, for Barnes soon developed a habit of sleeping with her wealthy male clientele, married or not, and, as fate would dictate to someone of her aggressive libido, she had been caught photographed with some of these men and ceremoniously slapped across the infamous Page Six of the New York Post.

Page Six was not-so-quietly known among upscale east coast females as "The Women's Sports Page," and placement in it was a guarantee of future notoriety. Priscilla Barnes loved it and lived for it—the men in her company, not so much. Page Six insertions probably ended more marriages than if nature had simply taken her course.

One paramour, whose family was deep in banking, had paid her $1.2 million dollars to keep her mouth shut and her face and words out of Page Six permanently. But Priscilla Barnes was a smart, savvy woman and more than happy to take the money and sidestep future plugs on Page Six.

She started a food blog with her erstwhile bankroll and proceeded to parlay her vast dining and culinary knowledge into a rabid foodie following. Her readers exalted in her reviews, specifically when a restaurant she disliked received a scorched-Earth critique. Some never survived the online evisceration and had to close their doors. Within a relatively short period of time, Barnes had gained a reputation for being *the* food critic to read and her original investment grew handsomely.

Now, she was a free agent, jetting to all four corners of America and even across the pond to review those cutting-edge restaurants she felt required her literary attentions and seal of approval. Her eye-catching website, detailed food blog, and her juicy, jaw-dropping podcasts drew hefty advertising revenue clicks and rumors swirled that Google was dangling major dollars at her with designs for taking her white-hot brand and making it their own.

Though Barnes was wildly successful, her Achilles was a simple one—she was mean to the bone. Mean for sport, mean for kicks; she was mean because it made her feel good to make others feel worse. She relished making servers, hosts, hostesses, and restaurant owners squirm with discomfort. She would even barge her way through the swinging doors of the kitchen, often bringing her plate and slamming it down on a stainless-steel prep table as if they had served her dog shit on a shingle.

More than a few chefs and sous chefs had been forced to stand, toque in hand, in full view of his or her staff and be dressed down by the mercurial Barnes. Finally, after all that gratuitous abuse, she would get on her laptop and cook up the nastiest review as a final handful of salt smeared in already bloody wounds. An upcoming visit by Priscilla Barnes was as welcome as having rats in the kitchen and word of her pending visits sent otherwise splendid restaurants into a chaotic, paranoid frenzy. For her, it was nothing more than lucrative recreation.

Worst of all, she shamelessly violated the single canon of ethics for food critics, long considered sacred: Barnes never paid her own way, hadn't bought a single dinner once her website launched and went viral. This practice reflected on the soul of the woman. Her former casual prostitution had been confined to what went on between men and women behind closed doors. Now, the whoredom of her labors was paraded in full view for all to read, and she loved every minute of it, wallowing in the celestial misery of others' pain while making heaps of cash.

Jacques had received word of the pending Barnes invasion via a heads-up text from his dear friend and fellow Frenchman, Chef Eric Ripert of Le Bernardin in New York. Ripert shared that Lady Barnes was coveting him, that it was rumored she was "...dying to try the *Poisson Avril* at Chez Rousseau. Can you get me in? You're his friend, after all." Ripert had told Jacques in the closing of his text: "Be careful of this woman, my friend. Her teeth are beautiful but razor sharp, as are her words and reputation. Not a nice person at all."

Jacques thanked his countryman and then made plans to sit Remy down for a chat to figure out how to handle a Barnes incursion. That sit-down was now.

Chapter 27

"Goddammit!" shouted Priscilla Barnes into her cell phone. "You get me that fucking reservation at Chez Rousseau CONFIRMED! NOW! You hear me?" she screamed again and hung up.

Patti O'Brien, the hostess and office manager at Chez Rousseau, had told Barnes's assistant that reservations were booked for the next four months. She could, however, have her boss placed on the waiting list, but she would need to be available within a 24-hour window in order to have the reservation honored. Patti, the hostess-supreme and a consummate professional, had giggled to herself as she hung up the phone. Take that, Priscilla Barnes. Remy had brought her in on the scheme, and she had been more than happy to play her part.

Barnes's assistant, a very young Hunter College graduate named Chloe, began perspiring at the thought of telling her boss this news; it was unheard of, that the world-famous food critic Priscilla Barnes would have to wait for such a small detail as a reservation. She was afraid it would send her into a state of apoplexy.

It had been Remy's idea. He and Jacques had sat at the window table and conjured up idea after idea on how to piss Priscilla Barnes off. Making her wait was the winner. Rather than pander to the food critic, they would deflect her…make her play by their rules. It was textbook Sun Tzu: *"If your enemy is of choleric temper, irritate them."*

The plan was to reduce the acidic Barnes to nothing more than a whining, shrieking shill—or so they hoped.

JACQUES ROUSSEAU, WHY DON'T YOU LOVE ME? screamed the headline on the laptop screen. Priscilla Barnes read the blog entry one more time and smacked the send button. She nodded to herself in satisfaction, hissing quietly, "Oh, dear Jacques, you don't want to mess with me." She didn't want her assistant Chloe to hear that, because she was truly good and pissed off at the treatment she had been given from Chez Rousseau the past two weeks.

Five times Barnes's office had called Chez Rousseau for a reservation and five times they were relegated to the reject pile, aka the "waiting list." After the fifth rejection, Priscilla's blog post screamed out to her readers.

"Bonjour, my darlings! For some time now, you and many others have insisted I absolutely MUST get myself to Chicago for the best salmon dish to be had in this country. Alas! Chez Rousseau, and more specifically, its notorious owner, Jacques Rousseau, will not grant me a reservation! I must wait for his divine *Poisson Avril!* Can you believe…I have been placed on the *waiting list*?! Oh, dear Jacques, what are you hiding from me?" she wrote.

Priscilla Barnes closed her blog with the following sentence, in French, for Jacques to absorb. It was more than a teasing statement about secrets; it was a shadowed promontory of threat.

"*Ce n'est pas comme s'il y avait des corps stockés dans les catacombes de Chez Rousseau? Ou y en a-t-il? Appelle-moi! Je t'aime, Cilla.*"

****

"DID YOU SEE WHAT THAT BITCH WROTE?" asked Remy to Jacques, laughing.

"*Oui*. I saw it. She really is full of herself," said Jacques.

"And that line about bodies in the basement!" said Remy. "What the hell is that?"

"Your guess is as good as mine," said Jacques. "Okay, we've had our fun. Tell Patti to give Mademoiselle Barnes a reservation. For tomorrow night only. *Vous comprenez?*" he asked.

"Understood," Remy chuckled. "At this late hour, it'll cost her two grand to fly from New York to Chicago," he chuckled.

Jacques nodded at Remy, then swung his hand towel over his shoulder and started humming as he turned his attention back to the huge pot containing a vegetable stock fortified with Sauvignon Blanc wine. It had been simmering all morning long, and the raft of chopped shallot, celery, carrot tops, and onion skins bubbled lazily on the surface and the aroma was as welcoming as coming through the front door at home. At moments like this, the chef's brain and singular focus moved everything out of his field of thought and vision and that especially included the likes of Priscilla Barnes.

Jacques dipped a spoon and taste-checked the broth, then added a pinch of kosher salt and cracked Malabar pepper and two more sprigs of thyme as he lowered the flame. His mind was going 90 miles-an-hour in a 30 an hour zone thanks to the Queen, but he was still King of the consommé.

Chapter 28

"That's what she said, Miss Barnes. Tomorrow night, only," said Chloe, the assistant. She stood at her boss's desk with the notes from her conversation with Patti O'Brien, taking severe care to appear calm. She was anything but; she was nearly prostrate with anxiety at having to tell Priscilla the bad news.

Barnes stood up and went to her window. "So that's the way you want to play it, eh Jacques?" she said lowly. She fairly growled, "Fine. I don't care if your precious *Poisson Avril* is the best dish on Earth – I'm going to destroy it. You'll close Chez Rousseau by the fall...you *fucker*," Priscilla seethed. She turned to see Chloe standing in the same spot.

"Book it," she said, "and get me Vincent Cribaldi on the phone, now."

"I don't think he's back from Chicago yet, Miss Barnes," said Chloe.

"I already *know* he's back in New York, you idiot!" Priscilla thundered. "Book the flight for tomorrow afternoon, get Mr. Cribaldi on the phone, and then take the rest of the day and tomorrow off!" she yelled.

"Oh," squeaked Chloe, shrinking a little. "Won't you need me in case something happens while you're in Chicago?" she asked. She asked only because that meant the time off would be unpaid. Priscilla Barnes was a very cheap woman who would only allow Chloe to work 39 hours per week because working 40 hours meant Priscilla would have to pay for her medical insurance.

"I'll be fine," Priscilla snapped. "Now get to it!"

Chloe said quietly, turning to go, "Yes, of course. I'll go and book your flight, Miss Barnes." She then stopped dead in her tracks, gasped, and wheeled around. "Miss Barnes! What about your reservation for tomorrow night's review of Café Santo Domingo?" she exclaimed.

"Oh, that. You write it," said Priscilla with a wave of her hand. She looked down at Chloe's suit and pulled a series of hairs off the sleeve and examined them.

"What is this?" said Barnes.

"Oh, I'm sorry Ms. Barnes. That must be from my cat. He sheds," she said meekly.

"I fucking hate cats. Keep that damned hair away from me. So, you're good to write the review? You should be. It won't be the first time, and God knows I don't want to be seen or photographed pressing the flesh with that flaky Dominican poseur Bryan Verais," she said.

Chloe, lightened immediately at the thought of writing a review, nodded at Priscilla and turned to go, her steps becoming lively. Chloe knew Verais, and he would treat her right and the food would be memorable, no matter what her boss thought of him. It was a night out amongst the glitz and glitterati *and* a fine meal. Chloe always paid for her own review dinners and was happy to do so.

"Oh, Chloe? Make sure you write the byline under *my* name. That's all for now," she said, pausing for a moment. "And don't forget Mr. Cribaldi. Go," she finished, coldly.

"And Mr. Cribaldi," echoed Chloe, her mood dampened. "Yes, Miss Barnes. Right away."

****

Jacques stood at the elaborate coffee station at Chez Rousseau, sipping an espresso in the mid-afternoon lull before service. His espresso machines looked like something from an Elon Musk daydream. Unfortunately, his mind wasn't focused on great coffee at the moment, because it kept circling around and around to the Barnes visit. He was bothered at having to deal with the additional pressure she brought, and the fact he'd be forced to be cordial to someone as nasty and sour as she. There was more to it than that, but he didn't want to get ahead of himself. The staff was emotionally strained, walking on eggshells and Jacques would have to do something about it.

His staff was his family, and Jacques was loyal to his core.

Chapter 29

The phone rang in the large suite at the St. Regis Hotel in New York City. The lone occupant, whose father was the head of organized crime in the city of Chicago, lay on the king-sized bed fully naked and coated in sweat. He had just finished a rough bout with a garden-variety call girl, flipping her over and yon numerous times on the bed while plying her in different subservient sexual positions and leaving her with bite marks on her upper back, thighs, and buttocks. He paid the woman an additional hundred bucks beyond her fee as an incentive to return, but the consort had not been pleased with the treatment and left the room— vowing never again to engage in business with this particular customer. She even entertained the idea of stopping by the CVS on the way home for some iodine and a tetanus shot.

Vincent Cribaldi was a full-bore psychopath. He differed monumentally from his father Anthony in that he completely lacked any of the manners or discipline or business acumen that had made his father and his grandfather rich. Simply put, Vincent was crazy-in-the-head with no filter, no money sense, and no real civility. Completely batso...an *idiota—Lui non capisce niente*. He loved gambling, especially the horses, he loved drinking expensive wines and spirits, and he loved fine cuisine. He especially liked fucking small women in a pounding, relentless ritual, sometimes five or six times during a paid session. He liked having fun and if someone got in the way of that? *Marrone*. If anyone looked at Vincent the wrong way, there emerged a sickening transformation. It was as if a spigot turned on in his chemical brain, and he became uncontrollably, irrationally violent.

For women, it was terrifying to be out in public with Vincent Cribaldi. One minute, they would be enjoying a nice, calm dinner in a restaurant and the promise of a big boned lay and the next, their date is hurling a bottle of Far Niente Cabernet at the head of a guy whose only offense was smiling courteously as he passed the table.

Vincent was reputed to be an expert with a knife, and numerous times over the years, Anthony Cribaldi had had to employ various powers and favors to keep his son out of jail. Vincent Cribaldi had nothing to offer an educated, cultured woman.

But for those women of questionable virtue, he was the total package. He had access to the family money, lots of it— none of which he ever earned—and Vincent sported a very large penis. Women of true refinement wouldn't look twice at Vincent Cribaldi. Priscilla Barnes needed but one look and her libido sang out. She had heard the rumors about Vincent, and they turned out to be true. After their first time together, sexually, Priscilla spent an hour afterward soaking in the tub and basically relearning to walk. They saw each other whenever she ventured west or he east, to New York.

Vincent slithered across the bed and picked up the phone on the 12th ring.

"What!?" he said.

"Uh... Mr. Cribaldi? Ms. Barnes for you, sir," said Chloe the assistant.

"Yeah, put her on," said Vincent. There was a click on the line.

"Hello there, darling," said Priscilla. "I can always tell when you're in New York—my antenna starts buzzing. "Where are you?" she asked.

"I'm in the middle of a meeting, Priscilla. What do you need?" said Vincent, leering.

"I need a favor, Vincent. Can you meet me?" said Priscilla. "Or I can meet you, say, the St. Regis?"

"Nah, that's no good. I'll meet you at the bar at The Radcliffe, instead," said Vincent. "One hour…you know the rules."

"I'll be there," she said and hung up.

Chapter 30

Jacques was down in the dry goods area in the basement at Chez Rousseau, checking inventory on supplies and sundries; he wanted to make sure they had all the proper ingredients in quantity for the next several nights' service. He had carefully hand-inspected the meat, seafood, and produce in the walk-in coolers upstairs and found them all to be excellent. Another shipment of salmon and other seafood was slated to arrive that day from Olson Fish Company, but it was always wise to make sure freshness was verified—something Jacques, Remy, and the other *commis* did regularly.

The next evening's visit from Priscilla Barnes had the entire Chez Rousseau staff on edge. They all loved Jacques and relished working for him, but the hard truth was they all knew what Priscilla Barnes could do. She had closed restaurants before with a bad review, even long-running establishments with a Michelin star in their galaxy, just like Chez Rousseau.

Jacques had decided to put those fears to rest with a staff meeting in the dining room. Everyone from both the front and back of the house was in attendance—this included the night porters, who came in and deep-cleaned the entire restaurant each night from top to bottom. For interrupting their sleep, Jacques made sure Remy gave each porter an envelope containing an extra $50 cash on top of their regular pay.

Remy quelled the buzzing in the dining room and got everyone's attention with a loud finger whistle.

Jacques gave Remy a playful swat with a hand towel, whipped it over his shoulder, straightened his chef's coat and stepped forward so that everyone could see and hear him. "Every night, you all give our customers a great experience. They come here because of you, because you all take such wonderful care of them, like they are your own family. They are loyal because of that," he said. He looked around the room and met all their eyes, his own growing misty at the action. "I love you all for that. You make it easy for me to come to work each day," he said, taking no credit for himself.

He continued, "Tomorrow night is just another night." Here the room began buzzing again, the pending invasion from Barnes truly had everyone on edge, and Jacques held up his hand, while Remy issued a terse little whistle-chirp, silencing everyone and bringing them back to attention.

"I don't care if Vice-President Harris comes to dinner. Or Bradley Cooper or Lizzo or Michael Jordan or Drake or whomever. Hell, I don't care if Oprah Winfrey comes to dinner, although we see her here so often, she may as well be picking up her mail." Hearty laughter at this, Oprah was a regular customer and a joy to serve—everyone at the Chez *adored* Oprah. Jacques would occasionally serve her a special dessert of a flaming maple crème brulee with Grand Marnier, which he would personally make ahead of time just for her. It was an inside joke the two shared from her earlier days, before she became *the* media icon in America.

"We will extend everyone the same distinct courtesy and respect, and that includes Priscilla Barnes. She's just another customer and we will treat her as such. She will receive our gracious service and enjoy our best food *and* she will have our deepest respect," said Jacques. He was a captivating speaker and the whole room seemed to drift toward him. Jacques wrapped it up while he had them in the palm of his hand.

"Let *me* take the pressure. Me. Not you. Not even Remy," Jacques said, and at this, Remy fake-frowned briefly, before smiling. Everyone laughed again. The mood was lifting.

He closed. "Remember that. I take the pressure. Otherwise, it's just another night, same as every night here at the Chez," Jacques said. He was a master of control.

"Any questions?" he asked and, of course, there were none. "Okay, thank you everyone, so much. I love you with all my silly, devoted French heart," he said and smiled broadly, tapping his hand on his chest in little fluttering heartbeats.

The entire dining room erupted in applause. Man and woman alike, cheering, celebrating a boss they truly loved— he was protecting them to do their work and keep their jobs. It was an inspiring moment. Remy thanked everyone quickly as well, adjourning the meeting so everyone could begin dispersing. Some went back to their workstations or similar duties, others who were off for the night headed to the bar for a quick refreshment, and a few others went back home. They were all going to be fine. Their leader had their back, as always, and more to the point, he had proved it, taking the heat alone and facing the oncoming double barrels of Priscilla Barnes.

Remy joined Jacques and put his arm in his as they walked back to the kitchen, a move everyone saw as complete solidarity between their two leaders. Once behind the swinging doors and away from other ears, Remy spoke.

"You think they bought it?"

Jacques stopped Remy and said, "I was dead serious when I told those people I loved them, and I know you do too." Jacques began to choke up. "Remy, my friend…I've worked hard all my life, ever since I was a little boy. Take my word—if…if Priscilla Barnes gives us a terrible review tomorrow night for no reason…for spite…if she tries to shut us down, I…" and his voice cut off.

"What?" asked Remy. "You'll do what?" He had only seen Jacques this emotional once before in their time together, when he had spoken of his mother.

Jacques said, "I-I will not be happy, Remy. I can't let Barnes close us down."

I could kill her, Jacques thought.

****

Barnes sat at the bar at The Radcliffe Hotel, an elegant throwback to luxury hotels of the 1980's. Unfortunately, the hotel now suffered from terminal design cancer, and the décor had faded desperately out of date. The bar and restaurant still served decent food and solid drinks, though, and Barnes sipped a chilled Ketel One martini with an anchovy-stuffed olive as she waited for Vincent Cribaldi. Her flight to Chicago was scheduled to depart the following morning, and rather than handle Jacques Rousseau in the conventional way for his disrespect toward her, she wanted to deliver an additionally direct and brutal message—one that guaranteed his future fear and compliance.

Vincent Cribaldi, dressed in Armani's finest, moved through the hotel lobby toward the bar, spotting Barnes on a barstool, knowing full well she was going to ask him to commit a felony. In the past, dispensing violence on someone had never deterred him. He was a physically imposing figure and had no problem shedding blood. He had grown up with violence as a first reaction, rather than discussing whatever matters the parties may have disagreed on before fists or other weapons were engaged. Such were the vicissitudes of Mafia life, and although he was no longer part of his father's empire in a day-to-day business sense, he knew the many nefarious resources that were available to him at any time.

In Barnes's case, though, he was more concerned with the method of payment. He was no longer satisfied with taking sexual favors in trade along with cash. She was no longer enticing to him in bed, anyway, because she was in her late 40's and not as pliable as he needed his sexual partners to be.

This meant payment needed to be in straight cash, which Cribaldi knew could be a challenge, considering Priscilla Barnes still owned her first nickel. Her reputation for stinginess preceded her. Vendors and other business owners who dealt with her company often found themselves with invoices that were months and months old. As a final bargaining tactic before selling the account to a collection agency, the vendors would negotiate with Barnes herself on a pennies-on-the-dollar basis just to get any money for their trouble. The list of those who would no longer do business with PB Media, Inc. stretched around the block. Vincent had decided to play it cool with Barnes and see exactly what she wanted, then decide whether or not it was worth his time or trouble. Besides, he needed a drink.

As he approached the bar, the bartender spotted him, and quickly poured a lowball glass full of Glenfiddich 18year-old, setting the drink, Vincent's favorite, down on the bar the moment he arrived.

"Now that's what I call service," said Cribaldi, "having your drink waiting for you right when you sit down. That's class." He took the glass and a long gulp of the whiskey, not bothering to formally greet Barnes first.

"What the hell, Vincent? I don't even rate a kiss?" she griped. Vincent smiled, took her hand as if to give it the gentleman's greeting kiss on the back and instead licked it.

Barnes withdrew her hand in disgust and scowled. "Jesus Christ, Vincent! Don't do that here! Do you have to act like an ass *all* the time?" she scolded.

"Sorry, baby, I was hungry is all...now I'm thirsty. What can I do you for?" he said as he licked the Scotch off his lips and smacked them.

Priscilla took a sip of her martini and regained her composure. She flashed her fake charm smile at Vincent, a sure sign she wasn't waiting to ask her favor.

"I need you to take some men—some very big men—and pay a visit to someone in Chicago who treated me very rudely," she said. "I want them to give him a real good beating. Don't kill him, but make sure he hurts. Send him to the hospital and then let him know I'm the one who set him up," she said. "Can you do that?"

Vincent said, "Who's the guy and what did he do to you?"

"I just told you...he was rude to me."

"You gotta do better than that. Shit, you take offense with everything. You remember those Jimmy Choo shoes I got you?"

"Yes, I do, Vincent. They were the wrong size...and they were *used*."

Vincent took a long pull on his drink and finished it and motioned to the bartender for more. "Yeah, were they?" he said. "I hadn't noticed."

"Vincent, are you going to do this for me or not?" Barnes pressed.

"You still haven't answered my question." Priscilla was now irritated and took a big gulp of her martini, finishing it as well and motioning to the bartender for a refill.

"The owner of a restaurant I want to review wouldn't give me a reservation," she said. "He's ducked me five times, and then told my girl that I would have to be put on a waiting list. You don't put Priscilla Barnes on a waiting list," she hissed, speaking of herself in the third person, something that had been a long-standing joke around town.

"What else did he do?" asked Vincent.

"*What*?! That's not enough? He was rude. He *disrespected* me, Vincent. You of all people should know the importance of that," said Priscilla indignantly.

"First of all, let's get something straight between us, and it ain't my dick. You're not in my business, Priscilla. You disrespect me in my business? I make you disappear or I put you in a tub of acid or I break your face. Disrespect in your fuckin' racket means someone brought you the wrong oyster fork," said Vincent. "It's apples and bocce balls. It don't compute." He turned to her and answered Priscilla's question flatly. "Breaking this guy's legs will cost you twenty grand."

Priscilla almost jumped. The number was far more than she had imagined. She said, "I was thinking more like...you know...a nice, hard roll in the sack, Vincent. Just like old times?" she said, twirling her finger around her earring, and then stroking the sleeve on his Armani.

This was not sexually enticing to Cribaldi at all.

"And maybe, oh, say five grand?" she cooed.

Vincent stared at her as his second drink was set in front of him. Rather than answer directly, he downed the whole glass of Glenfiddich and put it back on the bar. He looked at Barnes for a short moment and then got up to leave.

"Let me think about it, Priscilla," he said coolly, changing the subject. "Look, I got a meetin' over in Brooklyn I gotta take. I'll let you know. When did you say you were going to Chicago?" he asked.

"My flight is tomorrow morning, Vincent," she said, not pleased with his decision. "And my reservation for the review is at 8:00 p.m. at Chez Rousseau. Are you going to leave me hanging on this?" she asked, dumbfounded.

Vincent got up and straightened his tie. "I'll think about it, baby. Either way, it's a straight cash deal. You know the drill—half now, half when it's done. I'll see ya," he said, and without so much as a kiss or a touch goodbye, walked away from the bar and out onto West 57th. Barnes didn't know it, but she had just supremely offended a Mafioso at his own business, and something like that is never forgotten, at least until it is "reminded" in some way.

Little did Priscilla know, but as soon as she mentioned the name Chez Rousseau, Vincent knew it wasn't going to happen. Chez Rousseau was his father's favorite restaurant. Apparently, their langoustines reminded his father of Vincent's great grandmother Luisa's. She also made a mean risotto in her day—he had heard a thousand times. There wasn't a chance in hell he was going to get between his father and sacred Cribaldi family memories. Besides, Barnes was beginning to get on his nerves. It would be better to just walk away and let her think he might help her.

Priscilla held her drink in her right hand and nearly threw it at Vincent's head but stopped herself and let him walk away without another word.

"I guess I'll have to deal with you myself, Rousseau," she said under her breath as she gulped down the martini in a single swallow. She got up and left enough money on the bar to barely cover the drinks.

Chapter 31

The man in black walked up the street near Wicker Park at a moderate pace. He needed to slow down—kept telling himself to *appear normal*. His radar was up for someone tailing him, and he had always made it his personal gospel to be aware of his surroundings, but today was different. He much preferred moving under the cover of darkness. It was invariably safer, but a timetable had suddenly been expedited and he needed to make a pickup in broad daylight.

This put him at risk of being observed by someone who might later be able to tell police, "I saw a man in a black jacket and tam o'shanter cap walking up Walker Street by the pawn shop," or words to that effect.

No matter how sharply he tuned his inner instrument, he couldn't track the other eyes watching him. There was always a witness he couldn't account for. This bothered him to no end—why didn't people mind their own damn business? He was trying to eliminate bad people from the planet, people that in their own way had truly done things deserving of death. Rudy Tufton had been one of them. Dmitri Vasileyich was another, along with a dozen more who over time had met the Standard for elimination, because they brought untold misery and personified evil. This was the game he played, and it wasn't Parcheesi.

Defining the Standard on a prospective kill took great care and analysis, along with weeks, or even months, of planning and tracking in some instances. If someone eventually died at his hand, they had it coming—the world was surely better off without them. The man in black had calculated that he had made the lives of some 9,400 people better by eliminating certain individuals. That value was about to multiply by a factor of 10 and he had to be ready.

He let himself into the basement apartment at Mrs. Chlopicki's house, but not before making three different passes from alternating directions to ensure he hadn't been followed. Once inside, he went to the bedroom and checked his stash of equipment behind the baseboard in the closet. All was safe. He could hear Mrs. Chlopicki's classical music station through the floorboards upstairs. Then, he went to the kitchen, opened the freezer door, and took out the package behind the baguettes and the bottle of Tito's vodka. He was tempted to pour a quick shot to calm his nerves, but he knew the immediate relief might compromise his faculties later and he would need them for the task at hand.

He had worn gloves this time—light, black leather driving gloves—so there was no need to wipe anything down for prints. This might have seemed suspicious, given the warm Chicago weather that day, but there was no time to worry about that now. The retrofitted soles on his shoes were still doing their job and he slipped out the door and locked it, rejoining the Chicago public in the bright afternoon daylight. He removed the gloves nonchalantly and walked as if he hadn't a care at all.

Once again, the world was about to become a better place.

Chapter 32

Richard Baldwin, in addition to being a rich real estate scion, was also involved in many cultural endeavors in and around the city of Chicago and the Upper Midwest. He owned the Dell'art Theatre in Cicero, a multi-use facility that could stage everything from concerts to large musical theatre productions to a Saturday night movie double feature, complete with popcorn, pop, and snacks. He also kept a large row of offices on the second floor, including a spacious bedroom that served as both a means of rest and, on a more intimate level, entertainment, if he so desired.

Baldwin also sat on the board of directors of the prestigious Chicago Museum of Modern Art, where he was a generous donor and benefactor to scores of individual youth artists, musicians, and dancers. It was all a ruse. He claimed to enjoy giving them a leg-up in their young careers, and, in many cases, took a deeply personal interest in their professional growth from an early age. A very early age.

Baldwin sat up in bed now, sweating profusely. He had always loved a good bout of after-lunch sex, and, at 58, claimed it was good for his heart. He leaned over and lit a cigar, puffing contentedly and blowing out long streams of smoke as he grunted with satisfaction. He sat and smoked, occasionally reaching for the Scotch glass on the nightstand.

He looked over at the female figure in the bed next to him and gave her a poke from behind.

"What do you say there, honey?" he said.

The voice that answered was not the voice of Mrs. Baldwin. Genevieve Baldwin had a low, silky murmur that caressed a man's ear and soothed like nothing else. This voice was much, much younger.

Richard Baldwin liked having sex with young teenage girls, the younger the better. Sometimes, he employed a numbing agent, in the form of Rohypnol or some other Mickey Finn concoction. Sometimes, he simply lured them to his place under the guise of money or promised artistic stardom, and then had his way with them.

He had done this for years. Some of the young girls or their parents were paid hush money. Some who refused the money had threatened to report Baldwin to the police. Bad idea, he would say. He was connected to the Mafia, they were warned. Say one word to the cops, and you'll be at the bottom of Lake Michigan, you and your spouse and your little girl and your whole fuckin' family. The threats had been carried out on a number of occasions.

Improbably, he was never caught. No one ever called the police or took any measures, and Baldwin went on having his jolly way with little girls. They were his personal fountain of youth. They energized him, kept him young. He loved their smell, the way they moved, and he especially enjoyed the way they ultimately released unto him. He exulted in never getting caught and had beaten the cops' case last year, even with the two dead girls being found on his property. He was bullet-proof. He still marveled at the alibi he had given them, about his computer being hacked and the evidence destroyed or stolen or whatever. They bought it because they had no other proof in hand. Baldwin hadn't done the killings himself, but he did dispense the order to one of his men, who strangled them with gloved hands. The gloves and any other incriminating evidence had then been burned.

But now, there were two girls who had recent evidence they could use against him, or so they threatened. The evidence was a pillowcase that contained Baldwin's semen. One of the girls had spat his seed into the pillow following a forced fellating and had quickly concealed the folded pillowcase in her backpack while Baldwin relieved himself in the bathroom. The organized crime threat apparently hadn't deterred them.

Baldwin knew both girls came from broken homes and had no money—they were simply young dancers who had been studying ballet at the academy he sponsored. Baldwin thought he had been charitable enough, giving the girls money each time that they met. Paid rape. The missing pillowcase was a ticking time-bomb, and Baldwin needed to take immediate action, lest the authorities come to his door with irrefutable evidence. He wasn't about to let that happen. He knew fully well what they did to child rapists in
Joliet.

His mission remained clear: Stay out of jail if it was the last thing he ever did.

****

Good afternoon. This is a special bulletin from the WGN Newsroom. I'm Alyssa Rogers, reporting live. Police were called to a rural property outside Aurora this afternoon, where the body of 13-year-old named Cheryl Lange was discovered in what appears to be a shallow grave scene. Police and K-9 units were dispatched to the remote ravine location when an anonymous report to police indicated that there had been suspicious activity on the property yesterday evening. Lange had been missing for several days, following her disappearance from a dance recital in the Chicago area. Police have not yet commented on a cause of death, pending autopsy results from the Cook County Medical Examiner's Office. Stay tuned to WGN for continuing coverage.

****

Good evening, I'm Alyssa Rogers, and we have breaking news from Aurora. WGN News has learned that police are now seeking Chicago real estate developer Richard Baldwin for questioning regarding the discovery of the body of 13-year-old Cheryl Lange. The location of Lange's body was on property allegedly linked to the Chicago developer. Baldwin is considered a person of interest in the case although police are pursuing other evidence and possible suspects. We'll have more on this story as it develops.

Chapter 33

Barnes's flight the following morning to Chicago was delayed due to rain squalls over JFK, and Priscilla now sat on the tarmac without so much as a single drink to steady her rising nerves and temper. She was extremely annoyed at the lack of attention given her. Didn't these idiot flight attendants know who she was? Her name was printed right on the boarding pass, for Christ's sake! She tried to calm herself by going into her phone and retrieving old files of particularly harsh reviews she had written over the years, summoning some of the venom she would be unleashing on Jacques Rousseau and his merry little restaurant—especially his Cajun cornpone sidekick, Remy Thibodeaux. This made her relax a little, but some vodka would certainly have helped more.

Regardless of whether the food was spectacular, as she was sure it would be, Barnes had no intention of giving Jacques a fair review. She was a resourceful person, and she knew the restaurant business backwards and forwards, which meant she had ample ammunition from which to draw. When she was done, the whole world would know that the *Poisson Avril* at Chez Rousseau was nothing more than expensive fluff. A lark. The fake gold at the end of an even faker rainbow. Totally overrated. And then, she would take great umbrage in hearing reports of Chez Rousseau failing and going under. It certainly wouldn't be the first time she ruined a perfectly good operation, and it wouldn't be the last. She *was* The Queen of Cuisine, after all.

Priscilla Barnes had been wrong about a number of things that day. First, her read on Vincent Cribaldi had been off by a mile. She usually had him wrapped around her little finger, but that time had passed long ago. Booking a morning flight to save money was her second mistake, which was why she sat, trapped, on the tarmac in New York at JFK, badly needing alcohol. Had she taken the more moderately expensive early afternoon flight, the weather would have cleared, and her plane would have sailed without incident into O'Hare.

Now, her flight would arrive late and the limousine service would have to double-back to pick her up, costing even more money. Worst of all, on top of the phony review she was going to publish, she had been imagining with great excitement the headlines that America's top chef was in the hospital after being brutally assaulted. Now, that was up in the air. She could only hope that Vincent would come through for her.

Little did Priscilla Barnes know, fate was not on her side. Not one bit.

Chapter 34

Richard Baldwin sat behind the wheel of his Mercedes 500-S and drummed his fingers on the steering column. His car was parked a block away from his real estate office in a swank downtown building on the Chicago River. He and the two other passengers in the car watched as two unmarked city vehicles sat parked on the street directly in front of the entrance to Baldwin's building.

The man in the passenger seat, one of Baldwin's thugs, Denny Renaldo, spoke. "So, who's in the car there, boss?"

"That would probably be Mr. District Attorney, Joseph Ellison," said Baldwin.

"What the hell is he doing at your office?"

A voice shot from the back of the car, "Quit asking questions. I don't even live here anymore, and I know *why* he's here. But, Jesus, Richie, who *is* this fuckin' guy?"

District Attorney Joe Ellison had always relished seeing his picture in the papers or his face and creamy voice on the evening news. He was a politician's politician, a pure animal of narcissism, especially when he smelled a hot case. Unbeknownst to the good citizens he claimed he worked to protect, and thanks to loose lips in the police, he was going to expedite a press conference that there was a serial killer in the city of Chicago. It was Ellison's plan that his office would both release the news and simultaneously announce an arrest had been made, and that he, Joe Ellison, had been directly responsible for the killer's capture. Ellison could see the headlines already. It was all part of his master plan which ultimately led to the attorney general's office, the governor's mansion, and beyond.

The fly in the ointment was Baldwin. Ellison had done dozens of shady, even brazenly illegal, real estate deals with him for years and reaped millions of dollars in ill-gotten profits in the process. Baldwin was about to find himself in the crosshairs of the police on suspicion of murder and first-degree criminal sexual assaults on dozens of young girls. This meant Ellison needed damage control, now. It was time to take drastic measures to distance himself from Baldwin and ensure his political career and his freedom stayed afloat.

He had reason to be fearful; if caught and convicted, he would be sharing the same living quarters with hundreds of men he had put in prison over the years. These criminals would be only too happy to welcome their new housemate into the world of prison life—through whatever means they deemed as justice. The thought of such a potential future swirled discomfortingly through the DA's mind.

Luckily for Ellison, Baldwin had come up with a contingency in the form of evidence—six hairs belonging to Remy Thibodeaux. During the melee with Baldwin's thugs at the theater in Cicero, one of them had managed to grab a handful of Remy's hair, despite getting his ribs broken in the process. The entire plot to abduct Lisette D'Argent had been a ruse from the get-go. The real plan was always this: to set Remy up for murder.

Now, Ellison would plant Remy's hair at the scene of the latest crime and consequently charge him with the other murders. It would be an open and shut case. Remy was completely innocent, of course, but Ellison would be able to use the evidence to get himself and Baldwin off the hook. As skillful as he could be in a courtroom, the DA was unmatched when it came to using the court of public opinion. He would carry off a guilty verdict against Remy and further demand a life sentence as punishment for the heinous crimes. Remy being perfectly innocent was inconsequential to Ellison's and Baldwin's current plight and a boon to the current plan. Someone had to go. Who better than some no-name Cajun cook?

The complexity of these machinations had obviously escaped the dimwitted Denny Renaldo. It was not the first time Baldwin questioned why he had hired him. Carmine Tratella had told the business mogul that Denny was a good, blunt tool, and he had fallen for it.

"If I knew what the DA was doing, why would I ask?" said Renaldo.

"Because you're a dumb fuck," said Baldwin, irritated.

"Do what the man says and shut the fuck up, Denny, before you get us both killed."

Denny did as he was told and left the car, returning soon after.

"Okay, you got the bag?" asked Baldwin to Denny. "Now you can talk. Go."

"Got it right here," said Denny, producing a small, snack-size Ziploc bag. Inside the bag were numerous lightly colored strands with what appeared to be human hair.

"Let me see it," said the voice from the back seat. Denny turned and handed the bag back to Vincent Cribaldi.

Cribaldi examined the bag without opening it and held it out to Baldwin in the front seat. "You better be sure about this," he said. It wasn't a question.

"Denny?" said Baldwin. "The man's asking you a question. Answer him."

Denny now sensed he should choose his words very carefully. "Uh, yes, Mr. Baldwin, and, er, Mr. Cribaldi. It's just like the boss said. I already got a handful during the fight and then me and Frank got on all fours and searched the whole floor where we was fighting after we got out of the hospital. We got these hairs from the blonde guy. They were the only ones. They ain't my color and they ain't Frank's. We put 'em in the bag just like you asked, Mr. Baldwin," said Denny.

Baldwin carefully eyed Vincent Cribaldi in the rearview mirror. "Good enough for you, Vinny?" he asked.

Vincent Cribaldi had also partnered with Richard Baldwin and the DA on those same *fugazzi* real estate deals, using family influence and muscle. It was before either of them knew what Baldwin got up to in his spare time. Even though Vincent's father, Anthony Cribaldi, ran Chicago from an organized crime perspective, if Baldwin went down, chances were he would take Vincent down with him.

Anthony Cribaldi openly despised child molesters more than any single thing in the world. *You don't harm children, ever*, he had said many times. He had dealt with such people in the past, in ways beyond brutality. Vincent knew that if the plan failed, he would be as good as dead to his father. Though he wasn't guilty of raping the innocent children, his father would maintain that Vincent should have put a bullet in Baldwin's head himself, knowing the family law on the subject.

Vincent nodded once at Baldwin and said, "Okay, Richie. You know what to do," and handed back the bag to him, who put it in the inside pocket of his suit, nodded at Cribaldi in the rearview mirror, and got out of the car. He walked up the street and stopped on the opposite side from his office building, waiting. The driver's side window of the cruiser rolled down and the driver motioned for Baldwin to approach. He jaywalked and stopped at the car.

"Hey, Billy, what do you know?" asked Baldwin to the man behind the wheel, who looked at him and turned away without a response.

The rear passenger window slid down and a voice from the back seat said, "Well, hello there, Richard."

The District Attorney for the County of Cook in the State of Illinois was indeed the other member in the car.

"Do you have something for me?" asked DA Joseph Ellison.

"Yeah, right here," he said, patting the side of his jacket.

"Get in," said Ellison, "we're going for a ride. I'll talk to Vincent later."

Baldwin said nothing but hurried around the car and got in the back seat opposite Ellison. It sped away from the curb with the second car falling in behind it.

Denny Renaldo, rattled, turned and said to Vincent Cribaldi in the back, "Jesus, what the fuck was that, Mr. Cribaldi? Why did Mr. Baldwin leave with the DA?"

"Hey, Lenny, move over and drive us out of here," said Vincent, ignoring the question. "I can't be seen on the street. I ain't even supposed to be in Chicago right now."

"It's Denny," said Denny quietly, but he complied, jumping out and climbing back in on the driver's side. He started the Mercedes and waited for instructions from Vincent's image in the rearview mirror.

"Get us out of downtown, will ya Lenny? Head south to Decatur Avenue and turn west. We got a warehouse a few miles from here where I can lay low for a while," Vincent said.

Denny drove. He didn't want to ask any more questions. Something in his Neanderthal mind registered a flicker of intelligence and he suddenly understood why he didn't want to be going to a warehouse alone with Vincent Cribaldi. His bowels began to gurgle.

Vincent said, "Hey, what's your name again? Lanny?"

"Uh, it's Denny, Mr. Cribaldi. D-e-n-n-y."

"You know what, D-e-n-n-y? I gotta take a leak. A couple blocks up on the left is Cecil's Tavern. Pull over there and park on the side street. I'll head in the back door. Won't take two seconds," said Vincent.

Denny turned the corner and tucked the Mercedes into a space between two large box vans, taking care not to scratch the fenders. Baldwin would have his head if he found a single mark on his new Mercedes. He made it cleanly with room to spare and put the car in 'park.'

A single shot fired from the back seat propelled a silenced .45 caliber bullet into the back of Denny's head, scattering the dashboard and windshield with whatever remaining thoughts he might have had about scratching Richard Baldwin's Mercedes.

Or what was in the plastic bag.

END OF PART ONE

Part Two

Chapter 35

Patti O'Brien came walking briskly into the kitchen at Chez Rousseau. Remy was busy plating four simultaneous orders of the *Poisson Avril* and motioning to a *commis* for a final saucing and a plate wipe. Patti leaned in and asked Remy quietly, "Where is Jacques?"

"He was here a minute ago, Patti. Why aren't you out front?" asked Remy, keeping his voice controlled. "We're slammed right now—who's covering?"

"Don't worry, *cher*. Wendy Lynn's got it. We're fine," Patti said, then took in a deep breath. "Remy, she's here."

"Who's here?"

"Who do you think?"

"Oh, shit," Remy said. "Barnes? Already? It's only 7 o'clock...isn't her reservation for 8:00?!"

"I got a text from one of my driver buddies at the limousine service—he said she wanted to get here early," Patti explained. "And he said she's in a foul mood. Checked in at her hotel late and went down to the bar there. He saw her order four martinis when he was bringing in her bags."

"So? She knows we won't serve her until her reservation time," said Remy. "What is she going to do, sit at the bar here and get even more plowed? Jesus, Patti, you need to find Jacques *now*. Let him run interference or play host or whatever. Just keep that bitch out of my kitchen," he finished, agitated.

"Bitch indeed!" said Priscilla Barnes, standing in the doorway. "Mr. Thibodeaux, is that any way to refer to a lady?" She had been standing there for quite some time, having followed Patti at a distance. It had been unwise to leave the Queen of Mean unattended and unsupervised at the hostess stand.

Remy stood, frozen, unable to speak. Patti was equally worthless.

Before they could even think of conjuring something to cover Remy's gargantuan *faux pas*, a voice in the kitchen boomed.

"Why Ms. Barnes!" Jacques said loudly from behind her. "How can I help you? You have surprised us all with your early entrance! Why, you have even jumped your cue!" Jacques moved over to Barnes and adroitly took her arm in his, wheeling her around in one motion to lead her back to the dining room.

Barnes shook herself off Jacques' arm violently and straightened herself. "Well, Monsieur Rousseau! It's so good of you to join us!" she said, teeth bared. "For a moment there, I thought you had decided to duck and run back to France to hide under your mother's apron!"

Barnes gave an icy smile at the jab and Jacques winced internally, revealed nothing.

"No? Well, here I am, the Queen of Cuisine!" she continued, crooning. "And I'd like to be seated. Now." Barnes's eyes burned at Patti and Remy.

"Oh, I am so sorry, Priscilla," Jacques said warmly, his teeth also flaring with fake civility. "I'm so sorry," he repeated, "But your reservation is not for another 55 minutes, and our policy is firm on that. Also, no one is allowed in the kitchen except employees. Safety precautions, you know," he said. "I could seat you at the bar, but I am afraid it is full of people waiting for their table, *patiently*," he said, "unlike you."

"Monsieur Rousseau? Either you get me a table now, this very minute, or I leave. And believe me, if I leave, you have my solemn guarantee that the world will know how badly you mistreated me. My fans never forget, and I never forgive," Barnes threatened. She leaned in and motioned to Jacques so she could whisper in his ear.

Jacques leaned forward and immediately detected a dense fog of vodka on her breath, trying his best to school his face.

Barnes whispered, huskily, "And I'll just bet you didn't know I knew about your poor, dead mother? Poor little Jacques," she teased as she moved away from his ear and said audibly, "A murdered mother…that is so sad! But life goes on, so get me a table, garçon. Now," Barnes mocked, while she studied Jacques to see how well she had driven her dagger.

Remy and Patti stood nearby, completely stunned by the sheer cruelty of the emotional grenade Barnes had just detonated upon their leader. Remy knew the story about Jacques' mother, but Patti did not and how Barnes knew was a baffling mystery. Tears formed in Patti's eyes, and she turned to Remy to burrow her face into his shoulder.

Remy stood stock-still and fumed. He wanted to pick Barnes up and heave her down the flight of stairs to the basement and break her fucking neck in the process, but he knew the restaurant would surely be doomed if he did so.

Jacques simply stood there, taking the blows from Barnes and saying nothing. His face had morphed to marble—no emotion whatsoever—and he held himself together, standing perfectly erect as he slowly offered his arm to Barnes again, which she took.

Jacques spoke to Patti in a low, controlled voice. "Ms. O'Brien? Do we have a preferred table for our guest? Please, Priscilla, allow me," said a sanguine Jacques and he walked with her slowly back to the dining room, holding the door with his other arm while Patti led the way, dabbing at her eyes quickly.

Remy went back to the pass and continued with the dinner service. They would have to juggle tables. "Jaime!" Remy yelled. "Fire Table 12, *immediamente!* Rodrigo! Table 14's order is coming right behind that one! Let's move, people! We're juggling tonight!"

The whole kitchen staff snapped to attention and held their collective breath—it was the first time Remy had ever raised his voice to anyone during service. Something was terribly wrong.

Chapter 36

Young Jacques was coming from Montreaux's shoppe with his father's bottle of *vin rouge*. His face hurt terribly, and he couldn't see out of his left eye. He had looked at his reflection in the window glass at Montreaux's and touched his face gently with a finger, wincing at the bolt of pain. His father knew exactly where to hit to register maximum effect. It was his gift.

Jacques walked a block around the café so he would not have to pass Anton's friends again. He knew that by now Anton would be at work at Letreuce's, but he did not wish for the men to see his face. It looked much worse than before.

As Jacques walked up the Rue du Gaspard toward home in the afternoon sun, he heard the sirens from a couple blocks away. His heart jumped, and his feet took off in a mad dash, moving as fast and as hard as his 11-year-old legs could propel him, given the fearful thoughts that ran through his young imagination.

He sprinted to his block and saw two ambulance drivers attending to his mother, who was sitting on the steps of the Rousseau home—a tiny, dreary cottage—and holding a large cloth to her face. The police had been called as well, and two of the *gendarmes* were seen corralling Jacques' father on the small porch.

A third *gendarmes*, the senior officer in charge, had been managing the growing crowd and blocked Jacques as he approached the sidewalk.

Jacques said, "This is my home, monsieur, and that is my mother," he said. "Let me pass." The man led Jacques aside, keeping an eye on the crowd.

"What is your name?" he asked.

"Jacques Rousseau. That is my mother, Clarice Rousseau, he said, pointing a finger.

"Is that man your father?" the officer asked and motioned toward the porch.

Jacques paused, and a thought occurred to him. For the first time in his life, he was presented with an opportunity to punish his father. Both he and his mother had endured an almost-daily cruelty together under that same roof for as long as memory lived. Jacques certainly wanted to punish his father for what he did earlier that day—striking his mother and himself and taking his hard-earned money.

"What did the man do?" asked Jacques, bypassing the policeman's question. His father, who had continued to struggle and resist the other two gendarmes, had been placed in hand restraints.

"Jacques! You will say nothing to these men!" Gilles Rousseau bellowed loudly from the porch. "You will tell them nothing! Or I swear I will…" and with this, one of the policemen gave Gilles a sharp rap on the back of his head with a sap. Gilles became instantly quiet.

The officer asked again, "Is this man your father?"

Jacques dodged the question once more. He was learning the game. "He beats us, monsieur. My maman and me. He hurts us. He does not work, and he takes my money for his daily *vin rouge* and drinks it and makes us suffer," Jacques said calmly, rationally.

But the words, once they had begun, gained in speed and urgency. This confession to the police officer was, in essence, Jacques purging all the bad memories his father had delivered upon him in his short life. At the same time, it gave the police a reason to take him away. Oh, he wished they would take him away. Take him and throw him in a dark place where he could not hit his family and they would feed him wet, moldy bread and no cheese and no wine, only cloudy water and mushy bread. Not having any wine would cause his father to shake.

Jacques remembered many days when his father had had to go without drink because there was no money. Gilles would pace the floor, back and forth, sweat covering his face and making large, wet shapes on his shirt, front and back. He would not leave the house. On those days, Clarice would keep Jacques with her, away from their home, to take interminably long walks until they had no choice but to return.

Jacques wanted his father to suffer now. For the first time, he wished his father was dead. It would be better for them, he knew it. Their lives would be better, more peaceful. He looked into the officer's eyes and pleaded as if it were his last act on Earth.

"Will you take him away, monsieur? Please…take him away!" cried Jacques.

Gilles heard his son's words and shot to attention, coming alive, full of anger and fire, "*Vous petit bâtard putain! Je te fera du mal à mon retour! Je vais te faire souffrir!*

Jacques did not feel afraid, despite his father's threats of vengeance. Now, more than ever, he was assured he had made the right decision.

He watched in silence as three quick blows were delivered from the sap in the policeman's hand to the back of Gilles Rousseau's head, knocking him unconscious. The two strong men grabbed his arms and legs, hauling Gilles like a slaughtered boar ready for the coals. The only missing piece to the image in Jacques' mind was the long stick threaded between his father's bound hooves, and, of course, the ceremony of placing the bastard over a hot fire and roasting him. Instead, the *gendarmes* threw him in the back of one of the squad cars and rejoined the senior officer speaking to Jacques.

Jacques moved to his mother on the steps. "Maman? Are you alright? What did he do?" he said, taking conscious effort not to refer to Gilles as his papa anymore.

Clarice slowly lowered the cloth she had been using to dab blood from her face. Her son's eyes glazed over with tears at the sight.

Clarice Rousseau's left eye was completely closed and swollen with blood. Her lip was savagely cut and would require stitches. It left no doubt that Gilles Rousseau had used his closed fist this time. She tried to smile at Jacques to show it was not as bad as it looked but stopped, the pain from her gashed lip was so great.

Monsters really did exist.

She mumbled, "Do not worry, *mon Tati*. I will be alright," and replaced the cold, wet cloth on her bulging eye, which had continued to bleed.

Jacques' heart wilted at the thought of his father's huge, stony fist landing on his sweet mother's face. Surely, she had done nothing—had never done anything—to deserve this kind of treatment from the devil that was his father.

That...beast! thought Jacques. *I will make him pay this time, now that his heart has turned to granite. I will make him suffer, oh, how I will make him suffer,* Jacques vowed to himself. He would find a way.

Jacques lightly hugged his mother, careful to touch her so as not to create pain, then he stood and said to the three policemen, "I wish to press full charges for my father's assault on my mother."

The three men looked at each other and the senior *genderme* said, "Were there any witnesses?"

Clarice Rousseau sensed a miscarriage of justice was about to occur, and spoke up, tears in her voice. "Is not my face evidence enough for you, monsieur?" she asked.

The officer shook his head and said, "I'm afraid not, Madame Rousseau. And as your son is a minor, this makes his claim inadmissible without corroboration. We will need a third party to prove it. It is a very serious charge. Your husband would go to prison for a very long time if it were true."

Then a voice came forth from the sidewalk path.

"I am a witness, officer."

The people in the crowd all turned and saw the great chef, Pierre Letreuce, and they all moved as one to make a wide opening for him. He continued, "I saw the man you have in custody, Gilles Rousseau, strike his wife. Many times, he hit her with his fists and, as you have seen, he is a very strong man." Pierre stepped closer to the officers, avoiding eye contact with Jacques.

"Who are you, monsieur?" asked the junior officer.

The senior officer shot the young man a stern look, and began to say, "This is Monsieur Pierre Le…"

"My name is Pierre Letreuce," he said, finishing the introduction. "This boy is Jacques Rousseau, and he helps out at my restaurant each morning," said Pierre. "Today, I had forgotten to pay him and came here to his home to do so. As I was about to knock on the door, I heard loud noises inside. I looked in the window and that is when I saw Monsieur Rousseau beating his wife. I knocked on the window to stop him, but he ignored me and continued striking Madame. Surely, my word as a witness will satisfy you gentlemen now?" he asked.

Everyone in Marseilles knew the name Pierre Letreuce, if not by face, certainly by name and reputation. The officers stepped aside to confer with one another, and Jacques' eyes did not move from Pierre, who carefully put a finger to his lips as a signal to Jacques to not speak, while the officers kept discussing what to do about Gilles Rousseau.

With a stellar witness, they would have no choice but to charge and jail him for the crime. Pierre's confession had changed everything. Jacques moved to join Pierre's side, but he communicated to Jacques by moving his head imperceptibly side-to-side. *No, Jacques, stand still and say nothing,* it said. *Let this play out.*

"Madame Rousseau, will you come with us, please?" said the officer in charge. "We will take you to the hospital for your injuries and we will be pressing formal charges against your husband. You will not see him for at least 2 or 3 years, and possibly longer. Tomorrow, if you are feeling better, we would like you to come to the police station so that we may complete the necessary documents," he said, tacking on, "But only if you feel you can do so," after a second of thought.

Clarice motioned for Jacques, and he went to her. "I think this would be best, Jacques. You think so too, yes?" she asked.

"*Oui, Maman,*" said Jacques. "Three years will not be long enough for him," he finished, refusing again to attach the title of "Papa" to the monster who had hurt his mother. "I don't want to see him *ever again,*" he said with a forcefulness that made his mother sad.

She felt responsible for all of it. It was her fault. She had not loved Gilles enough to stop his drinking, nor save him from the anger that grew inside him daily. No words could be more wrong, but Clarice felt she had failed to keep a happy, loving household. Now, she worried about what would become of her and her precious boy.

She stood finally, lifting herself with care so as not to make her pain flare. "Officer, I cannot leave my boy alone in the house. He is too young to be by himself in the night," she said.

The officer in charge replied, "We will take him to St. Catharine's Orphanage. The nuns of the order will be good to him."

"No," Pierre Letreuce said, stopping the man. "He can stay with me, if Madame Rousseau will permit," and Pierre looked at Clarice for her approval.

She looked at Pierre and then away, thinking deeply for a moment before she nodded solemnly, a tear appearing in her good eye.

"Do not worry, Madame," Pierre said. "I have a comfortable home above my restaurant, and there is plenty of room for Jacques, if he would like to stay with me." Pierre then twisted the corner of his mouth and a glint twinkled in his eye. "But I wonder if we will have anything good for him to eat?" he said with the lightest wry touch. To hear such ridiculous words from the greatest chef in France made everyone look twice at him, but the soft, coy humor had been conveyed.

Clarice began to weep, at both Pierre's generosity as well as his good heart that knew when light humor was permissible to soften an otherwise horrible day. It was a very French thing to do. She gave Pierre her hand in gratitude, which Pierre, ever the Son of France, took, placing a kiss on the back, and bowing as he did so. Clarice then reached up and kissed Pierre lightly on both cheeks, favoring her gashed lip, and looked in his eyes with the deepest gratitude.

She turned to her son. "Jacques, you must go with Monsieur Letreuce for tonight and perhaps longer. You will be alright, my darling?" she asked.

"Oui, Maman. I like it at Monsieur Letreuce's. I will be fine. Do not worry," Jacques said.

He took her by the hand and squeezed it for emphasis and uttered his first words as a young man. "I promise, you and I will be fine from now on, Maman," said Jacques. "I am going to work even harder for Monsieur Letreuce. We will need the money, and I like it in the kitchen. I like learning to cook from Pierre. *Je t'aime, Maman. Je t'aime.* Go now," he commanded lightly and let go of her hand.

Clarice went with the *gendarmes*, who helped her carefully into the back of the ambulance and then it moved slowly out of the Rue du Gaspard. Jacques went with Pierre and the crowd dissolved as everyone moved on with the remainder of their day. The cafes in town would soon be buzzing with the news of the assault as well as the heroic gesture of Pierre Letreuce.

Chapter 37

The first course Jacques served to Priscilla Barnes for her review meal was a luxurious *Pâté de Campagne*, a cold pate made of finely ground meat, which included slow-roasted pork and cold pork belly, minced onion, salt, thyme, allspice, garlic, pepper, and a generous splash of cognac. The mixture was pulverized into a fine paste and piped into ornately shaped ramekins that had been generously greased inside with duck fat and then chilled in the refrigerator to firm them up. They were served *en croute* with three whisper-slivers of spring onion and it was a simple but formidably civilized way to begin the menu.

Jacques had served the first course personally, so as to set the stage for the entire dinner and give the reviewer his undivided attention. Barnes held their futures in her words and Jacques sensed his people knew this. For the first time ever, the staff at Chez Rousseau saw their boss was not himself. He was nervous and defensive, not calm and confident. He looked like a waitron on their first night, clumsy and ham-handed—grappling for purchase on a slippery slope.

Barnes sat, perfectly erect, no longer showing signs of her earlier intoxication; rather, she looked completely in her element. She lived for these moments like no other, taking her first bite of the *pâté* and closing her eyes, letting it warm in her mouth before slowly chewing and swallowing.

This is so delightful, she thought, taking another bite. Barnes had placed a small note pad on the table for jotting down observations and now made notes on the *pâté*. She took another bite and finished the single *en croute*, leaving the other two on the plate, untouched.

"Chef Rousseau, that was very nice," said Barnes, jotting down another note. She looked up at Jacques with an expectant expression. "Next?"

Jacques bowed and said, "Oui, Mademoiselle. The next course is a micro-portion of *Salade Niçoise* with my special dressing and the inclusion of quail eggs. Finally, I have your signature entrée, the *Poisson Avril*, a salmon fillet prepared with....well, I'm sure you know what it is and how I make it. I have paired the salmon with a 1970 Cheval Blanc, a superb vintage that is in prime condition to drink. Although, now that I think about it, I should change the name, *Poisson Avril*, because, of course, it is no longer April, you see," Jacques said, reverting his original intentions of being unique by forever keeping the name *Poisson Avril*. He sounded so oafish tonight! It was astounding to see and hear him fumble about so dreadfully.

"Yes, chef, I see. I see everything," intoned Barnes in a dead voice. She made a note and as she wrote, spoke to Jacques without looking up. "Menu items do not accurately verify or reflect the current times," she said, "server appears unconfident," and made a tisking sound with her mouth, chiding the great chef. She finished her note and looked up at Jacques, waiting.

"Please proceed with the next course, Chef," she said.

Jacques bowed and left to return to the kitchen, where no doubt, Remy had received intelligence from Rodrigo on her progress throughout the meal. The salad had been delivered by another runner as Jacques returned to the kitchen. Though he did not see it, Priscilla took a bite of the *Niçoise* and closed her eyes for a long moment, savoring. She then shook her head softly and engaged in three more forkfuls, each visibly captivating her palate.

Her every move that evening was not lost on nearby diners, who fully recognized the food critic in their midst. It was, obviously, a very important night, and the whispers soon swept throughout the Chez Rousseau dining room, that after a long *tete-a-tete* between Jacques and Barnes on social media, the battle royale was now waging forth right in front of them.

The salmon was being started in the sauté pan by Remy as Jacques came through the kitchen doors.

"How's it going?" Remy asked.

Jacques shrugged and said, "She is being prickly, but she clearly enjoyed the *pâté*."

Jacques was showing his stress, thought Remy. He tried to keep things light and straightforward, but he was failing.

"Well, here is the *Poisson, mon ami*. It'll be ready in 6 minutes. Let her sip her wine and enjoy the *Niçoise*. In fact, have a sip of wine yourself. You need it."

Jacques shook his head and dabbed beads of perspiration from his forehead with a handkerchief.

Jacques stood next to the pass, a mere 4 feet from Remy, and said not a single word as he prepared the *Poisson*.

Remy plated the salmon and slid it across the pass to Jacques, who didn't move. Remy snapped him to attention.

"Go, Jacques," he said.

Jacques nodded at Remy with a wan smile and took the plate, turning to go and running smack into Rodrigo, the plate flipping from his hand and crashing to the floor and shattering. Salmon, sauce, and bits of bone china scattered everywhere across the clean floor. Jacques was so off his game now; he simply stared at Rodrigo as if he had just urinated on the lobster bisque. Being unable to defend himself against Barnes had clearly put him back on his heels, but Remy saved him.

"Jacques! Ami!" said Remy, as quietly as possible. He did not want the dining room to hear any disturbances in the kitchen. "Chef!" he hissed. "No worries….I can switch another *Poisson* from another table. Here! It is ready to go! Take it, Jacques," Remy said, ready to lose his mind right along with his partner's.

Jacques took the plate, and this time, made sure his path was clear to the dining room. He moved through the swinging doors and disappeared. Remy had a backup plan ready for this very reason. His best friend was lost tonight, and Remy offered up a quick prayer that there would be no other miscues, if not for his friend's sake, then certainly for all of theirs.

Barnes had taken several pictures of the *Poisson Avril* and was now jotting terse notes. Jacques stood at stiff attention off to the side of her table, in anticipation of her next request, or, more likely, another jab. If this were a boxing match, Barnes would definitely be ahead on points. She took a large first bite of the salmon and chewed so deeply in thought that Jacques wondered if she might have dozed for a second. Then her eyes opened, and she took another bite, before closing her eyes again, savoring. She finished chewing, set down her fork, and picked up her pen, an almost robotic movement, then quickly set it down and picked up her fork again—treating herself to a third

bite. She chewed and swallowed, dabbing her lips with a napkin. She looked at Jacques, a beatific look on her face.

"Chef?"

"Oui, Mademoiselle?"

She spoke in clean French as she praised the dish: *"Jacques, ce saumon est paradisiaque. C'est le meilleur saumon que j'ai jamais goûté. Vous connaissez vraiment les secrets des dieux,"* Barnes said, in a kind and genteel tone. Her face was aglow.

Jacques smiled and bowed, regaining some of his confidence, and responded as well in his native tongue, to thank her, *"Merci, Mademoiselle Barnes. C'est très gentil à vous de dire. Je suis si heureux que vous l'appréciez."*

Barnes took one last large bite, chewing thoughtfully, and then daubed at her lips with her napkin. She picked up her pen and jotted some final notes. Jacques felt much better. She had liked the salmon very much and told him so to his face, and perhaps loudly enough for other nearby guests to hear?

Barnes put down the pen and looked up at Jacques.

"Chef?" she said.

"Oui...Priscilla," Jacques said. "If you will permit me to call you by your first name," he said, smiling. It was a genuine smile. He liked it when people truly enjoyed his food. He leaned in further to his guest, a respectful gesture.

Barnes's eyes transformed from soft and kind to devil's fire right in front of Jacques. She lowered her voice a full octave so the other tables could not hear her and fired one last mythical bullet into the chef.

"Your salmon is simply the finest I have ever eaten. It truly is otherworldly. But if you think I'm going to tell that to my millions of readers, you are sadly mistaken. I will instead be telling everyone that my journey to Chez Rousseau has been a disappointing waste of my time. I will write that your *Poisson Avril* is for shit. Overcooked. Pretentious and flavorless," she said. "I will tell them to avoid it and you and this posturing dump of a French restaurant at all costs…and they will believe me, even if it is a lie," Barnes said in a flat, contemptuous assassin's voice. Jacques said nothing, merely taking the last salvo from the Queen.

She had no intention of paying her dinner bill – why start now? Instead, she reached for her purse, removed a $20 bill, stood up and moved over to Jacques. She leaned in and slid the folded bill into the front pocket of his chef's coat, then air-kissed both sides of his face and whispered, "*Au revoir*, Rousseau. I must go now—I have a review to publish! Oh, and you may keep the change! You will need it now, no?" she said musically and then began to walk out of Chez Rousseau, but as she passed him, Jacques whirled and gently took her arm and placed it in his. This time, Barnes could not throw him off in the dining room as she had done in the kitchen, without starting a scene and appearing out-of-control.

"Please allow me to escort you," said Jacques with similar fake kindness. "I have reserved a car to take you to your hotel, the airport, wherever you wish to go!" and the two of them walked arm in arm past the hostess stand and a dumbstruck Patti O'Brien and out the front entrance. The entire room witnessed the exit and then returned to their conversations, albeit slowly. The battle, it appeared, was over.

Jacques and Barnes stood under the large red awning, waiting for her car, nothing but cold silence between them; Priscilla Barnes had expected her last words to be the guillotine in any future discussion she and Jacques might have had. This move by him was a surprise, but no matter. Jacques spoke first.

"I wanted to ask if you had been able to taste and identify all of the ingredients in the *Pâté de Campagne*?" he asked innocently.

Barnes eyed Jacques for a moment and thought, *Okay, I'll play along with this.*

"Hmmm....the pork AND pork belly...very delicious, I might add...perfectly cooked, just the right texture and ample fat for richness...the spice palette was pure symmetry," she said, rattling off each one correctly. She continued, "I enjoyed the essence of the cognac and you used duck fat to grease the sides of the ramekins," she said.

Jacques nodded. She was correct on every point. It was sad to see such obvious culinary instincts become so wasted and misdirected. "You're missing one, though," he said. "Another flesh mixed with the pork, but which kind?" he asked with a salacious wink.

"Rousseau, this is boring. You're trying to get back in the game, which is impossible. I've already won," Barnes said.

"You have heard the phrase, 'you are what you eat,' no? Of course you have," said Jacques.

"Everyone knows that phrase. Get to the point, my car is pulling up," Barnes said, growing annoyed now.

"*I fed you a ground up anus,*" said Jacques. He didn't wait for Barnes to respond and continued, "That's right. I won't say from which animal—but it was ground up and mixed
with the port and meat and spice mixture and I fed it to you. But you did not know! It's beautiful, you see? Now, you truly *are* what you eat…an asshole!" and Jacques started laughing loudly. He was relishing the moment, and the arched, frozen look on Barnes's face was priceless to see.

Her eyes searched Jacques' for a bluff and found none. She swallowed deeply, emitting a slight groan. "You didn't…I mean, you wouldn't?" she said in an almost pleading voice, seeking some kind of reprieve from his eyes. There was nothing of the kind, only a masked delight at her pained disgust.

"Priscilla. Get in the car," said Jacques softly, still smiling. "Go and write your review. And may you choke on it," said Jacques, leaving Barnes to get in the car unassisted as he strolled back into his restaurant.

The driver had popped out of the car and held the door open for her and she stepped in haltingly, sliding onto the back seat as he closed the door behind her. Back inside the car, the driver awaited instructions. After several seconds of silence, he finally spoke.

"Where to, ma'am?" he asked.

Priscilla Barnes was silent. She was fighting to wrap her mind around someone feeding her something so wholly repulsive and then cheerily boasting about it. She stopped thinking, because if she pondered it any further, the driver was going to have to clean up a mess of pate', salmon and wine…and anus…and she promptly leaned over and threw up on the taxi floor.

The driver seemed nonplussed by it all. "That rich food got to you, huh? Don't worry about that, ma'am. Slide over to the other side and I'll clean it up later. Now, where can I take you?" he asked warmly, turning to look at Priscilla Barnes while awaiting her orders.

Priscilla tried to think through the maze of her blurred thoughts as she moved behind the driver. "Um…take me to my hotel and then the airport," she muttered. "I want to get back to New York, now," and leaned back in the seat, suddenly weary.

The driver nodded to her in the mirror. "Right you are, ma'am. The airport it is," said Carmine Tratella.

Don Anthony Cribaldi's ranking *capo de regime* and lead enforcer, Carmine Tratella, a stone-cold killer with 63 hits under his belt, was now posing as the chauffer for Priscilla Barnes. He winked at her, then turned back around and straightened his chauffer's cap, put the car in drive and accelerated quickly away from the curb at Chez Rousseau. Carmine's acting chops made him a very passable limo driver, which was good for business. He had used his formidable talents over the years to lure many an unsuspecting mark. Unfortunately, it meant bad news for Barnes, the very worst of news.

Carmine wasn't driving Priscilla Barnes to the airport, nor was she flying back to New York anytime soon.

Chapter 38

WHERE is Priscilla Barnes?

The headline leapt off the page in the following morning's Restaurant section of the New York Post. The same story had appeared in the Chicago Sun-Times, a copy of which Remy held out for Jacques to see.

"Did you see this?" asked Remy to Jacques.

"I have," said Jacques.

"I wonder what happened to her."

"After she left here? I couldn't tell you."

"Jacques? Are you levelling with me? And why did Oprah leave suddenly before her maple crème brulee? She didn't look happy," said Remy.

"Remy, I was here with you the whole night for heaven's sake. After Barnes left here, I have no idea where the driver might have taken her. As for Oprah, she can't stand Priscilla Barnes. When I brought out the *Niçoise*, I passed Oprah's table and she made the nastiest face at Barnes. I guess that's why she left."

"And what did you say to Barnes on the street? Patti couldn't make out anything you two were saying to each other, but from her vantage point, it didn't look friendly, but it also looked like you had the last word, judging by the way Barnes got into her car. So?" Remy asked.

Jacques lowered his eyes and said to the floor, "Let's go someplace else, and I'll tell you everything. These walls have ears."

Jacques had told Remy the truth. He did not know where the driver had taken Priscilla Barnes.

But he knew Don Cribaldi did.

Chapter 39

The room was cold. She had sat on the hard chair for some time now, but her ass kept falling asleep, so she would alternate between sitting on the chair and lying on the mattress on the floor. When she was first thrown into the room, seeing the multitude of different colored stains on the mattress made her nauseated again. *God knows what went on here*, she had thought to herself when they first tossed her in, believing it had been nothing more than partying and sex and other harmless shenanigans.

But as the hours crawled by, and night became the following morning, a sinking feeling began to invade her thoughts. Priscilla had had a fertile imagination going back to childhood, and the matter of how the stains got there was now playing on her mind. The room was small and reeked of urine. The man had left her in the room with nothing but a bottle of water. As he was leaving, she had shouted, "Wait! Where do I go to the bathroom?" But he was already gone. The idea of peeing in a corner seemed so gauche. Then her mind dove to a harsher reality: what about having to shit? It locked her bowels down, hard, like that of a heavy English castle door slamming shut. *Boom*.

It had to have been Rousseau, but her reasoning was taking on a desperate tone. He had to have planned this, but how? He was nothing more than a chef with a successful restaurant. He wasn't a powerful man, like Vincent. He didn't have armies of men at his disposal, nor the money to finance such a well-planned endeavor as the kidnapping of a world-renowned food critic.

But now a truly haunting thought hit Priscilla: *how the hell am I getting out of here?*

She was hungry. Starving, in fact, and scolded herself for her earlier lack of self-discipline, tossing up what had been the last substantive thing she had eaten, which was the salmon and the other…thing. She should have been stronger, saving the nutrients to keep her body and mind sharp. She didn't want to relive the moment under the Chez Rousseau awning again when Rousseau revealed that he had fed her *a sphincter in her pâté,* but her mind was obsessed with replaying it. Her stomach began to lurch at the thought, and she fought it down with all her might. The nausea passed.

She tried turning her mind to better thoughts, but all it could come up with was getting revenge against her captors. Revenge and hate had always been an endlessly renewable resource for Priscilla Barnes, but now it was turning against her.

She tried to think logically, unlocking the steps it might have taken to hire a car service and secure a remote, vacant building and, most of all, enlisting the help of the other men—the driver, especially—who had seemed so nice, so subservient at first, and then, once they had driven away from downtown, had turned into an utter monster. She postulated on how a simple French chef made it all happen, but the gears wouldn't mesh; the tiny tumblers would not click into place, opening the lock on the door to the room with all the answers. It frightened her, and now the image of the consumed anus reappeared and worse, the recalled sensation of her own lips touching it, tongue flicking over it, her teeth chewing on something so vile. Once more, it began running free in her mind. Her stomach faltering again, and she could no longer fight it.

Priscilla leaned over the side of the mattress and threw up, but without any food for the past 16 hours, the contents were mostly water and bile. It stung her lips. She sat up and wiped her mouth, beginning to shake with anger.

Oh, he would pay, she chanted in her mind over and over again. She was surely going to make them all pay. *You do not treat the Queen like this.*

Chapter 40

"You did WHAT?!" asked Remy. He sat and stared at his best friend, not believing what he had just heard. Then he started laughing.

Jacques explained, "I told her, quote, 'A nugget of cat feces had been incorporated into the *pâté*,' unquote," said Jacques, playing the straight man. "I thought they mixed rather well with the spices, don't you?" he said, smirking. He couldn't possibly tell Remy what he had *actually* fed Barnes. It would have been a turning point in their friendship because it would require an explanation and further conversation he did not want to have.

Remy wiped a tear from the corner of his eye, still chortling, and reached for his tiny espresso cup to take a sip. He shook his head as he set it back in the saucer.

"You're a damned sandbagger, you know that, Jacques? You had us all, hook, line, and sinker! Who in the world thinks of feeding cat shit to the number one food critic in America? You totally played her like a fiddle, my friend. And you had all of us on our toes the last 24 hours, what with all that mopey, 'woe is me' bullshit. Why the hell didn't you let me in on the joke? Hell, I would have gladly acted the part!" Remy said.

"Remy, are you kidding?" said Jacques, getting serious for a moment. "If it had backfired, I didn't want *any* of you involved, because she would get revenge on all of you. As it turns out, she may only come after me," said Jacques. "But I doubt it. I truly do. Now she can't dare give us a bad review, because I will let the entire world know she ate cat shit—I'll make sure of that. Don't forget, there are a thousand people she does business with who will avoid her like…well, like one avoids cat shit. She's a bitch and everyone will say she deserved it. It was the smart move," he said.

"What if she prints a bad review anyway?" asked Remy.

"And why didn't you tell me this last night?"

"She won't give us a bad review, Tati. I'll put all my money on it. And I didn't tell you, because—think about it— you wouldn't have believed me anyway, what with how damned serious everything had become. It was better this way. I wanted to protect you," Jacques said.

"Damn, man. I'm glad you're my best friend. I can't imagine what you'd feed *me*."

"Well, at least we can stop worrying about Priscilla Barnes and get back to business. I hated having to act like a wimp in front of you all, but it was the only way to make you believe I was trying to kiss her ass…"

Remy finished the thought, "…all the while knowing you were going to make her eat shit. Jesus, you're a brilliant savage, Rousseau, you know that?"

Jacques smiled. He liked that…brilliant savage or

Sauvage brilliante, S'il vous plait?

"Okay, Remy, let's get back to the Chez and start planning tomorrow's menu. Are we still going with a hanger steak and the *cassoulet* as prix fix entrees, right? And how about a Kahlua Bread Pudding for dessert with dried currants instead of raisins?" he asked.

"Yeah, we were planning that, until yesterday when you started acting like such a wimp!" Remy began cracking up all over again and threw his hands up in surrender. "Sorry! Sorry! Don't feed me cat shit, boss!" and he kept on giggling, unable to control himself.

Jacques sipped his double espresso and nodded, smiling, finally enjoying a more jovial moment with Remy, after the exhaustion of battle with Barnes. In all honesty, Jacques knew they were damn lucky—he had just defused a ticking time bomb. But the cat shit gag was a good foil, he had to admit, and the look on Priscilla Barnes's face, knowing what he truthfully had made her eat, was worth it a thousand times over.

Chapter 41

Vincent Cribaldi waited in the car outside the Dearborn Social Club, tapping his foot on the floor and training his binoculars on three of the men inside. He was trying to see if Silvio Arradondo, his father's consigliere, had come out from the inner offices to sit at one of the tables and sip coffee—or something stronger. Vincent wasn't about to go into the club, especially if that prick Carmine was there. He didn't want anyone to alert his father of his presence. Vincent was no longer allowed in Chicago, since his father had banished him to the confines of New York City for an unspecified period, all thanks to a huge fuck-up in Chicago last Christmas.

The incident in question surrounded Vincent and a prostitute. He had been engaged in his usual rough sex with a certain call girl at one of the many 'no-tell motels' the family owned and operated around Chicago, but when the woman was less than willing to consent to Vincent's many strange and disturbing sexual repertoires, he became enraged and threw the hooker off the second-floor balcony and onto the asphalt below. She survived the fall, but suffered a broken wrist, a broken leg with a compound fracture, and a broken pelvis. She did not press charges thanks to the delivery of a thick envelope and its implied code of silence.

Then came the delicate matter of explaining to his father, for the umpteenth time, that his overactive and warped libido had once again submerged him in deep, hot water. "We don't need that kind of attention," Anthony had said to Silvio many times before. "This time, he can let his dick get him in trouble in New York. I don't want to see him," and then, he dispatched his consigliere to hand down the sentence to his son.

Vincent, ever the legal tactician, claimed to Silvio that he shouldn't be responsible, responding, "I mean, who tries to break their fall with their arms from the second story, for fuck's sake?" when he delivered the news. Don Anthony's verdict was thus: Banishment from Chicago to New York City for one year, and only New York City, and nowhere else, and subsistence earning from the family teat and nothing more. Anthony had been so disgusted with his son, he didn't want to look at him, which is why he sent Silvio.

Vincent was in trouble of a much graver kind now. He needed consultation, even if it meant violating his father's parole. The real estate scams and the sexual assaults involving Richard Baldwin were about to blow up in everyone's face and he needed to get out in front of the whole mess and do damage control. This was the reason for the meeting with Baldwin, but now all calls to his cell went straight to voice mail.

Vincent knew that Baldwin had simply disappeared—'gone to ground' in Mafiaspeak. If he ever resurfaced, Vincent knew a bullet would find its way into Baldwin's head. Getting rid of the body was easy, but anyone with a brain knew that if Baldwin truly went missing, a trail would be left behind that would ultimately bring the cops straight to both Vincent Cribaldi and Joe Ellison. It might even draw the cops to Anthony Cribaldi, and, at that thought, Vincent actually shuddered and stopped speculating inside his own head.

Joe Ellison was a master at spin-doctoring. Unbeknownst to Vincent, he had already manufactured an iron-clad alibi for himself as well as damning evidence on his partners, and he was prepared to use it against them. The worst of it, of course, was concrete proof that Baldwin had had two barely teenage girls and one child murdered after having repeated sex with them. Vincent obviously knew about it, which made him equally culpable in the eyes of the law, so he was fucked either way. But Vincent had a gut feeling Ellison may have taped some of their conversations regarding Baldwin's despicable activities. In the eyes of his father and Cribaldi family doctrine, recording someone was never, ever done, so eliminating the DA was a strong possibility as well.

Then again, Vincent knew verbatim what his father had long sermonized on the subject of child sexual assault. Vincent knew about Baldwin and did nothing, so by his father's credo, he was as bad as the rapist and the punishment should fit the crime—especially considering his son should have known better.

By the Mafia code of *La Cosa Nostra*, all three needed to go, and they needed to die in excruciating, fiery pain.

There was movement inside the club. Vincent saw Silvio Arradondo seat himself at a small table directly in the *front* window. He sipped from a cup and then took a bite from a plate of *shvooyadell*.

This was not right, Vincent thought, and his instincts set off an alarm. Silvio, like his father the Don, always sat in the back of the club at the large oak table, protected from passing eyes and driveby bullets. They would never seat themselves in full view of the street, where a potential enemy could easily cruise by in a car and blast their guns through the glass. Silvio took another sip from the cup and then raised his hand to wave in the direction of Vincent's car, motioning for him to come inside the club.

Is he waving at me? thought Vincent, confused and wary. Then Silvio pointed his finger directly at Vincent and motioned inside again. *Shit, he knows it's me,* Vincent thought.

"Fuck it," he said and checked his shoulder holster, making sure the 9MM was still loaded and secured inside. He got out of the car and crossed the street, not bothering to watch for cars.

Further down the block, an SUV with dark windows had been watching the cross-communication between the Dearborn Social Club and Vincent. It pulled out slowly from the curb, then began rapidly accelerating. Vincent should have checked the traffic. Better still, he should have stayed in New York and not disobeyed his father. The iniquities of the son were not to be visited upon The Don.

Chapter 42

It had been three days since Priscilla Barnes had eaten at Chez Rousseau. Three whole days since she had eaten anything at all, and she was growing closer to insanity by the second.

The man who had abducted her would come in once a day to deliver more water and had finally brought a urine bucket, but no toilet paper. Each time, Barnes would beg for food, pleading to the man, though she did not know him by name. *Could I please have something to eat?* she'd ask, and each time, her request would fall on deaf ears as the door was once again closed and the lock snapped into place without a single word. The day before, she had offered a blow job to the man and more. He actually laughed at the offer and in reply, threw three water bottles at her. She drank some now, then slowly shuffled back to the mattress, collapsing upon it in a heap of exhaustion.

In her weakened state, she couldn't make her mind work to formulate a plan of escape. There simply wasn't enough energy in her body. It was making her hallucinate as well. Earlier this morning—or was it afternoon now?—she thought she heard voices outside the heavy, locked steel door and swore one of the voices belonged to Jacques Rousseau. She scolded herself: Snap out of it! He was a tiny, inconsequential cook! He was nothing! She was the Queen of Cuisine! She was impervious and the world bowed to her, as always!

Now, she couldn't even trust her own mind. She closed her eyes and drifted off to disturbed sleep, but the images that flowed in her delta-state only confirmed that she was not a worthwhile human being.

An ancient montage flickered in her dreams. She saw her 11-year-old sister, Bridget, her only sibling, who once, long ago, saved her babysitting money to buy her mother a large, magnificent bouquet of chrysanthemums for Mother's Day. *Mums for my mom*, she'd said brightly at the time. Priscilla was 13 then, two years older than Bridget.

It had taken her a whole month of weekends, but Bridget finally saved enough money, and she knew it would be worth seeing the smile on her mom's face the morning of her special day. Bridget did not brag she was doing this, merely shared the information with her older sister, as sisters do. During the night, Priscilla had gotten up and gone into the kitchen, where Bridget's beautiful flowers had already been placed in a vase large enough to hold the many stems and slender blossoms. The flowers' lovely fragrance had already begun to fill the kitchen and it disturbed Priscilla. Bridget had set a tiny Mother's Day card in front of the bouquet and in her simple but clean handwriting on the card, declared, *"I love you so much, Mother. Happy Mother's Day! - Love, your daughter, Bridget."*

Priscilla looked at the note and the flowers, untouched by the thoughtfulness, and went automatically to the cupboard to grab a coffee cup. She filled it with white vinegar and poured it into the vase then went back to bed. When her mother Angelica came into the kitchen early the next morning, the crown of chrysanthemums had wilted, spilling languidly over the outside of the top of the white vase, like an elderly poet who had written their last stanza, taken a final breath, and simply folded over onto the top of their desk, expired.

Her mother read the note from her youngest daughter and then paused. She smelled something and took the vase and blooms to the sink. There she smelled the vinegar. Her heart also wilted a little, for she realized what had happened. Bridget was only 11 but knew fully well how to care for plants and had often helped her mother tend to the Barnes' family garden. It had been Priscilla. Her own daughter—her sister's sister—had deliberately sabotaged this fine, precious gift. And it still was, for now she knew the warm, loving intentions little Bridget's heart had wanted for her mother and it made her brim with joy.

As for her other daughter, well…Angelica had known for some time that her eldest was a mean child. Mean for no discernible reason at all. Mean for sport, mean for kicks.

It was Mother's Day, of all days, when she realized that Priscilla's heart was unlike her little sister Bridget's—it was as hard and coarse as the gravel on their country road in wintertime. She was 13 years old but had been cold and cruel in that way since kindergarten. It was clear now that she would remain this way, and Angelica knew she would not change, ever. Her daughter Priscilla was bad to her core.

Chapter 43

Priscilla heard a voice. "Hey. Open your eyes." Was she still dreaming? Or hallucinating again? Her mind registered a form standing in front of the bed, which meant her eyes had opened. There the man stood, holding a sleeve of crackers in one hand and a bottle of water in the other. She could not make out the face, as her vision had not yet adjusted to the conscious world, but her exceptional olfactory system was tuned to the odor of the crackers, and it kick-started her salivary glands.

"Would you like something to eat, Priscilla? You must be hungry," the voice said. He held out the crackers and said, "Sit up if you want something to eat."

She couldn't believe her eyes or her good fortune. After days of nothing, she was finally going to be able to eat! It was something she had loved to do all her life, to take in food and chew and relish the wondrous tastes, textures, and aromas. She had a superior sense of smell and could discern every spice used in cuisine. She also loved the full feeling in her stomach after a great meal and, best of all, she loved the attention she received in a restaurant. In her career, she had taken great advantage of her position and had made hundreds, if not thousands, of people suffer her cruel bullying, along with the heartless words of her blog that had shuttered dozens of restaurants over time. But she didn't care about that now.

She struggled up from the mattress and managed to fight her way to a sitting position with her feet on the floor splayed out in front of her. She held out her hands, creating a bowl with her palms, like a Dickensian urchin pleading for gruel, and looked up at the man who had chauffeured her from Chez Rousseau some nights ago. "Please," she squeaked to the monster, "May I have a cracker…please?"

"Open your mouth and close your eyes, Priscilla." She did so. The man placed two crackers on her tongue and Priscilla folded them into her mouth and began to weep. She chewed, not aggressively or noisily, but slowly and with great care, making sure to distribute the particles around the entire inside of her mouth. It was a most poignant reunion, Priscilla and her food. It had always been the best relationship she ever knew. The hell with people—she and food would always be one. She finished chewing and swallowed the completely liquefied crackers down her throat.

"Would you like more?" the man said. Priscilla nodded dumbly and shakily as she opened her mouth again.

"Not yet, Priscilla. First, you must do something to earn it."

"What can I do?" her voice croaked softly.

"I'm going to give you a laptop and you are going to write your review for Chez Rousseau. It is not going to be the review you told Chef Rousseau you were going to write. If you do that, I will kill you now and it will be painful. The review you will write is going to be a warm and inviting review, the nicest review you have ever written, and you are going to do it now or you won't get another cracker for the rest of your life. I will leave you in this room and starve you to death. But I will beat you bloody first," said the man. "So get to work," he said, pointing to the corner of the room.

Priscilla turned her head and gazed upon a small table that housed a wooden chair and a laptop. *Had that been there before?* she wondered. It may very well have been, given her fractured state of mind. Now it didn't matter. It would lead her to crackers. She got up slowly, hoping for power in her legs. They worked, and she stood, taking one tentative step toward the table and then another. She made it to the table and pulled out the chair, sitting down heavily, grateful her legs got her there.

The laptop was on, and a word processing program was ready for a command. Priscilla began typing, while visions of crackers and jam danced in her head. The writing at first was deathly slow; she was writing nice words, after all, and she had rarely written such before. She focused and kept writing, the crackers her holy grail.

After one hour, she was finished. It had taken all her reserves of thought and energy and she was ready to faint. She called out at the steel door, hoping the man behind it would hear her cries. "Hello? Hello? Are you there? Can you hear me? I'm finished! Can I have more crackers, please?"

A moment passed and the door opened, allowing the man to enter. He walked over and took the laptop, unplugged it, and walked back out the door, slamming it shut. There were voices behind the door and then silence. After a long moment, the door opened again, and the man walked in once more to set the laptop down on the table and plug it back in. The review was short—only five paragraphs in all—but it was sufficient, according to the person beyond the steel door. The man was satisfied.

"Priscilla? Would you like your crackers now?"

"Yes. Please. I've earned them…haven't I earned them?" she said meekly.

"Wait a minute. We have to send this to your blog publisher first, then email a copy to your assistant. Don't worry, it won't take long, and you can have all the crackers you like." Priscilla's shoulders sagged, but she obeyed the man because the crackers had told her to do so.

"Log into your blog account and paste the review into it and hit 'send.' Don't even try to pull anything funny, Priscilla, or I'll eat all the crackers in front of you and leave you to die," said the man.

Priscilla logged into her blog publisher portal. "Stop," said the man. "Let me check it first." Everything seemed in order. "Okay, Priscilla. Hit 'send,'" which she did, and then repeated the process and sent the email to her assistant, Chloe. When she tapped the last 'send' key, she exploded.

"*Give me my crackers now, you fucker!*" Priscilla screamed. Her eyes blazed in her head. She was crazed.

The man began laughing at her, holding out the sleeve of crackers and then taking one and eating it and then another. This made her even crazier, but, alas, she couldn't pursue the man in her weakened state, so she simply covered her face in her hands and began to weep.

"You won't get a cracker talking to me that way. Do you want a cracker, Priscilla?" said the man, holding out the sleeve. His voice was calm, yet icy.

A greasy tear moved down Priscilla's face, although it was a miracle she could make water of any kind, given her extreme dehydration. The water they gave her over the past days had been enough to keep her alive, but only barely.

"Close your eyes and stick out your tongue, Priscilla, and you can have a cracker. How about two or even *three* crackers?" he asked. The words steadied her, and she sat up straight, arms at her sides, and presented her tongue. "Keep your eyes closed. Here it comes," said the man, but now she heard another sound. The door had opened, and a set of steps whispered across the floor. They moved quickly.

A sharp, grinding pain pierced the front of her tongue and in her stupor, she now felt and saw a pair of channel-lock pliers latched onto her tongue, exposing and pulling it out much farther than it should go. As Priscilla commanded her weary eyelids to re-open, the puntilla knife hissed through the air and severed her tongue in one whipping swipe, severing part of her lower lip as well. The cut took more than half her tongue off and the blood began flowing, thick and fast.

The screams were incredible.

The room itself was small, and being made of brick, it reverberated the echoes exponentially. The man with the crackers was smiling with joy, he *so* relished this part of his work. Even if he wasn't doing the killing, he lived for others' pain. Those in the business who knew of his heartlessness had said, "This one's got a bloody mouth," and this was cold, hard proof. The other man, dressed in black, merely noted the puntilla had done its job properly. It had delivered a beautiful, clean cut.

The sound Priscilla made was as if young lambs had been set on fire. She didn't just scream, she squalled—a long, guttural siren noise—running lower to higher and back. But without most of a tongue to articulate the sound from her throat, she seemed more to bleat, screech, and bellow in a howl of horror. She stumbled about the room as if robotically possessed, pawing and wiping furiously at her mouth as she flung blood everywhere. Then, the last of her energy dropped to zero, and she stumbled amidst her tangled feet, pitching forward, striking her head on the concrete wall in the corner, and falling to the floor, unconscious. The blood still flowed richly out her mouth, covering the shoulders and chest of her crème-colored Chanel blouse.

The two men watched all of the action in bemused detachment. When she finally hit the floor, and was quiet, Carmine Tratella casually ate the rest of the crackers and packed up the laptop while the man in black wiped blood off the puntilla knife with the scrimshaw handle and restored it to its custom leather sheath inside his jacket pocket. He walked over and put two fingers on Priscilla's neck, counting to ten. There was a pulse, but it was irregular, thready, and fading quick.

The two then simply left the room, like sauntering out of a restaurant after a satisfying repast. Their project concluded, they closed the door behind them, and the lock snapped shut. Barnes died from shock and blood loss a mere 10 minutes later, though her body would not be discovered for a very long time.

Chapter 44

A year into his incarceration, Gilles Rousseau was a model prisoner within the French penal system. His attorney had finally lobbied successfully to have his sentence reduced and Gilles was transferred to a minimum-security facility in Montmartre. "Minimum" in France meant that there was no wall—not even an electrified fence—to keep the inmates on the premises. It was all on the honor system, a very strange practice given France's legacy of punishing its criminals. Devil's Island came to mind, as did the guillotine, though that method ended in 1939 with the last execution being the beheading of German serial killer Eugen Weidmann.

On the evening of Gilles Rousseau's first day in minimum security, he went for a walk after dinner and never returned. It took until well after 'lights-out' for the guards to discover his absence and by then, Rousseau was well out of the region. It never occurred to the warden to alert Pierre Letreuce or Clarice and Jacques Rousseau that Gilles had "escaped." As it stood, they kept communications within their ranks; they wanted to avoid the embarrassment of their very lax policy failing, though it was certain to find them in the coming days. The Marseilles Police would see to that.

The escaped convict, Gilles Rousseau, broke into his former home on the Rue du Gaspard shortly before sunrise the following morning and beat Clarice Rousseau unrecognizable before ending her life by breaking her neck with his bare hands.

He then proceeded to drink the only bottle of wine in the home, which he had stashed prior to his incarceration in a pile of rags underneath the kitchen sink. He sat down on the floor at the fireplace, downed the bottle, smashed it against the stones, and cut his own throat, drenching the Rousseau hearth with his blood and his shame.

It was Jacques' daily custom to bring his mother a warm baguette each and every morning, fresh from the Letreuce ovens. Young Jacques found both his parents there, dead, in those early morning hours, and proceeded to lose his mind.

Pierre eventually found Jacques, but word spread quickly and the police and the many neighbors in their Marseilles circle had already heard the devastating news about Clarice Rousseau; their collective hearts and sorrow went out to the boy. No one had seen Jacques since the news broke and no one could find him. Pierre knew the kitchen was Jacques' favorite place to be, his safe harbor, and shortly after news of the murder broke, Pierre found Jacques in a corner of the dry goods area in the basement at Letreuce, sitting on the ground in a puddle of his own urine, shaking uncontrollably.

Ever since the day Gilles Rousseau had been arrested, Jacques had taken command of the household and blossomed. His job at Letreuce was more than just work, it was his holy calling. He was able to support himself and his mother fitfully and kitchen life was his full-time obsession— Jacques was fast becoming a valuable team member and his skills soared, thanks to more advanced tutelage by Pierre and Andre Gaston and the other Letreuce *commis*. Now, that was all gone.

Pierre wasn't even sure that Jacques was still human, let alone a young man of 12. He didn't speak. He only sat wherever someone brought him; he would not take food or water unless they actually put it in his hands and motioned it to his mouth or fed him by glass or spoonful. Andre Gaston was immensely helpful and would sit with Jacques for hours, reading from his favorite book of poems or singing along with the radio. Jacques remained reclusive for months and finally, it was Pierre who cracked the shell to his inner darkness, slowly coaxing the boy back into some quieter version of his former self. While he at least ate and drank on his own now, real conversation was no more. Pierre tried to get Jacques to talk about what happened, but he would speak only in monosyllables and even then, only if had been asked a question by someone he trusted, mainly Pierre and Andre.

Eventually, Pierre thought it best that Jacques go to live with Clarice's cousins in America. It was the saddest time for Pierre, for having no children of his own, Jacques had become his adopted son and he loved him dearly. Clarice's family from Louisiana had visited Marseilles years ago, when Jacques was 7, and a friendly bond had remained. Strangely, Jacques did not object to the idea of going to America. Pierre's sadness for the boy was stained with the firm belief that Gilles Rousseau had killed three people that day and ultimately there was nothing he could do, except bid a tear-filled goodbye to Jacques, his beloved boy.

Jacques' young ego and his confidence had gained strength week after week since his father went to prison; now, his ego was a fractured, fragmented concept and his personality had seemingly split. It wasn't normal for a boy to not speak, but there was little anyone could do.

After three relatively brief conversations with his American aunt and uncle and only a few short months after the death of his mother, Jacques Rousseau watched his world disappear from the window of his seat on the Air France flight, bound for America.

Chapter 45

Chez Rousseau was not open for business on Sundays or Mondays. It was their time to recharge and regroup after a typically busy week and weekend. Today was a Monday, but Jacques and his core group had gathered at Chez Rousseau to eat, drink, and toast their recent, hard-won success.

Lisette raised her champagne glass and shared a touching toast to her love, Jacques, and the Chez team, and then clinked glasses with everyone else at the table, giving adoration to all of them. She had taken the morning off from her Bailey Farms duties because Jacques wanted to serve them all a luxurious Monday brunch in thanks and gratitude for the fine review they had received from Priscilla Barnes.

They all spread out at the large, round eight-top in the main window at Chez Rousseau and gorged themselves on a spare-no-expense feast for themselves, Patti, Jaime, and Rodrigo. The celebration was to recognize Team Rousseau's miraculous recovery from the acidic and acerbic Priscilla Barnes. The team was rejuvenated like a phoenix rising from ashes, thankful that she wrote what turned out to be a love letter of a review on her blog and in her New York Post column, instead of bitter malice. *"Jacques Rousseau Is Our New Food God"* was the headline that appeared in yesterday's massive Sunday morning edition.

It was a critique very unlike Barnes because she nearly *always* served some kind of detractive statement, even if she had enjoyed the restaurant's offerings overall. In the case of the *Poisson Avril*, no one had ever seen such gushing from Barnes. It was a masterpiece critique and worthy of the fare proffered on a regular basis from the Chez Rousseau kitchen. Jacques appeared pleased, certainly, but not exactly ecstatic and it had been noticed by the others. He must surely be tired, they all thought.

"I was wondering if she was ever going to write it. She ate here on Thursday night and the review came out just yesterday. Let me see the paper again," said Remy, and Lisette handed him the Lifestyle section from the Chicago Tribune. "Jesus!" he exclaimed as he read the review for the third time, shaking his head. "This is the same nasty bitch that waltzed into our kitchen and made my best friend nearly crap himself? I'm telling you—I was this close to tossing her down the stairs," said Remy.

"I'm glad you didn't, Tati. I had everything under control," said Jacques.

"Except for whipping that first plate of salmon straight into Rodrigo's chest, right?" said Remy, laughing.

"It was merely a fly in the ointment, sir! Is it not I who taught you the importance of having backup plans? You take direction so well now! Good lad! Perhaps you will have your own restaurant someday, just like me?" said Jacques, feigning offense as he teased Remy right back.

The two smiled warmly and raised their champagne in quick tribute to the other. Remy was indeed Jacques' second-in-command in the kitchen, but as for money, Jacques had rewarded Remy's loyalties long ago by giving him a generous ownership stake in Chez Rousseau. It was fun for the others to watch the comedic *tete-a-tete* between the two culinary bulldogs.

"So, it sounds like Ms. Barnes has also decided to take a vacation to France?" asked Lisette. "I think you inspired her, my love. Now she will go to where it all began? I mean, real cooking," she said, hiding her big grin behind her napkin.

Remy faked a throw of his own napkin at Lisette and chortled loudly. "Where it all began? Ouch! Yeah, we don't know anything about cooking down in Louisiana," he deadpanned. "Did the article say where she was heading first?" he asked.

Lisette re-read the section of the review and the critic's future plans. "It says she's flying to Paris and renting a sports car…heading for the country to do a 'culinary road trip of all the charming French inns,' from Paris to Lyon and beyond. She expects to be gone a month and gain 20 pounds in the process and may even write a book about it. I envy her, that sounds like fun!" said Lisette.

"Don't envy her so much, *chérie*. She almost tried to…" and Jacques, catching his tongue not a moment too late.

"She almost tried to do *what*, Jacques?" asked Lisette, a strange look on her face. Everyone at the table stopped eating for a moment.

Jacques quickly righted himself, "She *almost* tried to put us in our place, is what I was about to say. You've all read her reviews. She can be quite difficult, and she goes into kitchens and berates chefs all the time. That's all I meant to say," he said. Everyone seemed to buy it and the mood quickly returned to lazy joviality.

"May I have some more of that Kedgeree?" asked Patti O'Brien, and Jacques quickly and gladly took her plate, going to the adjoining table and spooning a healthy portion of the dish for his hostess before serving it to her. He seemed detached from the continued conversation about Priscilla Barnes, though this was understandable. Everyone assumed he had had enough of the critic and was merely relieved to be free of her. They were all glad it was over, and the Monday brunch was a well-deserved break.

Patti said between bites, "I had no idea Kedgeree was such a wonderful dish, but I must say, the British are onto something here! A breakfast of smoked haddock and rice and boiled eggs is *so* divine! And the curry! It just makes me feel so alive!" she said happily. "I'm going to spend the rest of the day at home, reading the newspaper and my magazines, then I'm taking a long nap with my cat curled up next to me. Then, I'm ordering pizza!" she said, and everyone joined her laughter.

Remy carefully caught Jacques' eye across the table and mouthed the word "meow" to him and then pawed the air with two fingers, grinning wickedly. Jacques did a double take, nearly spitting his champagne across the room. He, too, began giggling and then couldn't stop, having to hide his face behind his napkin, his face red from laughter. Damned Remy! He had almost spilled the beans, and though laughing about it was pleasant, Jacques wanted to keep the "cat shit sabotage" of Barnes between the two of them, and for good reason.

"What did I say?" asked Patti, talking around her food and covering her mouth. "What's so funny, you two?"

"Oh, nothing. Jacques just likes cats," said Remy, still giggling.

"Is this true? Oh, Jacques, do you really like cats?" asked Patti, which prompted Lisette to give Jacques a funny look.

Jacques gave Remy a quick stink-eye no one saw and replied, "Why, yes, I do. I like all animals. Especially the pretty ones with two gorgeous legs," he said, changing the conversation by leaning over to give Lisette a kiss, which she accepted and gladly gave back.

Patti was finishing her glass of champagne when she noticed activity on the sidewalk near the front door. While the restaurant was closed Sunday and Monday each week, there was always a small crew available, so the doors were left unlocked and open for deliveries. Now, two Chicago PD officers were able to take advantage of this, walking in to stand at the hostess stand.

"Jacques," said Patti, motioning with her head to the entrance and donning a serious look. "We have company."

Jacques turned and looked at the two cops and got up from the table. As he approached the men, he put on an imperious French look and greeted them with a mildly courteous, "*Bonjour, monsieurs*. Table for two?" he said.

They were not amused. A very short, squat officer—a lieutenant—took one step forward and said, "Remy Thibodeaux?"

Jacques felt pins and needles from head to toe. "No, Lieutenant, I am Jacques Rousseau, the owner of Chez Rousseau. What do you want with Monsieur Thibodeaux?" he asked.

The other officer, this one somehow both tall and wide, pointed at the far table. "Is that him with the blonde hair?" he said, making an attempt at some authority.

Again, Jacques deflected him and repeated his question. "Lieutenant, I ask again. What do you want with Monsieur Thibodeaux? If you won't tell me your official business, I will have to ask you to leave," he said, positioning himself in front of the two and not moving. "State your business, please, or go. Now."

"We have a few questions for Remy Carlyle Thibodeaux," said the Lieutenant coldly. "Is. That. Him?" he asked for the third time, punctuating his growing irritation by pointing a thick finger directly at Remy.

Remy saw all this and got up from the table, joining the men at the hostess stand. "I see this man was pointing at me, Jacques. Can I help you, gentlemen?" Remy said to them.

"Are you Remy Carlyle Thibodeaux?" asked the Lieutenant.

"Yes, I am, officer. What's this all about?"

"*Lieutenant*, Mr. Thibodeaux. Lieutenant Mark Longlet," he said with attitude.

Remy had no trouble with cops. He had a problem with *dick* cops, though.

"Sorry, *Leftenant*," mimicked Remy in a British accent, bastardizing the English phrase. The look on Lieutenant Longlet's face showed he was not receptive to comedy at the moment.

"Mr. Thibodeaux, we'd like a sample of your hair, if you don't mind," said Longlet.

"Yes, I do mind. What's this all about?" said Remy, not budging an inch.

"We have evidence from a crime scene. Blonde hairs. We need to take a sample of yours. The lab will see if we have a match."

"What crime are we talking about, lieutenant?" asked Jacques. "This sounds serious."

"It's a formality, sir," said the lieutenant. "Nothing to worry about." He motioned for Remy to turn around.

"Right here, Mr. Thibodeaux. I have to remove them, not you. Turn around please," he said.

Remy turned and let the cop take the hairs he needed, before facing the right way once more.

"Anything else, boys?" asked Remy. He was calm but on high alert. Neither cop said anything.

Jacques asked a third time, "What crime has been committed?"

"As I've told you, sir, I can't discuss the details of an ongoing investigation, but I am legally obligated to tell you, Mr. Thibodeaux, not to leave the state until further notice. You boys have yourselves a nice day now. We'll be in touch," said the lieutenant, tipping his cap and giving Remy a little smirk.

To this, Remy replied, "Hey, Barney Fife! The only state I'm in right now is the state of intoxication and I'm not leaving anytime soon!" Then he winked at the lieutenant. Longlet returned the stare but said nothing more, and he quickly left the restaurant.

Remy and Jacques stood at the hostess stand, absorbing what had just happened. The morning had surely felt like a Sunday, with the beautiful brunch and wonderful company, and a very real sense of *joie de vivre* in the air. In less than 5 minutes, however, it had deflated into feeling like a Monday.

Jacques put his hand on Remy's shoulder and patted it as he said, "Come with me. We need to make a phone call."

Chapter 46

Richard Baldwin, meanwhile, sat across the table from his companion and took a long drink from his glass of Johnny Walker Black. He preferred JW Blue, but the bar didn't have it and he needed some quick anesthetic, despite it barely being 11 in the morning. His companion was drinking ice water, and Baldwin had the thought this was likely the same substance that flowed through his veins.

"From this point on, for the next 48 to 72 hours, I don't want to see you in public, Richard," said the DA Joe Ellison. "Is that clear?"

"I thought you had this taken care of?" questioned Baldwin. "You got the evidence from the cook, the ME is running it through their labs or whatever it is they do, and they're going to prove the hairs are a match. What's the big fucking deal if I'm seen in a restaurant? And before you answer, be careful how you talk to me, *Joey*," said Baldwin, angrily. "I know you manufactured that evidence and it ain't the tenth time you've done that. More like a hundred, right?"

The DA hated being called Joey. It brought back bad memories from his childhood. He bristled at the jab and pushed it out of his mind. "I'll talk to you any way I see fit, *Dickie*," he said, sidestepping the evidence remark. "I could throw your ass in jail right now on a kiddie-rape charge and have you in Joliet by nightfall and you know it. You know what they do to people like you in Joliet, right? People who rape children?" said the DA with rising irritation.

Baldwin's face reddened at the thought. He forced himself to cool down by finishing his Scotch and signaling the bartender for more. "Joe, let's not let our egos get in the way here. If I go down, you go down. It's as simple as that."

"It's not as simple as that, Richard. Your evidence is merely circumstantial. We did a few real estate deals in the past, and if they were illegal, I certainly knew nothing about it. It's your name on the disclosures *and* the title docs *and* the banknotes. As for the little girls? Separate subject, but spare me your excuses," said Ellison.

Baldwin scoffed, "Banknotes? Are you high? Those were cash deals, dipshit. I don't need a fucking bank. I haven't had to go to a bank for years, remember that."

"What about the girls?" Ellison said, taking a second pass at the subject and the remark was answered with silence.

"That's what I thought," said Ellison. "Okay, here's how it goes. Finish your drink here, get up, go to your brand-new Mercedes and head for one of your many houses. Use one of your shell company properties and *stay out* of Chicago jurisdiction. I know how the cops work here and it'll take Chicago PD investigators at least a day or two to weed through a mountain of paperwork to come up with anything remotely linking you to any crime. Think about it. You've got some time now, you've some breathing room. Catch my drift? In the next 24 hours, I can have this Thibodeaux guy charged and you'll be in the clear. *We* will be in the clear."

"Then why'd you say 48 or 72 hours?"

"Don't be an idiot. The timeline isn't a fluid thing because life isn't fluid. You of all people know that. I just like to be careful. Don't try to be a stickler for legal details now, Richard, because you're no good at it."

Baldwin made a face. "I don't like the new Mercedes. The seat fits me all wrong and the sound system has no balls," he said.

"Well, you can't very well be driving around with blood and brain splattered all over the dashboard, now can you? You can thank your personal god that the Cribaldis have long arms and deep pockets, and that your fuckin' car was crushed and stashed where the cops will never find it," snapped Ellison.

"Hey, it wasn't my idea to whack Denny. That was all Vincent's doing. I had nothing to do with that."

"Richard? Never forget, those Cribaldi arms can just as easily reach out for you if you're not careful, and they *will* catch you, if they want to. Don't ever think they won't. Denny was a moron, and his mouth was going to get us in trouble eventually. Vinny did us both a favor."

"Fine, fine, fine," muttered Baldwin. He was tired of being talked down to by Ellison, who was nothing but a crook with good taste in suits. Baldwin picked up his fresh glass of Scotch and drained it in one gulp, then stood up. He reached into his pocket and pulled a $100 bill from a diamond-studded money clip, dropping it on the table. "Anything else?" he said.

"No. Just get your ass underground and don't come up until I give you the all-clear. Got it?"

"Yeah, right. I got it."

Ellison nodded, once. "You're a good lad...*Dickie*. Now get the hell out of town."

Chapter 47

Del Clayton stood over a Unitron electron microscope in the lab, examining evidence that had been brought in that morning by Chicago PD. He had received an email late that Monday morning by a very pushy Lieutenant Mike Longlet, who had *ordered* Clayton to fast-track it, though he had no such authority, and who stood before him in the lab now, as if Clayton were going to conduct the examination right then and there and give him the results immediately, fast-food style.

Longlet had no idea what went on in the forensic world and felt the MEs office was his own personal convenience store for information. Clayton had always found this imminently amusing and never altered his rate of speed for any matter involving the lieutenant. He knew Longlet was aware of this, and it pissed him off to no end.

"Who's fast-tracking this?" Clayton asked Longlet.

"This comes from the top, Clayton, so don't ask questions," said the lieutenant.

Del had been in his position much longer than the lieutenant had his and had several brushes with him over the past few years—all of them entirely due to Longlet's hugely overinflated self-importance. The lieutenant had zero authority over anyone in the MEs office.

"That doesn't answer my question, Lieutenant. Who?" said Clayton.

Longlet paused and said, "This order comes straight from the District Attorney's Office."

Clayton scoffed at this. "Ellison? Give me a break. Lieutenant, I take my orders directly from Chief Erickson, and by proxy, Police Commissioner Groenke. I do not take them from Joe Ellison or any other attorney, for that matter."

He continued, not budging an inch, "You should reintroduce yourself to the chain of command, you've been a cop long enough," said Del.

"I'll make sure to pass your sentiments along to the DA."

"Please do, Lieutenant. And add a personal message for me while you are at it."

"And what message is that, Clayton?"

"It's *Doctor* Clayton, if you don't mind, Lieutenant. I believe I've earned it. And you can tell him this: Shove it. I don't work for him, and I most certainly do not work for you."

"Don't press your luck, Doctor. This is a high-profile case." Now, he was really pushing it, which was a mistake. Clayton played politics like a chess master wielded strategy—always four steps ahead. He set down his pen and took off his glasses to look at the lieutenant squarely.

"High profile? In what sense or universe? Be specific, Lieutenant. Which politically connected ne'er-do-well has dipped their whatever into the wrong honey jar and whose official political hind quarters are now in a proverbial sling as a result? Let me guess...Mr. Ellison has managed, with his brazen political and financial aspirations and his self-serving and bloviating press conferences, to finally annoy a few certain individuals belonging, among others, to our secret Italian subculture here in Chicago? Those members shall remain nameless for purposes of this discussion, of course," said the senior ME.

Longlet's mouth had dropped open at the last part and now he simply stared ahead. He was suddenly and completely out of his depth, he realized, though he tried to keep himself in the battle, nevertheless. "That, I'm afraid, is none of your business, Doctor."

"Well then, Lieutenant, I'll have to ask you to accompany me to Chief Erickson's office so we can have a clarification session on the inner workings of the chain of command here at One Police Plaza and the necessity for following the detailed communication protocols therein. I say that because you are essentially forcing me into breaking the law. Come with me, please," finished Clayton, motioning as he turned to walk out of the lab. This caught Longlet off guard, but the ME kept up the offensive.

"Lieutenant? Are you coming? Or would you care to reconsider your position?"

Longlet gave him a long, hard stare. His bluff had been called and Clayton had forced him to fold the hand. He cleared his throat, saying, "When can we have the results, Doctor?" in a far more docile tone.

"As I told you previously, it depends, Lieutenant. I'll let your superiors know. Now, if you don't mind, I have work to do. Your superior officer, Captain Fairley, will be notified as soon as I have a determination. Good day, Lieutenant," said Clayton, who shooed him away with his hand and resumed his place at the microscope.

Longlet turned and stalked out of the room. Clayton chuckled to himself and took up the plastic evidence bags.

It was a simple fiber analysis of a human hair, which took mere minutes. He slid a glass slide containing two of the hairs under the lens, adjusted the fine focus and looked into the eyepiece.

Satisfied at his findings, he picked up the phone and dialed Captain Fairley's office.

"Fairley."

"Hello, Captain. Del Clayton here."

"Dr. Clayton, what can I do for you?"

"I have completed a basic analysis of the two samples of human hair fibers, one from the crime scene in Aurora and the other from the suspect, Thibodeaux, and they appear to be a match."

"Good work, Doctor. Thank you."

"Wait a minute, Captain. I'd like to do a mitochondrial DNA test for absolute certainty."

"That won't be necessary, Doctor. Would you excuse me? I'm going to be late for a lunch meeting. Thanks for the info," the captain said, and hung up. He turned back to his desk and typed a very quick note, hit *send*, then stood up and left to get his bag lunch from the break room refrigerator.

District Attorney Ellison's phone soon vibrated with a single text message: "Hairs are a match."

Chapter 48

Jacques and Remy left the brunch, went back through the kitchen to their office, and closed the door. The last time that door had been closed was nearly two years ago, the very first day Jacques and Remy had ever walked into the empty space at Rush and Division and envisioned the genesis of what would eventually become Chez Rousseau. They were checking out the dimensions of the kitchen and both had stuck their heads in the small office at the rear. It was tiny, barely big enough for two chairs and a very small desk, yet it still had a door. Remy had dashed outside and retrieved a large, broken chunk of concrete block alongside the building and used it to permanently prop the door open.

The closed door was a symbol of implied superiority, which is why the door stayed open after that first day and was never, ever closed. Now, it was closed because their privacy was a necessary means of keeping the other Chez doors open in the future.

"I'm calling Silvio Arradondo," said Jacques. "He might be able to help us."

Remy's face blanched. He wanted nothing to do with anything involving the Cribaldis. "Jacques, I don't want to do that. We don't know them. They come into the restaurant and eat the langoustines and gush over the risotto and Don Anthony asks you every time for the recipe for the *Niçoise* dressing and you smile and say, 'maybe some other time' and you all laugh and smile, but, Jacques...we don't *know* them."

Jacques had been looking at the ceiling, but now he looked at Remy. "I know them, Remy. I know him...the

Don. I've been teaching him to cook for a while now," he said.

Remy's face dropped and he thought Jacques had lost his mind. "You've been doing *what*?"

"Giving cooking lessons for Don Anthony," he said casually. "He said he wanted to learn some secrets on how to better cook seafood, and a few other things. I've been showing him over at his social club over on Dearborn. Actually, Tati, I was impressed; it's quite a nice kitchen," said Jacques.

Remy looked at Jacques and shook his head as if there were bugs in his ears. "Cooking lessons?! For Don Cribaldi?! You never said a word! And, anyway, how do you think that buys us protection from the biggest boss in Chicago?"

"Not protection. That would be asking too much. But the Don trusts me, and he said if he could ever return the favor, I should simply ask. We'll make a phone call to Silvio Arradondo, his consigliere, and he will know what to do. I don't want the police showing up and hauling you away in handcuffs."

This made better sense to Remy, since it was he that would be hauled away. He nodded at Jacques. "Go ahead. Make the call."

Jacques dialed the number and waited. "Voice mail," he said to Remy and waited for the tone.

Beep! "Hello Silvio, this is Jacques. I'd like to ask your advice over a little police matter concerning my sous chef, Remy Thibodeaux. Would you call me back when it is convenient? Thank you," said Jacques, then rattled off his cell number and hung up.

"I hope he calls back with good news," said Remy.

Jacques nodded, "So do I, my friend. Come on. Let's get back to the others before Patti kills the rest of that Kedgeree."

Chapter 49

Richard Baldwin didn't actually mind the brand-new Mercedes. The sound system might have had no balls, but the engine had balls the size of church bells, and Baldwin had a lead foot. He revved the engine and burned the tires out of the side street from the bar, heading west out of downtown. Within 20 minutes, he had reached the outskirts of the city and jumped onto Interstate 55 West. He owned several properties outside of Plainfield, and he planned to hide out in one of them for the next couple days.

He called and left a message for his wife, Genevieve, that he would be gone overnight for a business meeting the next day. It wasn't as if she didn't care, at one time she did care and very deeply, but Genevieve had long ago lost any illusions that her husband was a decent or considerate man. He would sometimes leave for days on end, with only the flimsiest of explanations once he returned. Business, always business, was the old refrain. It seemed all he did was work and make money. She didn't mind the money, but she certainly missed having a husband around, or at least someone to talk to after a long day and as the shadows lengthened into night.

It took only an hour for Baldwin to arrive at his destination—the Mercedes performed marvelously. No one was going to find him outside the city, he told himself. Fuck Ellison. He texted the DA's cell number and sent a single message: "*At the Plainfield property.*"

Unfortunately for Baldwin, the Cribaldi Family's love for technology once again proved someone reachable at their wont. Cameras along the route had monitored

Baldwin's progress out of the city, and they tracked him onto Interstate Highway 55 West, shortly thereafter establishing him on a heading leading to Plainfield.

The trailing car had kept a safe distance from the Mercedes the whole way. When Baldwin arrived at his final destination, the car then U-turned and followed the road back into town. From there, a phone call was made and instructions were issued to the driver to stay in Plainfield and monitor Baldwin's every move for the next 48 hours.

The driver came supplied with numerous articles of lethal weaponry, along with the training necessary to employ them, including a heart encased in ice.

Chapter 50

After the visit from the police and the phone call to Silvio Arradondo, Remy decided to get *really* drunk.

When he and Jacques returned to the table, Jacques feasted on more of the Kedgeree, chasing it with the Belle Epoque champagne, and Remy poured a glass and made a long toast, paying tribute to his brother-in-arms, Jacques, and the rest of the group, for keeping the ship sailing smoothly throughout the Barnes episode and emerging with the best restaurant in America. But the toast rang hollow for the both of them.

Undeterred and motivated to chase the police from his mind, Remy ran behind the bar and pulled out a bottle of Patron Silver tequila, before cutting up limes into wedges. He returned to the table with a tray containing six shot glasses, along with the bottle, dish of lime wedges, and a silver salt shaker.

"What's going on, Remy?" asked Lisette. "Turning up the party a notch or two?" She was smiling, but something seemed off. "Remy?"

Remy said nothing and kept his focus on the tray.

"Jacques?" asked Lisette. "What's going on? What did the police want with Remy's hair?"

"Nothing, love. It's nothing at all. Some investigation going on, about an assault that happened downtown, and someone thought they had seen a person fitting Remy's description. They wanted to rule him out as a suspect, that's all," said Jacques.

"Remy? Our Remy? Jacques, Remy wouldn't hurt a fly!" She joked, "Unless the fly pulled a knife on him, or on you." She smiled fondly, remembering the story Jacques had shared with her of the night the two first met outside Ripp's Bar.

"I know, love. Everything's fine," said Jacques. "Just a formality, the police told us, just a formality."

"Okay, everyone!" said Remy, a little louder than normal—the tequila was working. "Here's to us! Here's to you and here's to me and if ever we should disagree..." at the last second, Remy caught Jacques eyes, which said no to the last part of the vulgar toast. Remy nodded and simply finished his toast with, "I love you guys!" and pounded the entire shot of Patron in one swallow.

Next, he raced behind the bar and turned the restaurant sound system on to stream raucous songs from Chicago's own Old 97's, which came pounding out of the speakers. He began dancing around the restaurant, bouncing between the tables, and spinning around and around. He hustled over to the brunch table and poured more tequila for himself and Jacques, and he tried to get Jacques to dance with him, but the man was glued to his chair. Jacques knew Remy was worried, obviously, but the release was a good and necessary thing now. Let dancing and drinking take the pressure off. He hoped for his friend's sake that it helped.

The brunch party was winding down and everyone enjoyed Remy's little show toward the end, as it had been a good way to wrap up the celebration. Jacques thanked everyone again for their monumental efforts, and Remy kissed everyone right on their cheeks, including the normally reticent Jaime and Rodrigo—both blushed fire red at the Cajun's outward affections.

Jacques took Lisette aside and said, "I think I'll stay here with him until he winds down. You are going back to work, no?"

"Actually, I think I'll just go back home and work from there. I don't want to parade around the office with champagne on my breath," she laughed. Lisette kissed him deeply and waved goodbye to Remy, who sprinted over and gave her a massive hug and a kiss on both cheeks.

Jacques knew Remy would probably be very drunk by nighttime and therefore worthless the next day, so while Remy wasn't looking, Jacques took Jaime aside and said, "I think you're going to be head chef tomorrow. Get Pedro to help you, as your sous chef, with my blessing. Okay by you? Don't worry about cleaning up. We'll let the porters handle it."

Jaime smiled and nodded. "Oui, Chef. *No problemo. Hasta luego,*" he said and left with the others, radiating pride at the idea of being in charge tomorrow.

Jacques checked his phone. No message yet from Silvio Arradondo. This disturbed him, but there was nothing he could do about it. He had made the call and did what he could for his friend. The only thing left to do now was pour another glass of tequila and babysit Remy, but something was not right, and his sixth sense knew it.

The arrival of the police later that afternoon was still a shock.

This time, six police officers appeared, with Lieutenant Jackass Longlet leading the way, and filled the entry vestibule at Chez Rousseau. Jacques had spotted the officers in the street and went behind the bar to turn the music off. Remy had been sitting on a stool at the bar talking with Jacques and didn't see them come in. Jacques steeled himself, and when Remy turned around to see the horde of police in the restaurant, his shoulders sagged.

Remy stood anyway and brayed in false confidence, "Come on in boys! What are you all having? Jacques! More wine for the horses and hay for the men!"

The newly emboldened Lieutenant Longlet approached Remy with two patrolmen close behind and stated his business loudly, "Remy Thibodeaux? You are under arrest for the rape and murder of Cheryl Lange. We need to take you into custody now, sir. Please turn around."

Jacques tried to intercede on behalf of Remy, but two large cops stepped into his path. "How is this possible, Lieutenant?" asked Jacques with a look of pure anguish. "I have known Remy for many years, and he would never, ever do something like this. It is not in his soul," he said.

The officers had already placed the handcuffs on Remy, who had not uttered a single word. "His hair is an exact match for the hair found at the crime scene, Mr. Rousseau. The DNA report confirmed this as well," said the lieutenant, lying. Only the rudimentary physical examination under the microscope had been done, and not DNA testing. "Now, stand aside!" Longlet commanded.

Urgency had been in the air at One Police Plaza that day, driven hard and fast by the District Attorney, and the lieutenant had been given orders from his superiors, who had taken only partially correct information from Clayton, which was not the senior MEs fault.

Such was the nature of political machinations in Chicago; once again, as it had been for generations, something dirty was going on, and that dirt had been laid at the feet of Jacques Rousseau, who wasn't about to let his best friend go to jail for a crime he didn't commit.

"Gentlemen!" shouted Jacques. "There has to be some mistake! Monsieur Thibodeaux is the sous chef here, a very responsible individual, and as you can see, very handsome as well. He has more girlfriends than the White Sox and Bears combined! He does not need to rape anyone!" said Jacques, pleading with the officers and working his mind feverishly to find a solution that would keep Remy out of jail.

Murder charges don't just go away, and this is what drove Jacques at that moment, but he was failing, because Remy was turned and marched out of Chez Rousseau, leaving Jacques at the bar alone, dumbfounded and paralyzed. He stood, frozen in his spot, unable to move, unable to think. Remy, the best friend he ever had, was being taken away from him. The look on his friend's face as he was led away was the same look on his mother's face from long ago, the day his father beat her so badly it put her in the hospital. Jacques had buried the image deep down in his memory, but it came rushing back from the ether, haunting him all over again. Jacques buried his face in his hands and cried hard, hot tears for the first time since that day in France so long ago.

Lisette was home, reading, when her phone chimed a text from Jacques. She tapped the notification and read in horror: "Remy arrested. Murder of the little girl in Aurora. He's being held without bail at the police plaza. Going to see what I can do to help him."

Chapter 51

District Attorney Joseph Ellison was moving quickly through the halls at One Police Plaza, flanked on either side by two police officers. He was walking briskly, a single piece of paper folded in his right hand. The group behind him had trouble keeping the pace, and it included the Chief of Police Daniel Erickson and Police Commissioner Stephen Groenke. Ellison had obtained confirmation of the evidence around noon but needed ample time for his flunkies to contact and assemble nearly every media outlet and reporter in the city of Chicago, which is why, in typical slippery fashion, he had called the press conference for 4:00 p.m. so it would lead the 5 o'clock broadcasts.

"Ladies and gentlemen, if I could have your attention, please!" said the DA, loudly. "Earlier this morning, our forensic team uncovered evidence that linked a suspect in the Chicago area to the recent murder of 13-year-old Cheryl Lange. Today, my office has issued a warrant for the arrest of one Remy Carlyle Thibodeaux on the charge of rape, kidnapping, and murder in the first degree! I received word moments ago that Mr. Thibodeaux has in fact, been subdued and taken into custody by officers from Chicago PD!"

He continued, "It is believed that Ms. Lange's murder and the recent string of heinous murders have indicated the presence of a serial killer within the City of Chicago, and we believe strongly there is sufficient evidence to link Mr. Thibodeaux to those other murders. You will sleep safely tonight, Chicago! I would like to acknowledge Chicago's Finest for their heroic work. I would also like to thank the members of the forensic community for their fast and diligent efforts in bringing this arrest to fruition. Finally, I would like to credit the fine legal minds who work for me in the District Attorney's Office. I will have further information on this case for you in the coming days. Thank you all!" he closed. What a circus act.

The line of reporters wanting to question the DA took nearly an hour before everyone got their juicy sound bite from Joe Ellison, who stood in the middle of the throng like a painted-up whore standing at the pier greeting a fleet of boats filled with sailors coming back to port.

Meanwhile, Remy Thibodeaux sat all alone in a special holding cell in the bottom of One Police Plaza, wondering why his best friend had not yet come to see him, to help him, at the worst moment in his life. Perhaps he was trying to get help from Don Cribaldi? *But what could the Don do?* he wondered. He couldn't just make a magical phone call and *Abracadabra, Remy, you're free to go!* It didn't work like that. Remy paced back and forth in his cell, trying to keep his mind right, which was difficult to do because he always got emotional the more he drank, and he was starting to feel sorry for himself. Besides, nightfall was fast approaching, and Remy did not like the dark.

There were over 100 people at the DA's press conference: Police and other law enforcement personnel, firemen and EMTs, reporters, even a few of Del Clayton's staff were present, though neither Clayton himself, nor Liz Keller appeared. Out of all these people, only one civilian observed the proceedings firsthand: Jacques Rousseau.

He stood and watched the television monitors inside the lobby at One Police Plaza and stared at the DA, listening to him smear, besmirch, and attack someone he truly loved, accusing gentle, fun-loving, kind-hearted Remy Thibodeaux of something that had neither happened, nor could ever happen. The DA had wrongfully accused and incarcerated Remy in the name of politics, money, and covering of his own ass and in doing so, had now presented himself as a person of interest to the man in black.

He had met The Standard.

Jacques knew, from his association with Don Anthony Cribaldi, the DA was linked closely to Richard Baldwin. Ellison knew full well that Remy had not killed anyone, let alone innocent young women. Jacques would deal with the DA and then he would deal with Baldwin. The former did not concern or frighten him; the latter did, because it would mean placing himself in Don Cribaldi's hands and in his presumed debt. The Don's earlier implied favor toward Jacques was one thing—what Jacques was now asking far exceeded the Don's offer, and it scared the living shit out of him. Now, he was not only bargaining for his best friend's life, but his own head would also be on the chopping block if something went wrong.

No one acknowledged Jacques' presence, although it might have seemed strange to see a man with his hat on inside a government building, even though it was a Chicago outerwear staple—a tam o'shanter-style cap. The cap matched Jacques' black windbreaker perfectly. The fake thin moustache was an additional touch. Inside his jacket pocket was a tiny canister. A puntilla knife was strapped to his ankle inside a custom leather sheath and a third weapon was ensconced in his other inside pocket. He watched the last few seconds of the press conference and left the building, wanting to avoid the outrushing throng of reporters and other potential witnesses. Jacques wracked his brain for a plan, but it was difficult. All his thoughts were on Remy, who would be spending the night in jail, and it broke Jacques' heart.

****

The district attorney savored his latest public relations victory with the others at the Ice Bar in the Plaza downtown. Every TV channel from superstation WGN down through the dial had spread Ellison's breaking news about the captured serial killer and the DA was euphoric. He hadn't bought a drink all night, not that he would have paid for them anyway, and the liquor flowed heavily. He held court at a large table in the back, where everyone from his office, a few cops, and a large pack of fellow legal eagles from several law firms, had all joined in the celebration, which went deep into the night.

Chapter 52

Jacques left One Police Plaza and drove, slamming his fists into the steering wheel repeatedly, beyond angry with himself. Ever since the day at the café with Remy and Lisette, Jacques had made the decision that Baldwin had to go. He finally met the standard for elimination. Now, both Baldwin and Ellison were targets. They had fired a direct missile at those he loved—that was more than enough.

Jacques had even begun the process on Baldwin by doing his rudimentary due diligence. He had obtained Baldwin's movements down to a solid pattern; he had even selected Baldwin's final execution site. But he hadn't pulled the trigger, and this is what angered Jacques now. He should have taken him out. Hindsight was a vicious bitch, and tonight it was playing Jacques like a cheap banjo.

Jacques had no way of knowing that Baldwin and his partner, District Attorney Joseph Ellison, had planned on setting Remy up. At the time, Jacques also had yet to know that Don Cribaldi's son Vincent had been a witting party to the scheme, though that would ultimately be the Don's cross to bear.

Baldwin and Ellison. This was all their doing, and oh, was Jacques going to make them pay. This would not be a slow death. This would not be a kindness, releasing the two from their own inner demons, demons that motivated the real estate mogul to destroy the innocence of young women for his own pleasure and the DA to destroy lives to further his political career. No, this would be a righting of many wrongs on many levels. It would be a modern-day reckoning and bloody as hell.

Jacques dialed Silvio Arradondo for the third time that day.

Silvio answered with his usual, "Hallo?"

"Silvio? It's Jacques." His accent required no further introduction, as always.

"Oh, hey, there. Yeah, sorry I didn't call you back, kid. Me and Anthony were unavoidably retained. Whaddya need?"

"I need to know where Richard Baldwin is."

"What's the beef, chef?" This was a corny reference to the old television commercial with the elderly ladies, and it struck Silvio as immensely funny.

"Get it? What's the beef? You're a cook! *What's the beef!* Damn, I crack myself up sometimes," said Silvio.

He couldn't have picked a worse time to audition his Catskills routine on Jacques, who obviously wouldn't say a word in protest, because Silvio Arradondo was the consigliere to the most powerful Mafia figure in the Midwest, and Jacques desperately needed his help now. So, he laughed right along with Silvio, no matter how cheesy the material.

"That's a good one, Silvio. I like it." He changed the subject and upped the urgency. "My best friend is in jail. Remy. You have heard the news, yes? They arrested him for the murder of the little girl?"

"Yeah, we heard. We need to talk, kid. Come on by the club. Knock on the front door. Somebody will be there to greet you," said Silvio.

"I'll be there in 15 minutes."

Chapter 53

Jacques turned onto Dearborn Street two blocks away from the Dearborn Social Club and parked his Audi. He got out, making sure he kept his weaponry with him, and walked down the street, crossing Delancey Avenue to go up to the entrance. The daylight was fading and although the front windows were dark, Jacques was able to make out shadowy lighting in the back. The door opened before he could knock, and Silvio Arradondo greeted Jacques, without warmth. All business.

"Come on in, kid. The Don's waiting for you in the back."

Jacques and Silvio walked through the club, passing by dozens of pictures on the walls, the living, growing mural of Cribaldi family life and business.

The Don stood to greet his culinary instructor, his arms outstretched, bringing Jacques in for an embrace. "Jacques! How are you, Chef? You know, I don't want to boast, but my Dover sole is getting pretty damned good! I'm going to try to make it as well as you someday!" he smiled. "Have a seat. Can I get you anything? Espresso? A glass of this Rosé?"

Jacques waved a hand, "No, Don Anthony, I'm fine. Thank you for seeing me," he said.

"I understand your friend has a problem. Silvio mentioned it. What can I do?"

Jacques went through the details of Remy's first encounter with the police and his actual arrest. Along the way, he filled Don Anthony and Silvio in on the details surrounding Richard Baldwin, particularly his multiple hard sell moves on a new restaurant and the incident at the theatre, along with his theory that both Baldwin and the District Attorney, Joseph Ellison, are involved together in the murders. He also expressed his belief that Remy was set up by Ellison and Baldwin. He did, however, avoid mentioning anything about Vincent's involvement.

The Don listened, occasionally looking over at Silvio for either confirmation or negation on the facts related by Jacques and the overall story. When Jacques had finished, the Don nodded and took a long sip from his glass of Rosé.

"Are you sure you wouldn't like some of this, Jacques? It's quite good," said Anthony.

"No, Don Anthony, I'm fine, thank you," said Jacques. "But what can I do here? There has to be some way to prove
Remy is innocent and that Baldwin and Ellison are guilty."

The Don looked at Jacques and then at Silvio and spoke quickly in Italian, before melding back into English. "What do you think?" he asked his consigliere.

Silvio didn't hesitate. He was decisively exacting, which was why he had been the Don's consigliere for so many years. "Kill 'em both, Anthony. Ellison and that *strunze*, Baldwin. All we need to do is squeeze that fat, child molesting piece of shit, and he'll rat on Ellison so fast, it'll make his head spin. He'll make a plea deal to save his own ass, you can bet on it." Silvio thought for a moment and amplified his answer: "Just get a confession out of him and cut his fucking throat."

"I don't know where he is," said Jacques, referring to Baldwin.

The Don smiled cunningly and said, "Oh, don't worry about that. We do." He twisted the signet ring on his pinkie finger for a moment, looking over at the pictured walls, lost deep in thought. There was a question on his mind, and he was working his way around to asking Jacques something. He stopped twisting the ring.

"Jacques, can you keep a secret?" asked the Don.

"Of course."

"My son, Vincent knows about these crimes—the girls and your friend. This disturbs me. I don't believe he did anything directly to those girls, God no, because if I believed that, he would be dead already, even though he's my son and I love him as any father would."

The Don looked away, taking a sip of his Rosé and envisioning a time when both Vincent and the world were cleaner, simpler. "You must keep this to yourself, Jacques and never tell anyone," said the Don. "And you must keep to yourself, always, what we will do about *questi uomini avidi*, these greedy men. These pigs," he said.

Jacques nodded solemnly and said, "I will," and the Don reached over and patted his hand. The Don did not share with Jacques his knowledge that Priscilla Barnes had approached Vincent to have Jacques beaten. Jacques would hold a grudge against Vincent over this information, and Anthony knew he would be right to do so, but that was incidental to the current dilemma.

The Don remained focused on Baldwin for the moment. He said, "Jacques, these child molesters…what do you do with men like that? You can't teach them, because they already know that it's wrong, and yet they think they are to get away with it. Poor, innocent children," he said, shaking his head.

He looked at Jacques and tightened his mouth. "I'm going to have to deal with my boy. It's not a capital offense, but he knew about the girls and did nothing. It's also obvious he was involved in the setup of your friend. He needs a good smacking around. I will do that, myself, with my own hands and then I'm going to send him back home to Caserta and have some old, childhood friends of mine straighten him out and when he comes back, he'll be as good as new," he said. "And he will make good on his sin to your friend and to you. In that, my dear Jacques, I owe you."

Then, he sharply changed his tone and shifted in his chair. "But this Baldwin character and his friend—we're going to deal with them Silvio's way, just like he said."

"May I ask a question?" asked Jacques. The Don nodded.

"Will you let me kill the district attorney for what he did to my friend?" asked Jacques. "I know it's asking a lot, and although I am not accustomed to killing, I need your help," he added.

The Don froze a moment, then looked slowly over at Silvio, who met his eye. They both burst into laughter, loudly. Jacques must have missed the joke, because he had no idea why they were laughing, and he did not join in.

"I must say, Jacques, for someone not accustomed to killing, you seem to have a natural instinct for it," said the Don, still chuckling.

He was referring to Priscilla Barnes, thought Jacques, but he had had help from Carmine Tratella, which the Don knew about, of course.

Jacques said, "Barnes? Anthony, I'm sure you of all people understand that was purely business, and I appreciated your allowing me the use of Carmine's services that weekend."

The Don nodded, slowly. "True, she was trying to ruin something for you, but let us be honest with each other, Jacques. You can always open another restaurant. You are a superb chef and a smart businessman, so you will be successful anywhere. But I am an old man, and I would not allow her to destroy the memories of my grandmother. That is the difference," he said and continued.

"You are French; I am Italian, yes, but your *Langoustine de Marseilles* is the exact re-creation of my grandmother Luisa's recipe, although she called it *Tesoro del Mare*— 'treasure of the sea,' if you will. And when I first discovered it at your restaurant, I knew you were a person of considerable worth and value," said the Don.

"I am touched. That is very kind of you to say," said Jacques.

"You are welcome. Killing that nasty *buchiac* was the right move. From what Carmine told us, you did a very good job. You have an instinct for it. I wonder, Jacques, if your talent for killing comes from the same place in your head…where you create your food?"

Jacques shifted in his chair. Did he suddenly want Jacques to become a contract killer? He deflected the question. "Cooking is creation, Anthony," he said, using the Don's first name exclusively. "Killing is creation of a different kind. I killed her because she was evil. I killed her to restore balance. But she was the only one."

The Don's face suddenly became very dark. "Jacques, you are a good man, and I respect you, and you have my support… but do not ever insult me again by lying," he said.

"What am I lying about?" said Jacques, interrupting the Don. Big mistake.

The Don slammed his hand on the oak table, hard enough to knock over the crystal vase with the single tulip and spilling water everywhere. The room stood still. Then Anthony Cribaldi bellowed, in an old man's scratching, growling, basso-profundo voice: "WHAT ABOUT THE FOOD INSPECTOR YOU KILLED, JACQUES?! WHAT ABOUT THE RUSSIAN?!"

He turned to his consigliere, and said loudly, "Silvio, what was his name, the fat one?"

"Tufton. Rudy Tufton," Silvio said, expressionless.

Jacques' mind nearly imploded. He had not expected this fiery outburst from the Don. Jacques had done right in his killings, but, for the first time since he was a boy, he was afraid. Jacques looked everywhere: at the floor, at the pictures, at his hands, anywhere but at the Don or Silvio. Nothing had made sense in what the Don had just said; it didn't compute. There remained only one question: how in the hell did they know he killed Rudy Tufton and Dimitri Vasileyich, among others?

"How in the hell did you know I killed those men?" asked Jacques.

The Don scoffed. "We saw you! In the alley! You ran your knife all the way up from his cock up to his tits! That was definitely you, Jacques. That was *you*. Tell me I'm wrong. As for the Russian, we keep a closer eye on them than we do the police. Nasty bastards, all of them."

Jacques didn't know what to say. He had been revealed. There must have been a video camera somewhere around the Sturehof Tavern, which should not have surprised him. The Cribaldis had cameras everywhere around Chicago. It made him want to crawl into a hole and never return. He was caught, dead-to-rights.

"So, you know about me," was all Jacques could say. He slumped in his chair and hung his head. "You know I am a killer. I am sorry, Don Anthony, Mr. Silvio...I am so very sorry. It was a secret I had wanted to keep to myself. It was not meant to be disrespectful, believe me. Someday I would like to tell you the story of how I became this way. I'm not sure you would understand."

At this, Silvio began laughing, a harsh cackle. With gravel in his voice, he said, "Jacques! You're doing it again! Who do you think you're talking to?! *There are only serial killers in this room!*"

The man rarely spoke without Don Anthony asking his input, so when Silvio opened his mouth of his own volition, it carried weight. The words echoed around the walls, swirling like a layer of smoke.

The Don's voice calmed the air, "Jacques, I understand why you did what you did, and I suspect you have done this many other times as well." He held up a hand. "Don't answer...the point is, Silvio is right. There are only murderers in this room. Sometimes murder is necessary. People will never understand that. Let me ask: these are only evil people you have ever killed, Jacques, correct?"

"Correct," said Jacques, "Only truly evil people, only people that met The Standard. I didn't choose them. Fate chose them."

"Well said. Then, we are in agreement," said The Don. He stood up and looked over at Silvio, then back again at Jacques and nodded, the venom no longer on his face or in his words. The storm appeared to be over.

"Jacques, you've been good to me. You've helped me relive some wonderful memories of my grandmother. When I asked if you would teach me, I felt silly. I mean, here is the great Jacques Rousseau…a master in the kitchen, a chef who has grasped more about food than most of us will ever know. What is this man going to teach an old *Italiano* like me?" said the Don. "But you are a kind and gentle teacher. You know so very much and I'm lucky to have you as my guide."

"It has been my great pleasure, Anthony," said Jacques quietly. "You are already becoming a very good cook. Your instincts are quite natural."

The Don continued, "But you showed up here, and you were not afraid of me or what I do. You taught me well—you showed me respect, but not out of fear. You respect people. You respect life! Do you understand now?"

The Don turned his head and looked at the wall, at favorite picture of his grandmother and the tulips. He stood up and reached over the table and set the vase upright, lifted the tulip from the table and brought it in for a long sniff. It made him glow, this killer of men.

He pointed the tulip gently in Jacques' direction.

"My grandmother was a kind and generous woman, and you are the same. You will always have my respect, my dear boy. And you will have my support and my protection. But Jacques?"

"Yes, Anthony?"

"Always tell me everything. Never hold back. Never lie. *Capisce.*"

"Yes, I understand. And thank you."

The Don smiled at Jacques. "You let me take care of this Baldwin fellow. I have a man watching him as we speak. It will be a simple job," said the Don.

"What about Remy?" asked Jacques.

Silvio answered this. "Oh, that's nothing. He'll be out of jail soon. Danny Boy will get a confession out of Baldwin and get it on tape. He'll rat out the DA just as we said." Jacques gave the Don a perplexed look.

"What should I do, gentlemen? I still wish to kill the district attorney."

"I'm going to leave that to you, Jacques," said the Don, "But you should let us handle him. And Jacques? Loyalty goes both ways, my friend. Remember that. If you get caught, you don't know me, and this conversation never took place. I believe you know what this means, so I won't ever say it again. Now, you need to go see your friend, you might still have time tonight," said the Don, looking at his Patek.

"I'm going to have our guy deal with Baldwin sometime tonight. If you don't hear from me, give me a call tomorrow and we'll see about the DA. Then again, you might hear about it on the radio or the TV first." Silvio said, and he began chuckling again. For such a serious man, Silvio picked his moments of humor well.

Jacques rose, and offered his hand to the Don, who took it warmly and embraced him, kissing both Jacques' cheeks.

The Don walked Jacques to the door with his arm around his shoulder and spoke one last time. "Come by next week, eh? I think it's time you taught me your risotto. Yes? Have your pretty girlfriend get me some of those Morel mushrooms, too, and please give her my best."

"*Absolument.* I'll call this weekend and set it up," Jacques said and smiled as he shook Silvio Arradondo's hand and thanked him as well, promising to call tomorrow if he did not hear from him before. Jacques had already decided what to do about the DA, and he would be honest with Anthony Cribaldi about it after the fact.

Jacques walked out of the Dearborn Social Club as if he had been paroled. The greatest weight had been removed from his shoulders in ways no one but he and the Don could possibly understand. He got out his phone and texted Lisette.

"Going to see Remy. Home soon."

Chapter 54

Jacques parked the Audi on the street one block from One Police Plaza and removed all of the paraphernalia in his pockets. He placed the tiny canister and the puntilla underneath his seat, careful to watch for suspecting eyes. The last thing he needed right now was to get pinched for having such suspicious equipment on his person, especially considering he was going to visit a suspected serial killer; it was quite the paradox.

He walked through the building and was directed to the basement level where the jail was housed.

The Sergeant-on-Duty sat behind a desk next to the counter, where he administered the daily operations of the jail, visitors in particular. The people in these cells were generally there for very bad reasons, so security and protocols were stringent. Jacques approached the counter and spoke to the well-armed sergeant.

"Is there a Remy Thibodeaux here, sir?"

"I'm afraid visiting hours are over, unless you're his attorney."

"I am not an attorney. I am a chef, and he is my sous chef…my assistant chef."

"Visiting hours are 8 to 5."

Jacques looked at the sergeant and asked, humbly, "Can
I deliver a message to him?"

The sergeant paused and said, "You do know he's been charged with multiple homicides?"

"I do, sergeant. He is innocent. I just want him to know I was here to see him and that I'm doing what I can to help him."

The sergeant reached over and took a piece of paper from a notepad, sliding it across the counter to Jacques, along with a pen.

Jacques knew the police sergeant and other officers would read the note before it got to Remy, so the message had to be transmitted in code. Don Anthony was on their side, working on a plan to get him out of jail. He wrote the following words:

Hello, Tati. This is Don. I am your friend, and I do not want you to worry. Remember, there are people who care about your safety. You have their best wishes. All will be well. Bonsoir, Tati.

Get some sleep. — Don

Jacques handed the note to the sergeant, who looked at it and read its contents. It seemed innocuous enough, nothing nefarious, so he did not ask Jacques for his ID, which would clearly state his proper first name, and not 'Don.' Remy would understand the code, all too clearly.

"That looks like French to me," said the sergeant in a courteous manner.

"It is."

"What's this…*Tati*?"

"Merely a nickname for Remy, Sergeant. It means 'tiny one.'"

"Oh, so you're French, Don? I could tell by your accent."

"*Oui*, Sergeant. *Merci*."

"You're welcome, Don. I know that one—'merci'— I'll get this to your friend. Have a good night."

"And you as well, Sergeant," said Jacques, turning and walking away. His best friend was spending the night in jail and it broke his heart. Then he turned his thoughts to those who did this, and how they would pay.

Chapter 55

"Danny Boy" Mackenzie hung up his throwaway cell. The phone call from Silvio Arradondo was only a short conversation with instructions to get a confession from Richard Baldwin and send it back to Silvio immediately. It was a toss-up on whether or not to kill Baldwin outright, but Silvio left it to Danny to decide the degenerate's fate.

Danny turned the key to start his car, a black Ford SUV with tinted windows, and headed back out of town. Baldwin's property outside Plainfield was a mammoth luxury home sitting tucked away in a large section of woods and, unless it had laser-pointed motion sensors outside, access would not be a problem for Danny. He had worked for Silvio and the Don since he was 17 and rose through the ranks, finally obtaining his button three years ago. Danny Mackenzie was a sharp weapon because he was powerful both physically and mentally. He was a good thinker on his feet, always weighing options and choosing well. This is why he was the one selected to work tonight.

Richard Baldwin had been fast asleep, passed out in his chair in front of the TV when Danny snuck into the lower level of the mansion. A nearly empty bottle of Johnny Walker Blue sat on the end table next to the chair, the glass of the scotch still in his hand as he rested. He had spilled some of the liquid on his crotch but had continued snoring away.

He stirred awake at a clicking sound and opened his eyes to stare directly down the barrel of a large pistol.

"Hello, Richard," said Danny Boy. "Don't move. When I tell you, get up out of the chair and put your hands behind your head, interlocking your fingers. If you make any sort of movement, I'll blow your head off."

Baldwin noticed Danny was wearing light blue surgical booties over his shoes and rubber gloves on his hands. The implication made Baldwin's sphincter clamp down tightly. He did as he was told, setting the glass down and getting up slowly out of the chair to lock his fingers together behind his head. He shot a quick glance down at the side table and saw that his own pistol was gone. He had kept it with him every second since he had been at the Plainfield property.

"Don't worry about that, Richard," said Danny, patting the bulge on the side pocket of his jacket. "Now, turn around and don't move." Baldwin complied, with Danny twisting Baldwin's hands behind his back and shoving them inside the zip ties, ratcheting them tightly.

"Okay, Richard. Where's the laundry room?"

Baldwin was mortified. This wasn't happening. It had to be the Cribaldis behind this.

"Who sent you?" he asked, frightened.

Danny smirked, "Why, a friend of yours. Do you know a Joe Ellison?"

Baldwin's ass clamped down even tighter, and he managed a hoarse whimper. "Who's that?"

Danny chuckled. "Now, now, Richard, let's not pull that shit. Take me to the laundry room," he said, jamming the gun in Baldwin's back. "Move," he commanded, as he reached into his pocket and clicked the record button on his tiny digital recorder.

Once inside the laundry room, the confession spilled out of the child rapist like a waterfall. He answered every question from his captor, who had written each one ahead of time on a small spiral notepad. He presented them to Baldwin to read and then answer. Danny's voice would not be on the recording, and this, paired with the structure of Baldwin's answers, would make it sound like a genuine confession. It was a coldly brilliant, tactical move by Danny, one used many times over the years in similar Cribaldi-led interrogations.

Baldwin's confession included everything under the sun about his involvement with the District Attorney over the past 10 years, including the phony real estate deals, quashed investigations, and bribery of public officials. The most damning evidence of all was the DA's knowledge of Baldwin's sexual assaults and the murders of the three girls. Danny danced around any possible mention of Vincent Cribaldi in his questioning, and Baldwin never named him directly.

Finally, he asked Baldwin about the bodies of the victims. Baldwin told him there were three bodies in all—13-year-old Cheryl Lange and the two other girls, 14-yearold Diana Baumgartner and 12-year-old Tiffany Edelman. Baldwin had ordered his bodyguard Denny Renaldo to do the murders and then bury the bodies deep on his property. He confessed he had also instructed the bodyguard and others he employed to sabotage his video and computer systems, a direct contradiction to what he had told police during previous questioning.

Baldwin had officially hung out his own ass to twist in the wind. There could be no turning back, and he knew it. He had been sweating profusely during the entire confession and now began to shake. So much for the uberwealthy, confident and cocky real estate mogul. In the end, he was nothing more than a cowardly, simpering fool. All the danger and bravado had leached out of him.

Danny wrote the next to last message on his notepad and showed it to Baldwin, "Do you want to kill yourself? Don't say anything. Just answer with a nod of your head, 'yes' or 'no.'"

Baldwin didn't hesitate, nodding 'yes'. Danny wrote, "Say the following..." Danny handed Baldwin the pad and as Baldwin started to speak the last message, Danny walked around behind him.

"Because of everything I've confessed here, I, Richard W. Baldwin, am going to take my own life, with my own handgun, registered in my name. I'm sorry for what I did and for what I am. May God forgive me." Baldwin finished the words on the pad and shrugged his shoulders to the air, as if to say: *what now?*

Danny clicked off the recorder, stepped to Baldwin's right side and fired, shooting him flush in the temple with his own .357 magnum. The explosion relocated most of Baldwin's head, blowing a large crevasse in his skull and scattering brain matter, blood, and other detritus all over the south wall of the laundry room and washing machine. Baldwin sagged and twisted down to the ground in a heap, nothing more than a pile of rotten debris. He had met his perfect end, according to The Standard.

Danny stepped carefully, avoiding the blood splatter, and wiped down the gun to put it in Baldwin's right hand, making sure his own prints were off the weapon.

He left the laundry room and followed his earlier path to leave the house, stopping before he got to the lower-level sliding door, and waiting for a full 10 minutes. He scanned the outside for any sort of movement. Nothing. Satisfied, he went to the woods leading to the road and stopped there as well, scanning the area methodically. No one was watching. He returned to his SUV, started it up, and drove slowly away, back to the highway. In an hour, he was back in Chicago, where he stopped at one of the Cribaldi's many safe houses. From there, he called Silvio Arradondo.

"Yeah."

"It's done. I'll bring you the cannolis in an hour," said Danny and hung up.

Chapter 56

Very early the next morning, Del Clayton was back in the lab. He had been going back and forth on re-testing the fiber samples from the Thibodeaux case but was sidetracked by more politics after yesterday's announcement. Second-guessing the chain of command was something Clayton occasionally did in his career, but it had been a long, long time since he had butted heads over politics from a higher level. Regardless, in the name of science, he was going to prove someone wrong today.

Clayton picked up the phone and called Liz Keller's office. Even though it was very early, he knew she would be there. Keller had transformed herself completely from her earlier days, becoming a valuable resource to the senior ME and to the department; she was once again a very sharp instrument and the best version of herself.

"Keller," she said.

"Liz, come on down to the lab, would you please? I'd like you to see something," he said and hung up.

Keller shot up from her chair, grabbed her lab coat and raced out the door. She came into the lab, out of breath. "What's going on?" she asked.

"Take a look at this and tell me what you see," said Clayton, moving back from the compound light microscope and motioning for her to look into the eyepiece.

Liz adjusted the fine focus knob. Two single fibers, side by side on a glass slide, came into view. After a few seconds of observation, she said, still looking into the microscope, "They're identical."

"That's what I thought as well, as did the District Attorney, given his fanfare of the trumpets yesterday," said Clayton. "Liz, flip the wheel and use the 400x lens. What's different about them?"

Liz took a second look. "I see the fibers on the right are a different color. Wait, not a different color. They look darker, but…they're swelled up and slightly abraded, like they've absorbed something, but what?" she asked.

"I think it's time we disobeyed an order," said Clayton.

The DA's fingerprints were all over this rush to judgment, and if Clayton and Keller could tilt the scales of justice in favor of the truth, then politics be damned. The captain had told Del not to do a mitochondrial DNA test on the fibers, but that is exactly what Clayton was going to do, with Keller's help.

"Liz, we're doing an mtDNA test on these fibers. Set up the equipment, will you, please? I'll be right back," said the senior ME.

"Del? What about the captain?"

Clayton turned and looked at Keller. "Oh, don't worry about him. I have his DNA."

****

Thirty minutes later, a zip printer connected to the trusty spectrometry unit was spitting out the test results on a single narrow strip of paper into Liz Keller's hand. She grabbed it and started reading to Clayton.

"Soybean oil, beta carotene, tertiary butylhydroquinone/TBHQ and sodium chloride," said Keller. "That's the breakdown of the compound the hair absorbed and made it look thicker. What the hell is TBHQ?" she asked.

Del said, "TBHQ is a preservative meant to keep colors from fading in many processed foods. Beta carotene, in this case, is an orange coloring agent. The last ingredient, of course, is salt. There's your clue. Add them all up and what do you get?"

"I give up."

"Ever been to the movies, Liz?"

"Sure, Del, a million times."

"Then you've probably consumed this a million times."

Her eyes lit up and she snapped her fingers. "Popcorn? Wait…popcorn oil…the *topping!*" she shouted.

Clayton nodded and actually smiled, teeth and all. Keller was spot on. "Want to take a walk?" he asked.

"Where to?"

"The basement."

"The jail is in the basement."

"Nothing gets by you."

"Why are we going down to the jail?"

"To pay a visit to an accused killer and ask some questions."

She nodded and smirked. "Great. You buy the popcorn."

****

Del and Liz waited at the sergeant's desk while an officer checked a computer screen for the holding cell of the accused serial killer Remy Thibodeaux. He clicked on his computer mouse three times and came up with Remy's cell. "He's in D4, but he's been sequestered, so he's all alone, Doctor Clayton."

"Thanks, Jay. We won't be long."

They made their way through several locked-door checkpoints, presenting their ME department ID badges each time. They finally arrived in front of D4 to find the suspect lying on his single cot. He appeared to be sleeping.

Clayton nudged Liz to talk first. She understood why.

"Mr. Thibodeaux? Are you awake?" she asked softly.

"Yes," Remy said, his back to them.

"Can we ask you a few questions, please?"

Remy turned over, sat up, and looked at the two as he rubbed his face. "Sure. I'm not busy at the moment, as you can see." He still had Jacques' message from last night in his pocket. It had been the only thing that kept him from madness as the evening's darkness had descended.

Clayton spoke in a friendly tone. "Mr. Thibodeaux, I'm Del Clayton. I'm the senior medical examiner for Cook County. This is the assistant medical examiner, Liz Keller. We've been analyzing your hair strands in the lab and were wondering something. When were you last in a movie theatre?"

Remy looked at them with utter surprise. He knew exactly what they meant before they said another word and smiled for the first time since he had been arrested. He got up off his cot and began pacing in his cell, telling Clayton and Keller about the fracas at Richard Baldwin's Dell'art Theatre in Cicero several weeks ago. He seemed to grow more animated as the story drew to conclusion.

Clayton nodded and asked him, "And at no time were you yourself ever on the ground during the fight, on all fours? Where your head would have made contact with or been rubbed or ground into the carpeting?"

Remy shook his head vehemently and said, "Not a chance, Doctor, Ms. Keller. You can check the shirt I was wearing if you like. I was on my feet the entire time." He grinned and looked at the ground, "I'm a pretty good fighter when I need to be."

Clayton looked at Keller and they both nodded at each other.

Keller spoke this time. "You see, Mr. Thibodeaux, it appears Mr. Baldwin planned to have one of his henchmen grab your hair with the intent of placing it at the scene of the latest homicide."

Clayton added, "The men had popcorn oil on their hands from being on the ground so much, scrambling about. Apparently, Mr. Baldwin doesn't clean the carpets very well, if at all, but it didn't take much, and this particular popcorn oil takes forever to break down on its own. When one of the men grabbed your hair, the residue from the oils on their hands permeated your hair fibers."

"How did you figure this all out?" asked Remy, a quizzical look on his face. He was still finding it hard to believe that he might actually get his freedom back.

"Simple deduction, really...and a kickass spectrometry sequencer," said Liz with a smirk.

Clayton added, "We can also verify this from the chemical makeup of popcorn oil in the carpeting itself. From what you tell us about the place, Mr. Baldwin had cameras installed at the theatre, inside and outside. Unless you have anything else to add, we need to go now, Mr. Thibodeaux. There is more investigating to do, but I'll go on the record now that the evidence presented by the DA is sketchy at best, and the charges will not likely hold up," said Clayton.

Remy was overjoyed. "No, I remembered everything exactly as I told you. My God, is this really happening?" asked Remy, shaking his head. He extended his hand to Clayton through the bars and said, "I don't know how to thank you both."

Clayton shook Remy's hand and said, "It's no trouble, Mr. Thibodeaux, but you need to be patient, and you need to be a model prisoner starting now." Clayton beckoned to Remy to come closer and lowered his voice.

He whispered, "Do not say anything to anyone here. Keep your mouth shut. Chicago PD doesn't like to walk back mistakes. We're not finished yet so be patient. We'll get there."

They bid goodbye to Remy and turned to go. Liz looked back and gave him a small smile and a toodle-oo wave with her fingers. Remy smiled back. And winked.

Chapter 57

Lisette reached over and shut off the alarm. Jacques was still sleeping soundly. He was normally the first one up, but, given the events of yesterday, she understood his obvious exhaustion and the need for sleep. She pulled herself out of bed and was making strong French-press coffee when she looked up to see Jacques leaning in the doorway, scratching his head.

"Good morning! You slept well."

"I'm glad I did," he said, yawning again. "I have a lot to do today."

"Are you going to see Remy?"

"*Oui*. It's my first stop," he lied, "And then I have to get to the restaurant. Jaime will be in charge of the kitchen today, but I already spoke to him about it."

"Surely Pedro or one of the others can cover for you, no?"

"Lis, I still have to take care of certain things, you know," Jacques said, annoyed. He rarely snapped at anyone, let alone Lisette, and it registered. He hoped she had bought the act.

"Are you okay?"

"No, I'm not okay! My best friend is in jail for a crime he didn't commit, and I don't know what to do!" he shouted, playing up the act even more.

"I know you don't want to, but perhaps now is the time to call Don Cribaldi?"

Jacques was hoping she would say that. He felt better about his lie already. "Yes…I think you are right, *chérie*," he said, drooping his shoulders, "I will give the Don a call. Who knows? Maybe he can help." He walked over and wrapped his arms around Lisette from behind and kissed her on the neck several times. *"Merci, chérie.* You always know what to say," he said. "I need to get in the shower."

She handed him a cup. "Let me know if there is anything I can do," she said, kissing him on the cheek.

****

Once in the car, Jacques dialed the restaurant and left word for Patti O'Brien that he was going to see Remy and take care of some other matters, and to please tell Pedro he would be Jaime's sous chef for the day and that Jaime was in charge of the kitchen. It was necessary that they know the chain of command began and ended with them, at least for the next day or so.

He also informed Patti that he was not to be disturbed in any way, even if the restaurant were on fire. She would know what to do anyway.

Chapter 58

Clarice stood over her son, Jacques, combing his wet hair after his bath. She had done this since he was born, and she did it once again tonight, because she could tell that her son, now 11 years old, was growing mildly quizzical, if not completely unsure, of why she continued this ritual. He was obviously old enough to comb his own hair, he thought, but he let his maman do this anyway, without a word of protest. She seemed to enjoy it, and, besides, the tines of the comb felt very good moving through his hair after a long bath, so he stood very still for her.

She did it because the end of an era was approaching, and she sensed it in her marrow. All boys grow up and become men. Clarice wanted to seal this moment in memory. Jacques was becoming a young man and would not need his mother much longer. He would be able to take care of himself, and this made her sad. Profoundly so.

Jacques was such a sweet, quiet boy, and he was so good inside. It gave her such pride and satisfaction that she thanked God at that very instant. *I will remember this moment for the rest of my life*, thought Clarice, smiling so warmly it felt like sunshine inside.

"Jacques, *mon tati?*" said Clarice.

"Yes, Maman?" he said, looking at her in such a way it made his eyes gleam. He loved his mother more than anything in the world.

"You must promise me to always be good. There are people in the world who are not good. They are sometimes very, very bad. You must always remember, whenever bad things happen to you, if you fight it, you will make life better for yourself," she said. "And you will make life better for others if you fight the badness. Do you understand?"

"Do you mean fight people like Papa when they do bad things?" asked Jacques. That day, Jacques' father had hit his mother in the face again. It left a mark and Jacques could see it now, reflected in the mirror, a streaked mass of purples and reds. Gilles had hit Clarice many times, so she did not hide her wound.

She also did not respond to her son's question. Her stillness was answer enough.

After a moment of silence, Jacques said, very quietly, "Yes, Maman, I understand. I will be good."

Clarice shook her head, "No, Jacques. Sometimes, you must do bad things to bad people in order for good to happen. You meet force with greater force, you see? You have that inside you because you are stronger than you could know." She continued to comb his hair as she spoke, "That does not mean I want you to become bad, because I don't believe you could do so. You are such a good boy," she paused, the words catching in her throat and making tears in her eyes, and she added, in a whisper, "…such a good young man!"

"Remember this, Jacques. Remember this for me," said his mother, fervently.

"I will, Maman," promised Jacques. "I will."

Chapter 59

From his Audi, Jacques observed the District Attorney with the help of a powerful, miniature single-scope lens. His tam o'shanter cap was pulled low on his forehead. The DA was sitting in the back of a place called Jensen's, a quiet breakfast spot in the Pilsen neighborhood on Racine Avenue. Jacques knew the place well. It seated 60 people and had access to both the alley and Racine Avenue from a long hallway the led to the restrooms, which were separated from the restaurant through this hallway. It provided Jacques with an excellent opportunity.

The DA was having a late breakfast alone, nursing a wicked hangover from last night's press conference afterparty at The Plaza. He had cleared his calendar for the morning as a result. After some 30-35 minutes, and two coffee fill-ups, he got up from his half-eaten, heart-healthy omelet and hash browns and headed for the men's room. Jacques got out of his car and followed, entering the hallway from the alley side.

Jacques pushed the door open to the men's room and walked to the urinals. The DA was three spaces down on the long trough and paid no attention to him. When the DA turned to go to the sink to wash his hands, Jacques got ready by palming the tiny canister. He zipped his fly and turned, walking toward the sinks to wash up as well. In the mirror's reflection, the DA looked at Jacques' approaching figure and said, "Hey…don't I know you?"

Jacques smiled and put his hand out, palm side down, as if he were reaching to shake the DA's hand. When the DA turned to face him, Jacques flipped his palm over and sprayed Ellison directly in the face.

"What the hell are…you…doinggggggggg…," slurred the DA, succumbing to the Rocurium and, as he slumped forward, Jacques caught him on his feet. With no time to spare before others came in to piss, Jacques hauled the DA by his armpits, hustled him into one of the open stalls, and sat him on the toilet seat, leaning him back against the plumbing. The DA's eyes looked straight into Jacques', as if he were trying to communicate telepathically with him.

It had zero effect: Jacques Rousseau was lethal now and vengeance was coming.

Jacques reached into his inside pocket and brought out a hypodermic needle filled with a dark blue liquid. In one swift move, he snapped the needle cover off with his thumb and jammed the sharp appendage deep into the DA's chest, piercing the breast plate, going straight into the heart. He thumbed the plunger rapidly and forced the liquid all the way into the muscle. The next few seconds would be excruciating, he predicted.

Jacques whispered savagely, "This is for Remy Thibodeaux. And Cheryl Lange. And everyone else you've fucked over in your miserable life, you prick. *Au revoir.*"

He pulled the needle out and glared into the DA's glassine eyes. Ellison's chest rose once, twice…and then he spasmed, violently, and his chest rose no more as the light behind the eyes faded into a dark mist.

Jacques put two fingers on his neck and started counting to ten. At the count of seven, the door to the men's room opened and two voices were heard conversing as they walked in and settled at the piss trough. Jacques heard the door open again, and a third man came waltzing in as well, proceeding to micturate with the others. They were chatting amongst themselves about the serial killer with the funny name. Tippytoe or Tibadoo, they all laughed. Jacques was not amused. He went into panic mode.

If he left the stall now, the men could physically describe him, or confront and tackle him, considering the dead body of the DA and him together in the same stall and the can of Rocurium in his pocket. It would give the police all the evidence they would need to convict him, and although Illinois had no death penalty, this would not apply in the murder of a United States District Attorney. The Feds would own his ass.

Or...Jacques could stay in the stall and risk being caught outright, in which case, he was vastly outnumbered. There was no possible way he could take out three men at the same time, even if he could subdue them physically with the Rocurium—that would mean killing them all, which was where Jacques slammed the brakes on his serial mindset.

His one true defining characteristic had been to protect those he loved. He took care of the bad people later in life because of the very scars he held from childhood and because, well, they deserved it in spades. He killed now only through firsthand discovery of evil and a hard confirmation of the person's horrid misdeeds. Every single criminal he had killed had been a nasty, brutal, soulless person who had deserved their fate; their disappearances from life had spared countless heartaches and made the world a better place. As he got older and better at his work, Jacques' tracking, thought, and planning on his projects had become state-of-the-art.

Today, he had run headlong into the mother of all ethical dilemmas: he didn't know any of these men. They had done him no wrong, and they could not be harmed. *The Standard must stay intact,* Jacques confessed to himself, even if it meant self-sacrifice.

So, that was it. Jacques was going to jail and would likely die there. He should have listened to Don Cribaldi, whose advice had been solid: "Let us handle it." Jacques killed the DA because it satisfied his singular barometer of justice, however loosely it had been planned and executed. Calm rationality should have prevailed, but his ego forced his hand here. He had lost the battle and now the war, all because of pride. It was a stupid move—he hadn't done any due diligence on the DA; he had *reacted*, not acted, and now it was going to blow up in his face at the expense of his friendship to Remy and the loss of his love, Lisette.

Remy was the best friend he'd ever had, the only real friend of his own age and experience. Jacques' thoughts drifted to the others who cared for him—the dear, gentle giant Andre Gaston from Letreuce so long ago in Marseilles, and, certainly, his beloved mentor, Pierre Letreuce. Pierre had been his real, true father, had discovered his immense talent and nurtured him in the art of the kitchen. He had given Jacques a life and a wholesome meaning within that life which had almost erased the damage his biological father had done. Almost.

But Remy was special.

They would never open another restaurant together. Jacques would never get to see Remy's own fine establishment and deep in his heart, he knew it would have been truly superb, possibly even better than his own dear Chez. Perhaps Jacques would be able to see Remy one last time, before his inevitable incarceration, so that he could tell him how hard he had tried to punish Remy's enemies, how he truly valued and relished their friendship—that he had given his own life for Remy's freedom. Finally…to tell his best friend that he loved him. After that, Jacques Rousseau would rot in a jail cell until the political machine that dealt with executing people finally got around to him.

He couldn't even begin to fathom the pain of losing Lisette. At this precise moment, his mind was slipping, because not only was he facing the fact that his one true love would be taken away, but his eventual punishment as well: a bag over his head and a paralyzing agent flowing through his veins.

He wept silently, repeating over and over in his mind, *I'm so sorry, Lisette, mi amour. I'm so sorry, Remy. Je suis désolé, Remy. Je t'aime, Lisette. Je t'aime."*

Chapter 60

All three men simply washed their hands and left the bathroom without another word.

Jacques sat in silent shock for a moment. Then he righted himself, dried his face, and made sure the DA was properly situated. He picked the hypodermic cap off the floor and flicked the lock on the stall door, so it appeared the DA was in fact performing his normal ablutions. He slid under the partition and eased his way casually out of the next stall, making sure to flush the toilet in case someone was just walking in. No one came, and Jacques moved out the door with forced calm.

He walked casually down the hallway and out the side door to the alley. Two men were walking away from him in the alley and paid no notice to Jacques. He moved down the narrow path and turned the corner, walking away from the restaurant on Racine and back to his car the other way from the crosswalk. Jaywalking would have drawn attention. He walked to his car, got in, and headed out of Pilsen and toward Wicker Park.

When he entered the basement apartment at Mrs. Chlopicki's house, he collapsed on a chair in the kitchenette and laid his head on the table, breathing in and out, trying to find his center once again. He made it. He was still free. He needed to call Silvio Arradondo and tell him about the DA. He needed to go see Remy, who must also be losing his mind right about now. He needed vodka.

He got up and grabbed the vodka from the freezer and poured three fingers of Ketel One and downed it, then added two more fingers and sat down. He was raising the glass to his lips when his phone rang. He thrust his hand into his pocket and grabbed the phone. It was Lisette. He didn't want to talk to her right now; he was morbidly ashamed with himself during those last frightful moments in the bathroom when he feared he had finally been caught. He didn't feel like himself right now, but he answered anyway.

"*Oui*, Lisette."

"Jacques! Where are you?!"

"I'm driving to see Remy. Why are you out of breath?"

"He's free, Jacques! Remy is free! The police found evidence that proved Remy didn't do it! They're releasing him this afternoon!"

Jacques couldn't speak, couldn't even think.

"Jacques, are you there?" Lisette asked.

"Yes, love, I'm here," he said softly. "How did you find out?"

"A man named Silvio called the restaurant and told Patti and she called me right away. You must have convinced Don Cribaldi to help, yes? And he did!" she practically sang.

"Lis, I cannot even think straight right now, I'm so happy. Forgive me, love, but let me get to the police station and pick up Remy. *Je t'aime, mon sucre*," he said, and hung up. He was so grateful to be able to say those words to her.

He quickly called Silvio.

"Hallo."

"Silvio, it's Jacques. Are you on a throwaway cell?"

"Always. You can talk. Whaddya need?"

"The district attorney is dead."

"Yeah, no shit? Where?"

"Jensen's over on Racine, in one of the stalls in the men's room."

"Nice. How'd you do it?"

"Gave him a heart attack with a needle."

"Subtle, Chef, subtle! Baldwin's dead too, bet you didn't know that?" he chuckled.

"No, I didn't. What happened, if I can ask?"

"Poor bastard shot himself in the head, right after he confessed. Recorded it and everything. Tragedy, ain't it? We're gonna leak it to the cops in a few minutes. I'll wait to add the DA part while I'm at it, but they'll find him soon enough. Call it a 'two-fer.' Hey, 'Two-fer Tuesday!'" Silvio was polishing his comedy chops again.

"Where did you get the news about Remy?" asked Jacques.

"Oh hell, Chef, we know about shit before the cops even think of it."

"That's a nice arrangement. Silvio, I don't know what to say. Will you thank Don Anthony for me, please? I'm very grateful to the both of you."

"Don't mention it. It was Anthony's pleasure. Just remember? If something comes back to you on the DA thing, you gotta take the pinch. You don't know us."

"Know who? Who is this? Just kidding, Silvio. *Au revoir.*"

"*Arrivederci,* kid."

Chapter 61

Jacques was sitting on the sidewall of the fountain in the middle of One Police Plaza, waiting for Remy. He saw him first through the glass, and then again as he was walking out the revolving doors and looking up to the sky. *For an innocent man, he looks terrible*, thought Jacques, but that didn't matter—his best friend was free.

Remy saw Jacques and waved madly. He jogged right into his arms and bear-hugged him. Both men were giggling, as silly as children.

"You okay?" asked Jacques, incredulous and wide-eyed, patting Remy on the face.

"Hell no! I've got a hangover that could kill a horse and I smell like an old Cajun's boot!" Remy cried. "Let me give you some advice—stay out of jails, man, the food here *really* sucks! Jacques, where's your car?"

"Right over there."

"It's gotta be on the radio by now! Ellison! Come on, let's go!"

They ran to Jacques' car, jumped in, and tuned the radio to WGN.

Once again, our top story from the WGN Newsroom—District Attorney Joseph Ellison was found dead earlier this afternoon, the victim of an apparent heart attack. His body was discovered shortly after the noon hour at a restaurant in the Pilsen neighborhood near downtown. Foul play is not suspected at this time, and an autopsy is pending. In related news, the man charged by the former District Attorney for a string of murders has been released from police custody. Remy Thibodeaux was initially charged in the murder of 13year-old Cheryl Lange, but breaking, new evidence from the Cook County Medical Examiner's Office confirmed Thibodeaux was not the killer. Chicago Police have resumed their search for...

Click! Remy turned the radio off. "Okay, that's enough of that horseshit. Let's get the hell out of here and get a drink and a bite. I'm starving! I've got the rest of the night off, don't I, Tati?"

"Yes, you do, and for the rest of the week if you like. I think it's only fair, don't you?"

"Absolutely! Where should we go?" asked Remy.

Jacques grinned and said, "How about that place they call Chez Rousseau? I hear the chef serves a wicked *pâté*."

Remy did a double-take, and they both started laughing, long and loud, as Jacques drove away.

THE END

Epilogue

The autopsy saw whined loudly, echoing off the walls of the primary forensic exam room situated deep in the recesses of One Police Plaza. Liz Keller was manning the saw, dressed in full autopsy gear. This included a thick, cuffed-sleeve lab coat, heavy-duty propylene gloves, surgical booties, and a fully protective face shield. Tiny bits of overspray in the form of liquid and micro-pulverized flesh from the dead body whipped from the spinning blade and spattered the face shield as she sawed her way through the thorax.

She shut off the saw and grabbed a set of rib spreaders, positioning them in the crevice of the chest cavity, and slowly beginning to crank. Larger and larger the opening was made, so she could gain access and remove the victim's heart for post-mortem examination.

She stopped cranking when she saw the heart, or rather, what was left of it. It was weirdly shaped and…partially dissolved? The interior cavity wall was a morass of congealed fluid and tissue, both a reddish and blueish tint. She steadied herself on the steel table.

"Holy shit," she whispered, the words catching in her throat.

She tossed off her gloves and grabbed the phone in the room and punched Clayton's office, speed dial #1 on the phone directory.

Del picked up on the first ring, as always. "Liz?" He had seen the extension light and known she was doing the DA's autopsy.

"Del? Will you come take a look at this?" Keller had long ago dispensed with the formality of titles when it came to the senior ME now, and theirs was a solidly symbiotic relationship.

Clayton sensed the urgency in Liz's voice. "Is something wrong? I'm in the middle of cleaning up the palace intrigue from yesterday," he said.

"You'll see," and she hung up. She kept her cool on the phone, but seeing a semi-melted heart was a jolt. She wasn't going to puke, though. Puking was for rookies.

She kept her gear on and stood in the doorway to the autopsy room. Clayton came jogging down the hallway at a good clip for someone in their mid-50's. He saw her at the door, fully clad, and exclaimed, "Liz, what the hell! You sounded like the Alien popped out of this guy's chest."

"Funny you should use that analogy, Del. This Alien took a bite out of the heart. See for yourself."

Clayton grimaced and walked over to the PPE cabinet and grabbed some gloves, a face shield, and an apron and suited up. He stepped over to the table and looked into the chest cavity.

Del Clayton had seen everything in his 25 years as the senior medical examiner, or so he thought. Homicides wore so many ugly masks and people never ceased to amaze him, how they could find new and innovative ways to destroy the human body.

This case would go right into the ME's Hall of Fame.

The dead body on the steel table belonged to the former District Attorney for Cook County, Joseph Ellison, deceased since yesterday afternoon—time of death, approximately 11:30 a.m., give or take an hour.

The mixture delivered by Jacques Rousseau in a hypodermic needle into Ellison's chest had pierced his heart with a combination of Acid Blue 25 and construction-grade muriatic acid. The former is an acidic used to dye fabric, the latter strips concrete down to its bare ass. Mixed together, it destroyed the DA's heart, very likely while it was still beating.

Clayton postulated the searing, unthinkable pain—pain on a level few humans have ever endured—was likely to have been fatal on its own. The remaining heart in Ellison's chest cavity was now nothing more than a soggy clump.

"Well, there's something you don't see every day," said Clayton, in deadpan fashion, the standard coroner's response.

"Pretty remarkable, really," Liz said.

"And we'll see this again, or variations on it, Liz. Did you notice the face…that sheen of residue around the mouth and nose?"

"Jesus, this one is good," she said. "I'll bet you a million bucks that's Rocurium."

They both turned and looked at each other and spoke in unison.

"We have a serial killer."

-JLL

Here is the *soft open* for the next installment in the Jacques Rousseau Mystery Series…

****

TABLE FOR ONE: The Dying Season

By

John Louis Lauber

"Sometimes...there's God...so quickly."

From "A Streetcar Named Desire" by Tennessee Williams

Chapter 1

When you work hard, success, in the form of many dollars, can come your way.

For some, success comes with an expiration date.

The young man walked down Michigan Avenue in a relaxed, casual manner. It was another beautiful Friday afternoon during an already superb summer and he appeared to be merely another young Chicagoan walking home from work or out to an evening's destination. The theoretical work whistle had blown and downtown had released its working citizens, and all were now ready to hop like their feet were on fire. The working week was done. Time to relax.

The young rogue could have been meeting a date or a group of friends out at one of the many popular pubs, whiskey and vodka bars and restaurants in and around Chicago's magnificent downtown. The sun had begun its long, fine downward arc toward the horizon line of Lake Michigan, casting rays off the water and setting a perfect visual prelude to the weekend, as Fridays usually do.

He was walking that distinguished American Boulevard known as The Magnificent Mile. Michigan Avenue—aka "The Mile"—remained as one of the most striking urban constructs in America, as it stylishly has done for over 90 years, its stunning skyline morphing subtly with the times, certainly, but it still continues to exhilarate visitors and residents alike, particularly the view facing cityward from the lake.

The allure of the natural and architectural endowments had zero effect on our friend; he paid no such attention to either the sight lines or the water or anything human, for that matter.

He strolled toward the Rush and Division district, in light microfiber pants and a tasteful button-down shirt, untucked, and in powder blue, the style and crisp press of his clothing conveying his job paid well. He looked like a techie, but could have been a marketing wonk or something equally lucrative.

His Cubs hat was turned backward on his head, with the requisite Bluetooth appliance plugged into his left ear. Wraparound designer sunglasses completed the ensemble, a thoroughly modern and Middle American Millenial's taste in fashion; a backpack of nondescript navy blue was slung over his right shoulder.

Nothing stood out to the casual observer that this young man was anything but pure Chicago, either in his gait or mannerisms. Even his accent was perfect—he had robotically and repeatedly practiced it on the nonstop flight from LRS/Lyon, France to ORD/Chicago, USA—speaking into a tiny recorder, listening and replaying back untold examples of the Chicago accent for hours, so that by the time he arrived at O'Hare, his voice was pure Chi-Town.

Witnesses on the street had not seen the eyes behind the shades, for if they did, it would have rendered a chill of pure cold and dread. Millenials from across the Pond can be quite different from their American counterparts, but this young man was quite rare; he brought with him a deadly wrath from Europe, sent to deliver a very brutal message.

The young man's backpack had a telling feature: A side compartment, easily accessible through a long Velcro strip. Inside was a Walther P38, complete with a silencer. The gun itself was highly illegal, the silencer, even more so; if caught, the young man would find the inside of a penitentiary for the remainder of his 20's. Accessing the gun would merely appear like scratching his back or fishing for a bottle of water. Deadly convenient.

Time was now approaching the height of the dinner hour and there was activity abuzz coming from the back patio of the restaurant known as *Chez Rousseau*. A steady, friendly murmur signaling high anticipation was the soundtrack of the evening there.

The alley path ran from the buildings behind East Bellevue Place within shouting distance of Chez Rousseau and the assassin walked past and gauged a wide, easy view of all the guests. He kept his eyes straight ahead, using his acute peripheral vision, never looking inward, simply walking at a leisurely pace, taking in the warm evening and then circling the block several times, using different routes so as not to be noticed.

He made four trips, once altering and once removing his Cubs hat to appear different each time. No one noticed him.

The kill would come soon, but perfection-through-patience was his only chance of success, and though the young man was only 24, he had spilled blood seven times in his early career as a paid assassin; cool and calculating resolve were his calling card and the proof of his skill sets would result in yet another dead body, this one destined to lie on the patio stones of Chez Rousseau. For now, he would wait.

Chapter 2

Jacques Rousseau and Remy Thibodeaux stood in the kitchen, surveying the preparation for the evening dinner service, while they worked alongside their team to prepare the sumptuous and ample buffet for a large group of special guests, all of whom had converged on Chez Rousseau for a special event, the unveiling of a new discovery in the food and wine world. The buffet was being served outside in the back on a brand-new patio expanse and 50 excited gourmands waited, in great and enthusiastic anticipation, for the announcement. It added a shot of adrenaline to the crew as well, who on top of the exquisite buffet, also had to execute and serve the regular dinner menu to Chez Rousseau's guests, who by now had filled the restaurant every night, expecting the highest cuisine served in the land. You could have fooled even the most astute gourmand, for the atmosphere in the kitchen was calm, professional and slick. Nothing new at The Chez.

Jacques and Remy both grabbed sterling oval platters containing individual plated servings of the entree that had made them famous: the incomparable *Poisson Avril*, a heavenly salmon dish consisting of a plump salmon portion poached in lobster stock fortified with *Pouilly-Fusse* wine and adorned with a creamy Sorrel sauce. The dish had put Chez Rousseau on the culinary map, and serving it tonight was merely a reminder of the good and fine things in life and what got them there.

But time is a fickle lover, especially in a cutting-edge restaurant. The *Poisson* aside, the highlight dish of the evening was a *Fluke Ceviche*, fluke being a member of the sole and flounder family. It was prepared in ribbon strips of the fish's flesh, the slices awash in a light bath of lime juice and seasoning, white wine and pureed shallots and completed with an adornment of tiny petals of carnation and fronds of saffron, which would add a bright, peppery note to the finished dish and a stunning color presentation. It was simple, yet ingenious in its preparation: the acids in the wine and lime juice "cooked" the fish by chemical reaction; no heat, fire or flame was necessary, and as such, each bite was designed to literally dissolve on the palate, leaving behind the essence of the ocean and a breeze of citrus and spice; it also left the diner wanting more, price no object…and yet another breathtaking creation of the fertile imagination of America's most famous chef and his second-in-command.

Rousseau and Thibodeaux could now command the greatest assemblage of cooks and chefs around the country, if not the world, to ply their trade at The Chez. Everyone who wanted Michelin stars in their galaxy desperately strove to work at Chez Rousseau, as if by osmosis, the intelligence and vision of R&T could pass to them and they, their gift to the dining world. Many offered to work for nothing, but the promise of tutelage.

It was a remarkable time, seemingly without the possibility of failure or disappointment.

Jacques came back to the kitchen and inspected the last trays of Fluke being transported out to the new patio area; satisfied, he strolled to the bar, where he grabbed a silver tray containing 6 flutes of chilled 1971 Dom Perignon and, using only his fingertips, brought it to his shoulder and walked briskly, not eyeing the tray and certainly not spilling a single drop. Though he was trained and lived his working life as a cook, chef and restaurant-owner-supreme, Jacques knew all the finer points of exemplary service and could certainly have opened a school for butler training, if that had been his vocational inspiration; instead, he made, arguably, the greatest food in the Western Hemisphere.

He walked with a smooth carriage through his own dining room, all guests pausing forks and glasses and noting the famed owner in their presence. True, he was both the proprietor and the renowned chef at Chicago's Chez Rousseau, but most notably, he had recently nailed down his 3rd *Michelin star*, a career achievement, and the awe from his customers was palpable...*Jacques Rousseau just passed by our table!* Jacques had received his first Michelin star at his Louisiana restaurant, *Clarice* and then his 2nd Michelin star the year he opened Chez in downtown Chicago, just off the Miracle Mile.

Two short years later, the 3rd elusive Michelin star had launched he and everyone at Chez Rousseau into orbit, joining them in that pantheon of the culinary gods around the globe, past and present. Their legend was now secure and their reputation and red-hot brand, was firmly entrenched in the world culinary consciousness. Jacques Rousseau had indeed become a god of cuisine, as the food critics and fine dining community had predicted and now loudly declared for all to see and experience.

The first congratulatory tweet came from his fellow Frenchman, and longtime friendly competitor, Chef Eric Ripert of Le Bernardin in New York, whom Rousseau had supplanted as the best chef in America: "Welcome to your 3rd Star, Jacques! We're all very happy for you!" said the tweet, and then Ripert texted Jacques privately, with a one word salute: "Bastard!"

No small credit for the 3rd Michelin Star was due to Rousseau's partner and best friend, Remy Thibodeaux, who had been with Jacques through the identical journey, having joined him when Jacques first opened the New Orleans landmark, *Clarice*, earning his first Michelin. From there Thibodeaux provided key contributions that helped build the new Chez empire, from carefully selecting the location to making those key hiring decisions, right down to the strident menu repertoire they sweated over each week; the two were the bricks and mortar of the stunning success that was now Chez Rousseau on this very evening. Remy had contributed much to their Michelin ascendancy, and it became not a question of *if*, but *when* he set off to plant his own culinary flag.

The Chez was as packed as any 60-seat restaurant could be, and the volume was not loud by any means, but the atmosphere was lavish and rich, heavy with joyous anticipation and an equal measure of release. Such was the heady nature of the wonder and expectation of being served the finest food in the land. Tonight, Chez Rousseau was the epicenter of North America's dinner. It also served as the evening's launch pad for a whole new brand destined for great success.

Jacques moved out the large quadruple-French doors next to the bar and stepped onto his new patio; it had been furnished luxuriously and with great functionality; al fresco dining at its comforting best. The lighting was intended for emotional soothing and was adjustable by remote control and by all accounts was doing its job well, because the vibe was humming and rising in the oncoming Chicago dusk, men and women engaged in and alert to the presence of each sex, such was the thrusting, intoxicative effect of superb food and sublime wine.

On the matter of the allure of the grape, Jacques' fiancée, Lisette D'Argent, was the star of the evening. She was there to be honored for introducing a revolutionary new hybrid grape of French and American domain she had pioneered through her employer, Bailey Farms & Garden. The early buzz from wine experts on both sides of the Atlantic Ocean had already predicted great success and word was spreading quickly. This information was welcome and exciting to oenophiles everywhere, but of a growing concern to competitors in Europe and France especially, a select few who wanted nothing but utter failure from the new American vintage.

The grape was birthed by cross-pollinating a rare Burgundy varietal and an American Marechal Foch, the marriage of which yielded a sumptuous red wine of sturdy constitution and bold flavor with mesmerizing, very nosey taste-leaps and a velvety, earthy finish of chocolate, orange zest and rosemary, with a whisper of tobacco at the end. Simply a phenomenal bouquet.

Best of all, the sturdy Foch lineage ensured the grape could be grown in the soil of the Upper Midwest and Great Lakes regions, where even the thought of a bitter winter's wind was enough to demoralize most other French grapes. It was aptly named by Lisette with the perfect *nom du vin*, for it embraced not only the individual seasons of the year, but imbued that every day of the year was *the* season for good and memorable wine.

Jacques stopped momentarily with the tray and scanned the crowd on the patio, spotting Lisette speaking to Charles Bailey, the owner and patriarch of the Bailey Farms family, as he stood alongside her parents, Simon and Julia D'Argent. Jacques moved over to them and held out the silver tray so each could take a glass.

In a playful mood, Jacques raised his glass and asked innocently, "So, to what shall we drink?" Over 25 years after coming to America from Marseilles, his voice still exuded a distinct French accent on the ear.

"What shall we drink to?" gasped Lisette, grinning, but slapping him lightly on the arm and leaning into him. Her accent was easy to spot as well.

"Allow me," said Charles. He took a glass of champagne from Jacques, turned to the crowd and spoke in a pleasing baritone:

"Everyone! May I have your attention, please?" he asked, raising a hand very briefly; the patio volume from all 50 people dropped to zero. He commanded the space.

"Ladies and gentlemen, we are here tonight to toast this incredible creation of our own dear Lisette's. I have known this young woman ever since she first came to America from France as our foreign-exchange student. Over the years, I have watched her grow and learn and stretch so very much with her work ethic and her imagination, yet never forgetting her exceptional French roots. We are so very blessed to see the result of it here…or at least we will in the coming year. We have to grow the grapes' inaugural vintage, after all, and then make some wine with it." He paused for effect. "You know...the easy stuff!" and Charles smiled broadly and winked at Lisette and everyone in the crowd laughed.

He continued, "But I believe every indication is present that this will be the grandest success and we are so fortunate to have Lisette leading us into this new aspect of our business. I think we can all agree this is a monumental accomplishment," and with this, Charles turned and faced Lisette directly and she began to register emotion, touching her hand to her throat and visibly forcing tears to remain in check. It was readily apparent she deeply adored Mr. Bailey and the entire Bailey family. Charles Bailey had long ago sensed in his young charge a grand potential, perhaps one that could exceed his own mastery of plants and Earth, which was considerable, given the wealth his years of toil had produced.

He continued, "And we would all be remiss, myself especially, if we were to not pause and recognize this moment, for it is a stunning achievement in our world," Charles said.

Charles finished with, "Lisette, my darling girl, if you were my own daughter, I could not be prouder of what you have achieved!" Charles raised his glass. "To Lisette D'Argent, ladies and gentlemen, and her singular discovery of the new grape...*Cote d'Fontrachet*!

Vive le Fontrachet!" he exclaimed, his glass high in the air.

****

About The Author

John Louis Lauber is a Minnesota writer and a self-described "foodie" since the 1980's.

TABLE FOR ONE: *The Standard* is Mr. Lauber's first novel. His Jacques Rousseau Mystery Series continues in 2023 with the sequel, **TABLE FOR ONE: *The Dying Season*.**

Mr. Lauber resides in Minnesota with a very large cat. Both are passionate about pizza.

Made in the USA
Monee, IL
24 January 2025